The
Irish Cottage
Murder

The
Irish Cottage
Murder

Dicey Deere

St. Martin's Press ≈ New York

Library of Congress Cataloging-in-Publication Data

Deere, Dicey.
    The Irish cottage murder / Dicey Deere. — 1st U.S. ed.
        p.   cm.
    ISBN 0-312-20552-X
    I. Title.
PS3554.E3553I65   1999
813'.54—dc21   99-12841
                                                    CIP

First Edition: May 1999

10 9 8 7 6 5 4 3 2 1

To my sister Edna,
and to the one and only Charles

The
Irish Cottage
Murder

1

Just past a castle glimpsed on a hill, he spotted the pond through a break in the hedgerow and stopped the yellow Saab. Shakily, he got out of the car.

There was a greenish scum on the pond the other side of the hedgerow. He knew it was only algae, but at the last minute, kneeling there on the bank, he couldn't drink it despite his thirst, the furnace in his throat. Vodkas and brandies and a couple of Irish whores picked up outside that pub in Rathdrum. What a night! The worst hangover since his wedding twenty-six years ago in Helsinki. Only thirty miles more to get back to his hotel in Dublin on the access road, but his thirst couldn't wait.

He drew back from the scummy pond. Through the trees he saw a shack. No, it was a small, decrepit cottage. Maybe they'd have a well, cool well water and a tin dipper, or even a refrigerator with ice-cold Cokes, or beer. He had traveler's checks and a few Irish pounds and some pence.

He stumbled toward the cottage. It was a dreary-looking, tumbled-down dwelling with a lopsided wooden bench by a low door that was scabbed with peeling green paint. Small, square open windows; dead silence. He stopped. Something odd. His brain felt fuzzy. He was remembering when he was in the army, coming into a supposedly empty village; the strange kind of silence. So instinctively, instead of knocking, he moved cautiously to an open window and looked in. At first, nothing. Then, his eyes probing, he saw.

"Christ!" he said aloud. A head turned; he saw the face, the eyes looking at him. He stood motionless. The door opened. He backed away. "Christ!" he said, again. It was the last word he was ever to utter.

2

The voice on the telephone from across the ocean rang like a dark bell. "Forty thousand dollars, Ms. Tunet," said a cultured Boston accent.

Torrey couldn't answer. She stood there, naked, shivering, hair dripping, clutching the towel, chilled from the shower, staring from one of the long bedroom windows of the castle. The voice from Boston dimmed the morning's view of the mountains north toward Dublin; it fuzzed the ragged edge of blackthorn that bound the castle's woods and hazed the leafy entrance to the bridle path. *Forty thousand dollars.* It brought a bitter metallic taste to her mouth, a copper penny from childhood on her tongue. Water from the shower slid down her legs and puddled on the rug; the damp towel was cold.

"Ms. Tunet?" Boston, polite, but impatient. In Boston it must be 3:00 A.M.

She swallowed. She'd find the money. She had to. "Please go ahead." Having said it, she felt a moment of panic.

She put down the phone. She picked up the towel she had let fall. She had run from the shower when she'd heard the phone; Boston calling back.

Today was what? Tuesday, July second. So she had three weeks. Forty thousand dollars. She didn't even have four thousand. Or three. Or two. Back home in North Hawk, north of Boston, population seven thousand, she rented a one-bedroom apartment above an antique shop. Her car was an old 1985 Cabriolet convertible Volkswagon with perennial engine trouble. "Wasting your money, driving this baby," Larry the mechanic said each time. What else? Lump all her jewelry together and it might bring five hundred dollars.

She had to find a way. *She had to.* She stood biting a fingernail. She'd get two thousand for her interpreting job this coming week. The Belgian-Hungarian conference in Dublin. But her next job assignment could be weeks away. Longer. She lived on the edge. She loved the risk of it. It was a high-diving kind of life. Maybe she was a gambler. Maybe she had inherited a love of adventure from her Romanian father, an explorer. "The ice floe was green and huge, and us a black speck like a bug in its lee. . . ." "They threaded the snake on a spit . . ." "The women's palms were tattooed in patterns like lace . . ." Her father. She, the same. Though her exploring was in languages, endless, absorbing.

But — forty thousand dollars!

She gazed helplessly from the window. In the distance, she glimpsed a flash of yellow, a yellow car on the road that went past the castle gates; it was going toward Dublin. She glanced at the clock on the ornate mantel. Quarter past nine. She'd better dress and get on the road to Dublin herself.

In the bathroom, brushing her teeth, she thought wryly that at least she had the luxury of staying in this castle when she so desperately needed money. Interpreters International had booked her into a second-rate hotel in Dublin. But here she was in Castle Moore. Funny, she didn't really know her host. She'd met Desmond Moore just once, a week ago, through that mishap with the spilled plate of soup in the restaurant in North Hawk. When he'd learned she'd be working at a conference in Dublin, he'd insisted she be his guest here in Wicklow. "It's only a half hour from Dublin," he'd assured her, smiling. *Why not?* she'd thought. A castle! So she'd cancelled the reservation that Myra Schwartz at Interpreters International in New York had made for her in Dublin. When she arrived at the airport, she'd rented a Mini-Cooper. With the slip of paper with Desmond Moore's directions to Castle Moore on the dashboard, she'd driven southwest to this castle in Wicklow. She had arrived late last night. Desmond Moore had not been there. A plump little maid named Rosie had shown her to her bedroom. Jet-lagged, she had slept until eight this morning. Rosie had brought her breakfast: black tea, brown bread, boiled eggs, sausages.

She glanced around the bedroom. It was bigger than her whole apartment in North Hawk. She'd hated it on sight. Heavy damask curtains she'd love to rip down, a bed canopied in swaths of raspberry satin, a furbelowed dressing table, tapestried walls, a fireplace filled with silk flowers, a scattering of priceless little cherrywood tables with Moore family photographs in gold and silver oval frames — all the marks of historic pretension via an expensive decorator. All this was presumably Desmond Moore's taste.

So Desmond Moore, an American of Irish antecedents. She knew nothing more about him. She guessed he was in his thirties. He was obviously rich. Certainly hospitable. Yet, oddly, she'd felt repelled by his assessing yellow-green eyes.

"Ma'am! — I'm sorry, ma'am!" In the bedroom doorway, hand to her mouth, giggling, staring, blushing, stood Rosie in her blue uniform and starched white pinefore apron. "I thought you'd left for Dublin, ma'am. I came for the breakfast tray."

"That's all right, Rosie. . . . Is Mr. Moore about?" Torrey held the bath towel to her breasts to cover herself. She was twenty-seven and felt she had no reason to be embarrassed. After all, she was sleek and slim in spite of eating so much pasta with gorgonzola and all those chocolate bars with almonds. She didn't care if Rosie saw her naked. But she'd once read that European aristocrats in earlier centuries thought of servants as animals and had no modesty before them. She wouldn't do that to Rosie. Or to anybody. Except on purpose. Out of malice. Or mischief.

"Mr. Desmond's gone to a horse sale in Wexford, ma'am. He and Brian Coffey, who's in charge of the stables. They left

5

over an hour ago. He said to tell you drinks in the library, seven-thirty, before dinner."

"Fine, Rosie."

"Anything else, ma'am?" Rosie picked up the tray.

"No, thanks. I'm off to Dublin."

Alone, she dressed quickly in her businesslike, navy suit and white shirt. She ran a comb through her hair, which was short, dark, and wavy. She slid a geranium-colored lipstick across her mouth. Her eyes were gray, with short black lashes, but they somehow looked better without mascara. She strapped on her watch, a man-sized Timex with date, day, and world time sweep. It was nine-thirty. The watch looked too big on her narrow wrist. But it was vital to her business.

"Ready?" She stood soldier-straight before the mirror. "Ready." Torrey Tunet, interpreter. She was proud of herself. She had struggled out of a morass. She had studied twelve hours a day for ten years to achieve this career. She knew, with a sometimes lurching heart, how lucky she was to be doing work she loved.

But now —*forty thousand dollars*. It was as stunning as a hammer blow on her head. Where would she get that much money?

She picked up her briefcase and headed for the door.

And stopped.

That claw-footed, gleaming mahogany table near the door. Silver-framed Moore family photographs. In an oval frame, a dowager, regal-looking, white hair piled high. Around her bare neck was the same diamond necklace that was in her portrait in the great flagged hall downstairs. The diamond necklace with a pear-shaped emerald at the throat.

Torrey's heart beat faster; her temples pounded; she shivered.

No, never that! Once she had been a thief. Recidivism. Once a thief, always a thief? *Recidivist*. From the Latin, *recidivus*, "recurring"; from *recidere*, "to fall back"; from *re plus cadere*, "to fall"; "to one who relapses"; "an habitual criminal".

No, never! It had taken years. But she had left the horror behind. She had become somebody. The past was over. Forgotten. Never to be exhumed or thought of. Buried. None of it could touch her now.

In the castle driveway, she slid into the seat of the Mini-Cooper. She put her briefcase on the seat beside her, drove down the winding tunnel of ancient oaks, and turned left onto the access road to Dublin.

Forty feet beyond the castle gates, she said, "Hey!" indignantly, and swerved to pass the empty yellow Saab that someone had left parked carelessly, half off the road.

3

Fourteen-foot-high bookshelves lined the walls of the library at Castle Moore. Arched windows soared. It was noon. A bronze clock ticked on the Florentine desk with its red leather top.

Fergus Callaghan, genealogist, working at the desk, flung down his pencil in exasperation. His wrist struck his teacup. Tea spilled onto the red leather desktop and onto Fergus's tweed trousers. "Shit!" Fergus said.

On his feet, swearing, mopping with his handkerchief, Fergus thought enviously of the American girl in the red Mini-Cooper he'd seen earlier this morning disappearing up the oak-lined drive. He wished he had such freedom from care. He sighed and went back to feeling angry and frustrated.

"Mine is a noble and ancient Irish family," Desmond Moore had announced to Fergus in his overbearing, pompous manner.

That had been at their first meeting. Desmond Moore had arrived by appointment at Fergus's state-of-the-art office in the Dublin suburb of Ballsbridge.

"I want my family traced, Mr. Callaghan. Our lands were taken from us in the seventeenth century, at the time of Cromwell. This box is my grandfather's records. It's all I have. Search me out my branch of the Moores, Mr. Callaghan. You'll provide a genealogical chart, of course."

"But—"

"And a coat of arms."

Fergus had swallowed. Integrity was his watchword. Genealogy was a tricky business. It had been his business for thirty years. He had a reputation.

That had been two weeks ago. From his office window on Boyleston Street, he had watched the retreating self-assured figure of Mr. Desmond Moore. He had found Mr. Moore unpalatable.

But he had accepted the job. He had accepted it because he was in love. He was in love with the widow, Maureen Devlin, who lived in a decrepit cottage in the woods a half mile from Castle Moore in Wicklow. Ordinarily, he would not have come to Castle Moore at all. He never worked on a client's premises. He kept a distance. But — Maureen. So here he was.

Working with the handful of barely legible documents, he'd scoured regional archives, parish records, land grants. He'd tracked back through both Protestant and Catholic records so as not to miss anything. But even the Genealogical Research Office on Kildare Street at the National Library, usually an unfailing source, had failed him.

Now here he was, unhappily righting a teacup in the library of Castle Moore.

He ran a hand over his balding head. He was fifty years old this past April. This was his third morning at the castle. Disliking every minute.

"Keep on," Desmond Moore had said at eight o'clock this Tuesday morning in the library. He had stood over Fergus, tall, hard-bodied, slapping his leather gloves against his riding breeches; he was off to a horse auction in Wexford. "Let's see some progress. Let's say, on the chart? Let's say by next week?" — and significantly — "I expect you'll come through, Mr. Callaghan" — hands in the pockets of his tweed hunting jacket, yellow-green eyes cold — "considering what I'm paying you."

Provide me a genealogy chart-cum-crest out of your own noggin, Fergus Callaghan. As though he, Fergus Callaghan, were a charlatan, a weasely faker of antecedents . . . so Desmond Moore, an arrogant thirty-six-year-old, could hang a tapestry coat-of-arms on the walls of Castle Moore in county Wicklow, Ireland. Fergus had blushed in shame at the veniality of mankind. A genealogy chart! Woven out of air.

Desmond Moore, with brassy fair hair and cold yellow-green eyes, had an eastern Massachusetts accent. He pronounced *chart* like *chaat*. His great-grandfather, Flann Moore, had been born in Hingham to Mary and Liam Moore, who had emigrated from county Wicklow in one of the "coffin" ships to escape starvation during the potato famine. "My grandfather, Erin, Flann's oldest son, got rich in America," he'd told Fergus when he'd hired him. "Cement, not politics. And not running booze through Canada during Prohibition," Desmond Moore, smoking a Havana cigar: "My father visited Ireland twenty-six years ago and bought Castle Moore. It was Castle Comerford then. The Comerford family were English. Anglo-Irish. Usurpers. Six hundred acres, riding to hounds, the sheep-rich lands of Wicklow, Irish renters in thatched huts. Around nineteen-seventy, the Comerfords touched bottom. Stupid management. Bad investments. Buying the wrong horses." Desmond Moore had laughed; he'd had a high-pitched laugh that had made Fergus wince. "They had to sell. Pa bought it. So the Comerfords were out. Likely weeping and rending their garments. I was ten then; I'm an only child. My mother felt lucky she'd managed the one. We spent a month here every summer after that. I own this place now. My parents died in a plane crash five years ago."

"Any other relatives who'd have Moore family records?" Fergus had asked hopefully.

"None. I've only got one cousin. Winifred. Winifred Moore. She's thirty-eight, two years older than me. A lesbian. Looks like a walrus. Lives in London. Writes poetry. Doesn't believe in antecedents, family stuff. If she'd had family records, she'd likely have torn them up. Or burned them." He shrugged. "A bitch. Doesn't like me any more than I like her." So that had been that.

Standing beside the Florentine desk, Fergus looked for the tenth time at his watch.

Quarter past twelve. *Now.* He shoveled the documents from the desk into his briefcase. His heart beat faster.

Outside, he put the briefcase in the basket of his motorbike. Getting on the bike, he felt sweaty and ugly. He was five feet, seven inches tall and twenty pounds overweight, and his belted tweed jacket was too heavy for the July day, though in this part of Wicklow the summer temperature was sometimes as low as twelve Centigrade, and this morning when he'd arrived at Castle Moore, he had shivered in the chilly air. Lately, he'd felt the cold more. He shrank from thinking of his age. He felt drearily that he had a nerve being in love with a widow who was only thirty-one.

In love. This morning, as always, he'd left his brand-new white Toyota in Dublin and ridden the thirty miles to Castle Moore on the motorbike. That way, returning to Dublin, he could take the bridle path that wound through the woods; he could leave the bike on the path, skirt the bogs, and a five minutes' walk through the woods would bring him to Maureen Devlin's cottage near the hedgerow. He'd just as lief not be seen visiting her; he felt a romantic fool. Others would agree. So he didn't want to leave his Toyota parked on the access road by the hedge for all to see.

He started the throttle on the motorbike and glanced at his watch. Almost twenty past twelve. Just right. Any minute, Maureen would be arriving back at the cottage from her morning job in Ballynagh. His excuse to visit her would be that he'd come for a loaf of her bread. It was always the same excuse. But the truth was that just the sight of Maureen Devlin would ease his heart.

4

Twelve-fifteen. On the narrow access road between the tall hedges of blackberry bushes, thistle, and holly, Maureen Devlin, six years widowed, wheeled her bicycle to a stop. In her bicycle basket were two five-pound bags of flour. In a few minutes she'd be home in the cottage with her feet in a basin of hot water. Then she and Finola would have a tomato sandwich for lunch and a cup of tea. After that, she'd bake the bread. She already had three orders.

Who had left that yellow Saab parked near the hedge? The car door was hanging open. Maureen looked around. Nobody. No sound except for birds and the rackety hum of a mowing machine in the McInnerny's field a quarter mile away.

She wheeled the bicycle toward the break in the hedge. She could feel the pebbles through the soles of her black sneakers, though she'd put on heavy woolen stockings against the early morning cold. The full skirt of her navy cotton dress came almost down to her ankles. She had rolled up the sleeves of her faded red sweater so that the raveled cuffs and elbows didn't show. When Desmond Moore paid her for the loaves, she'd buy the blue dress at Clery's in Dublin for Finola's birthday. Finola would be eight next month. Maureen would take the bus to Dublin on her next day off. She got one day off a month. Mr. Moore wanted six loaves. He had guests. He paid her two pounds a loaf. But the way he handed her the money!

Holding out the pound notes folded the long way, his head turned a little aside, as though to avoid contamination. Lord-of-the-manor dispensing largesse to a beggar. As though those Moores hadn't come up from a dung heap! Come *up?* What did she mean, *up?* Joyce to Desmond Moore was likely only a girl's name. And the poetry of Seamus Heany so much gobbledygook.

But baking bread was the only way she knew to make a living. Working in O'Curry's butcher shop in Ballynagh from six in the morning to twelve noon came to only thirty-five pounds a week. Still, what choice did she have? In Dublin they wanted young girls for the jobs. Besides, her looks were shot—her skin was no longer soft and creamy, and although her curly brown hair still had a burnished gold look, it was striated with crinkled gray strands. Gone was the passion, the surging love and wild whispering nights and her skin throbbing with joy. Now she had no husband. But at least there was Finola.

That yellow car. A Saab. Maybe a man had stopped to urinate behind the break in the hedge? A pity, a perishing pity if he was modest. She had to get home!

She gave a loud cough to warn the fellow urinating and made her way as usual through the break in the hedge.

5

Ah, my darlin' Sheila!" Winifred Moore said. "Look at that baby-sized castle! Eighteen bedrooms. Desmond won't dare protest that he hasn't room to put us up. Though he'd rather have a cobra than me!" The Jeep she drove with careless expertise through Castle Moore's iron gates was from Hertz, rented in Dun Laoghaire when the ferry arrived from England.

It was Tuesday noon, half after twelve, lunchtime. The sun was high. From somewhere in the distance came the sound of a mowing machine. A wind blew the faint sweet-sharp smell of cut grass from a meadow.

"I've a mind to say in front of Desmond's servants that I haven't got two pence to nestle together," Winifred went on. "Desmond'll start blinking his yellow-green eyes in a rage, hating me to say it before servants. 'Blinky' Desmond's how I always think of him." She laughed her full-throated laugh, showing strong white teeth. Her face was square-jawed. Her cheeks had a high russet color, like a stain. There was a look of suppressed humor about her mouth and in her hazel eyes. A worn, tan suede hat with a floppy brim was pulled down over her brown hair, which was twisted up into a knot just above the collar of her navy shirt. She was big-boned, but with little fat. She wore jeans and sturdy brown brogues.

"Winifred, *really!*" Sheila turned to look at her, "You *know* I can deduct our expenses, everything from London on." Sheila

Flaxton owned and edited London's well-known *Sisters in Poetry*, six issues a year, fourteen pounds annually. *Sisters* had published the four poems for which Winifred Moore, born and bred in Dun Laoghaire, this coming Friday, would receive the year's Irish Women's Poetry Award at the Women's Academy in Dublin. The prize was one hundred Irish pounds. A tea would be laid on.

Sheila was forty, short and wispy, with a blue-eyed look of innocence in a somewhat squishy-looking, pasty face. She favored long, flowered skirts and wore flat-heeled shoes that looked vaguely like ballet slippers. She recognized quality in literature and admired Winifred Moore's poetry tremendously. A pity there was little money in it and, often, none.

A maid in a white-aproned, blue uniform was washing a flower-filled iron urn on one of the pedestals that flanked Castle Moore's great curving sweep of stone steps. She turned and squinted toward them as Winifred Moore drove up.

"Rose?" Winifred Moore called out, "Is that you? Remember me . . . from last August? Time of the Kerrygold Dublin Horse Show? Winifred Moore, Mr. Moore's cousin, from London."

"Of course, Miss . . . Ms. Moore." Rose smiled, twisting the damp rag in her hands.

"I didn't phone. I thought I'd just come out. Need digs for a week." Cheap digs, free digs. She was the poor mouse, Desmond the rich one. The pity of it was that she would likely never inherit because Desmond was still young, alas, two years younger than she and healthy as a prize hog. And what if he were to marry? "I figured Mr. Moore would have room to put us up. This is Ms. Flaxton, from London."

"Yes, ma'am. How do you do, ma'am. Mr. Moore's off at a horse sale in Wexford. I'll just let Janet Slocum know you're here. She's the maid in charge. She'll see to getting you settled in."

"A sandwich first thing, if you don't mind, Rose, we're starved. And a lager. Orange juice for Ms. Flaxton, though." Winifred sprang from the Jeep, then reached back, yanked out two soft-pack suitcases, and went up the steps. Sheila followed.

In the great circular hall, Winifred asked, "Any other guests, here?"

"Just one, ma'am. An American young woman, Ms. Tunet. Ms. Torrey Tunet. She arrived last night."

Winifred's brows went up. She grinned at Sheila. "Desmond's latest, no doubt! — another eager young woman who thinks, erroneously, of marriage-cum-Desmond. Disillusionment, followed by tears enough to overflow the Liffey." And to Rose, "That's all?"

"Yes, ma'am. But there'll be a landscaping man. Architect is it? Coming this afternoon."

"Designer, you mean?"

"I guess, ma'am. For laying out the gardens."

"Gardens? What d'you mean, *gardens*, Rose?"

"Something about the taxes on the castle, ma'am. Mr. Desmond saw in an American magazine about how this architect, pardon, ma'am, *designer*, laid out a garden for Laughlin House in county Meath. So last month — June, wasn't it, when he was in America — he visited that architect — designer, I mean, excuse me, ma'am — and . . ." Rose stopped. It was getting too complicated. And Winifred Moore was looking at her as if she wanted to laugh. Rose herself wanted to cry. She so envied people who didn't get flustered but could explain things without blushing and being afraid of mixing everything up.

"Rose," Winifred said, "some fool, some *oaf*, has parked a yellow Saab a couple of hundred yards up the road on the wrong side. I almost ran into it. You might ring up the village police. If the car is still there, it should be ticketed."

"Yes, ma'am."

"What a clever apple, that Desmond!" Winifred said to Sheila. "Landscaping! Taxes. That's what Desmond's about."

They had unpacked and were drinking lager and orange juice and eating ham sandwiches with mustard on Irish soda bread on the stone-flagged balcony of the bedroom that Janet Slocum had chosen for Winifred.

"Delicious bread," Sheila said. "I wish I could gain." She was thin and anemic. "Taxes?"

"In Ireland," Winifred said, "if you have a Georgian house or castle or other historical gem and you open your gardens to the public one month of the year, on a certain day of the week each week of that month, you don't have to pay a property tax."

"So . . . your cousin, Desmond . . . ?"

"It'll save him a pile in taxes. But—" Winifred frowned down at her sandwich—"on second thought, I don't think that's exactly it with Desmond. I wish it were. I wish it were just money."

"You sound weird, darlin'. Maybe your cousin Desmond simply loves gardens. People do."

"Not Desmond. It could be more of his autocratic—that overlord obsession of his."

"What d'you mean, 'overlord'?"

"Oh . . ." Winifred shrugged. "His trying to be an autocrat like those Anglo-Irish Comerfords who once owned this castle." Winifred bit into her ham sandwich. "Getting even, somehow."

"I never can understand," Sheila said, "why people can't just be themselves." She took a last sip of her orange juice. "Anyway, I'm sleepy. I'm going to take a nap. Wake me in an hour, will you?"

6

In Dublin, at lunchtime Torrey left the four-star Shelbourne Hotel on Saint Stephen's Green. The first session of the Hungarian-Belgian conference had been long, grueling, exhausting, and exciting. It was always a high-wire act. Each time she was confident she could perform flawlessly. One misstep wasn't sure death to her career, but close. She loved it.

She walked fast, aimlessly, taking deep breaths. The conference promised to be a challenge. The Hungarian representative had been fussy, contradicting himself, stumbling and stuttering besides. Stock exchange was *tozsde* in Hungarian; gold was *arany*, government was *kormany*. She needed to keep her head clear.

"Oh, look! Lovely rings, aren't they, Albert? And look at those turquoise earrings!" A woman's breathy English voice; Torrey could see her dumpy figure reflected in the jewelry shop window, the man beside her. "Come on, Alice," the man said. "You think I'm the Bank of England?" The two people disappeared up the street.

Why was she standing here on Grafton Street staring into the window of this elegant jewelry shop? Why? Her eyes widened; her heart beat faster. In the back of her mind, was the question lurking: Did they sometimes buy jewelry, as well as sell it?

"*No!*" she said, aloud, vehemently. But —

Money, money, money. Money makes the world go round. . . . Liza Minnelli, spangled, strutting and singing in *Cabaret*. Joel Grey, deadpan, comic-grotesque stick figure mincing on a nightclub stage, rouged cheeks, white face, *Money, money, money.*

She bit her lips. Her theft in North Hawk those years ago had led to such terrible tragedies. But now she had a chance to make up for one of those tragedies: The new surgery for that particular kind of injury, the surgery that could make a person with useless legs stand up and walk again. It could be done. It would cost forty thousand dollars. But if she couldn't pin down the time frame by committing the money within the next three weeks, there would be the wait of a year. Another year of Donna's thin body in the wheelchair.

"Watch out, ma'am!" Two young boys on skateboards swooped past, one after the other. Torrey looked unseeingly after them, then walked slowly up Grafton Street away from the jewelry shop.

7

That goddamned plate of asparagus soup.

Luke Willinger swore under his breath. Jet-lagged, head aching, eyes grainy, he stood on a gravel path in the National Botanic Gardens in Dublin. It was Tuesday. A clock bonged the noon hour; he'd head for Castle Moore after a pub lunch. Desmond Moore had given him the directions. And he had a map, courtesy of the car rental company at the Dublin airport.

But, goddamn it! —

Torrey Tunet. The thief. She was far worse than a thorn in his side. Torrey Tunet. Destroyer of his family. Through her, destruction and death. His mother's tears, his kid brother's numbed little face, the black-bordered notice in the *North Hawk Weekly*.

And now, like him, she was a guest of Desmond Moore at Castle Moore. Tonight, and all week, he'd be sleeping under the same roof as Torrey Tunet. Christ!

All because of the asparagus soup that evening two weeks ago at the Waterside Inn in North Hawk. He saw himself and his new client, Desmond Moore, Massachusetts resident and owner of a castle in Ireland, being ushered by the headwaiter to his table, passing the candlelit table of the little thief, become so elegant a young woman . . . saw Desmond Moore's sleeve accidentally brush her table, rucking up the white tablecloth and sweeping the plate of cold asparagus soup into her lap.

Confusion, laughter, waiters, busboys mopping up . . . Desmond Moore apologizing, Desmond spotting the little thief's book of Gaelic grammar on the table, his curiosity, then his awakening sexual interest as he looked into the gray eyes with their rim of short black lashes.

"Gaelic?" Moore had asked, nodding toward the book.

"Just recreation," she'd answered. She was an interpreter and translator. She would be in Dublin on an interpreting job in a couple of weeks, French and Hungarian. Ireland was neutral terrain. "But I always like to be familiar with a few words of the language of any country where I'm working. Gaelic — I understand it's called 'Irish' these days? — is the official language of Ireland, isn't it? And still used mostly in the Gaeltacht parts of Ireland."

"Dublin? You'll be in Dublin?" Desmond Moore had exclaimed. "I've ruined your dress with that asparagus soup. You've got to be my guest at Castle Moore."

"No, really," with a laugh, "But thanks."

And Moore, "I mean it! Twenty minutes from Dublin. I've a stable, good horses to ride, a lake . . ."

The rotten little thief had slanted a glance at Luke, a malicious glance, cold as dry ice, smoking cold. Almost as though she were daring him to tell Desmond Moore what he knew about her. Or was she remembering the stone shattering the windshield when she was eighteen and necking one night with Jeremy Lowe in Lowe's car on old Forsythe Road? Who else but he, Luke Willinger, had flung it? Ten years ago. He was then twenty-two; now, at thirty-two, he flexed his fingers as though they were gripping another stone.

". . . dating back to 1795" — a Botanic Gardens guide leading a tour group past, was saying — "twenty thousand varieties of plants, also including a rose garden and a vegetable garden."

He left the Botanic Gardens. In a nearby pub he had a meat pie and coffee. An asparagus soup had ruined any pleasure in his forthcoming week at Castle Moore, where he'd be studying the terrain and working out landscaping plans. Desmond Moore was very rich. Luke swallowed the last of the coffee.

Sixteen acres of garden, a challenging project. A good fee was in order.

As for the little thief —

He swore under his breath. Whatever he could spoil for Torrey Tunet, he would spoil. Whatever he could ruin, he would ruin.

8

At half after twelve, Fergus Callaghan wheeled his motor-bike off the bridle path and propped it beside a stand of birches. He'd left his genealogical research for Desmond Moore in the Castle Moore library, and momentarily he felt happily free of it.

He walked through the woods. They were speckled with sunlight, leaves rustling in the breeze.

Fergus reached the cottage. A peaceful-sounding buzzing of grasshoppers came from the weedy grass. A rabbit stood on hind legs, eyed Fergus an instant, and vanished.

"Mrs. Devlin?" Fergus stood before the stone lintel of the cottage and cocked his head, listening. He could hear her singing to herself, an old ballad he couldn't place. The door was not on the latch but open an inch.

Had she heard him? He waited patiently, gazing at the peeling green paint on the door. He'd be happy to paint the door for her. He could bring his electric sander and get rid of the bubbled old flaking paint. He would smooth it down, slick as peeled birch. Or maybe she'd like a different color. He'd bring a color chart; she could choose the color. Dare he suggest it?

He glanced around. Each time he came to the cottage, with the pretense that he'd come for bread, he thought it a pity that Maureen Devlin had no time for a patch of garden. Vegetables, maybe; the pleasure of picking her own vegetables. Not much space for a garden though. There were only a few feet of uncut grass and weeds, enough so that the cottage was not engulfed by the surrounding woods. There was a grassy path worn by Maureen's going daily to and from the cottage, past the little pond and farther on to the break in the hedge in order to reach the road.

Fergus squinted at a trampled patch of weeds beneath one of the small windows. It looked scuffed; a clod of fresh earth was turned up. Perhaps a badger had been investigating, foraging for food. Anyway, that spot got plenty of sun. If ever Maureen had a vegetable garden, it should be there.

Low, her contralto voice humming now. Perhaps she hadn't heard him. "Mrs. Devlin?" he called again, louder.

"Fergus Callaghan? Come in."

He pushed open the door. She was in the old rocker by the stove, soaking her feet in a dishpan. She looked exhausted and beautiful. Her navy skirt was rucked up above her white knees, which showed blue tracings of veins. The water in the battered dishpan reached above her ankles. Fergus felt a painful rush of love and embarrassment. He blushed. "You're fine, I hope, Mrs. Devlin?"

"As fine as ever I'll be, Mr. Callaghan." Tired as she seemed, there was a teasing glint in her dark blue eyes. "You have a good reason for stopping by?"

"Reason? Stopping by?" He felt very warm. "Bread. Yes, I just left Castle Moore; I'd had an appointment. I was going past through the woods on my motorbike when I thought, *bread*. Bread. That you might be baking. Or have baked . . . might have baked . . ."

"You sound like a lad in a Latin class, Mr. Callaghan. What about 'would have baked'?" She reached down and rubbed one of her bare feet. "I suppose you think I have no shame, chatting with a visitor with my feet in a dishpan? I haven't a single loaf on hand, Mr. Callaghan. But I'm baking in an hour. Let's see . . . That's bread for tonight for Castle Moore; and baking in the night again for bread ready in the morning: three orders, two for in the village when I go to work. How many loaves would you be wanting? And when? The oven's only so big. Six at a time is what I can do. Sit down while you're thinking, Mr. Callaghan."

Fergus pulled at his tie. Was she laughing at him? "Well." Should he ask for two loaves? Two, at least. "I'm thinking two loaves. I could pick them up tomorrow noon . . . if that's all right? I have to be at Castle Moore again in the morning. So I can come by afterward." He looked away from her white knees with their delicate blue tracings. Was she ever lonely? Did she sometimes waken in the night and long for a man in her warm bed? Did she keen in the dark for her late husband? Emmet Devlin had been a carpenter. He had fallen from a ladder and struck his head and died two days later in the hospital. Six years ago. The little girl, Finola, had been only two.

"Yes, come by tomorrow. After Castle Moore." Maureen Devlin gave Fergus a sidewise look. "And how are you getting on with the genealogy for Mr. Desmond Moore?"

"Well . . ." Fergus wished she hadn't asked, "You know, like a lot of Irish Americans, Mr. Moore believes — But one can't always trace a family back to . . . ah . . . ahh . . ."

"To Celtic kings? Or only to lesser nobility?" Derision in Maureen Devlin's voice.

"Ah, well . . . ," Fergus said, awkwardly. He was remembering Maureen Devlin's own antecedents, those Anglo-Irish, who they had been. And it had come to this, an old groundsman's cottage with a fireplace kitchen for a living room, with its pine table and chairs and two worn chairs and a shabby couch. The black iron gas stove for the bread. Besides this main room, the cottage had a small bathroom and a bedroom, where Maureen and Finola slept. The cottage belonged to Desmond Moore, as did all the surrounding woodland, and the glens and streams and mountainsides.

Maureen Devlin took a clean, ragged towel from the arm of the rocker and began to dry her feet. So white, they were! "Did you see Finola outside?"

"No." He shook his head.

"She must still be picking blackberries," Maureen said. "I

should buy her a watch. She gets thirty pence a box for the blackberries. I bring the boxes to Ballynagh. She wants a set of doll's dishes with the money when she has enough."

Maureen put down the towel. She smiled at Fergus. "I'm so lucky. Finola's very capable for an eight-year-old. I go to work before six in the morning. Then she makes her own breakfast and does an hour's reading. She's afraid of not keeping up, for when the fall semester starts."

"Kids!" Fergus said, sympathetically.

"She's so good. She fixes us something to eat at noon, for when I get home from work. She makes sandwiches, peanut butter, or chopped egg, or tomato, and wraps them in plastic wrap and puts them in the refrigerator. She has the kettle filled, ready for tea."

Maureen Devlin folded the towel and put it on the arm of the chair. She slipped her feet into flat rubber sandals and stood up.

"You'll have a sandwich or two with us, Mr. Callaghan? And a cup of tea?"

"Well . . ." He wanted to. Oh, how he wanted to! "Thank you."

"I'll just add more water to the kettle," Maureen said. At the stove, she lifted the kettle. Then, motionless, she held the kettle. "Why, I don't—After all my bragging! Finola has forgotten to fill the kettle again. That's the third time. Her mind's off in the sky someplace. And not eating right. A bit worrisome." Slowly she filled the kettle under the faucet. "And where is she? She's always been so responsible."

Fergus, noticing that Maureen's hand trembled a bit as she put the kettle back on the stove, said comfortingly, "Even little kids change from one week to the next."

9

Six hundred acres of mountainous countryside, glens filled
with fern-lined brooks, wooded lands thick with pine and oak,
broad sheep meadows, the lake shaped like a whale, at least to
Rose's mind. Bogs and ponds, hare and quail. Most of the
Moore estate in Wicklow lay north and west of the castle.

Castle Moore itself was of gray stone. It had no turrets or
flying buttresses. It was a combination of styles and periods,
From the north corner rose a tower dating from the sixteen
hundreds. At the foot of the tower, roses and ivy covered a bit
of ruined wall, all that was left of a twelfth-century fort. For
three hundred years, the castle had been Castle Comerford
before falling into the hands of Sean Moore, Desmond Moore's
father. It was Sean Moore who had installed the plumbing
throughout, so that even the servants' rooms had a bathroom
for each two bedrooms. Rose shared her bathroom with the
senior maid.

Tuesday night at midnight in the west wing of the castle,
Rose sat bent over the writing desk in her bedroom. She was
writing to her younger sister, Hannah, who'd gone to London
two weeks ago. Hannah was staying in a bed-sitter in that vast
city. Hannah was a shy girl, fearful, and she knew no one.
Rose had promised to write. Anyway, Rose loved to write letters.

" . . . so that makes the four of them," Rose wrote.

Ms. Torrey Tunet got here last night. Winifred
Moore and her friend Sheila came from London
around noon today. The American landscape man,
Mr. Luke Willinger, arrived early in the afternoon
and went right out and tramped all over what was
once the parkland. He has a long, handsome face;
he's fiercely angry . . . the way he slung his bags into
his room, expensive bags they were, too. He came
back with mud on his brogues, but a little calmer.
He has eyebrows thick as mustaches. Hair like a
thicket, brown and curly. Dark eyes. He likes Winifred Moore, that cousin of Mr. Desmond's from
London. They got on over dinner.

But he, this Luke Willinger, didn't get on with
Ms. Torrey Tunet. Oh, no! I was serving the before-
dinner sherry, only Ms. Winifred's was vodka and
Mr. Desmond's was Jack Daniels, as usual; Ms. Tunet's was a martini and Mr. Willinger's was a Coke.
Ms. Winifred's friend Sheila had sherry. Anyway,
Ms. Winifred was talking very instructivelike about
how there had never till now been any Irish women
poets; it was the male Irish syndrome: "Women were
nothing in Ireland back then, good merely to cook
and breed a pack of kids. Irish poets exalted men
and wrote stupid, romantic nonsense about women.
Only one Irish poet ever pointed out a truth about
the sexes," and then Ms. Winifred quoted from a
poem. I wrote it down later in the kitchen: " 'Bloody
treason, murderous act/Not by women were de-
signed/Bells o'erthrown nor churches sacked/Speak
not ill of womankind.' "

"I get it," Mr. Desmond said, swirling the Jack
Daniels around in his glass, the way he does, "It
means men mess up the world and blame the
women. That it?"

"You're close, for once, Desmond," his cousin
Winifred said, ironiclike, and her friend Sheila Flax-

ton said, "Oh, Winifred!" reproving, as though Ms. Winifred were a naughty child.

Honestly, Hannah! Then Mr. Desmond said, a bit nasty, "Must have been a damned liberal, that Irish poet."

At that, Ms. Torrey Tunet (she looked like a mermaid in a skinny green wool dress) gave a kind of giggle and said, "Fourteenth century. By the poet, Gerald Fitzgerald."

"How did you know that?" Ms. Winifred asked, as though a frog had just spoken English, and Ms. Tunet said, "Oh, well," and shrugged her shoulders.

And then, such a look, sneering, you might say, that Mr. Luke Willinger gave Ms. Tunet, and he said, significantlike, quoting again from the poem, " ' . . . murderous act/Not by women were designed'?" like a question, and he added, staring at Ms. Tunet, "Mr. Gerald Fitzgerald was not wholly right."

I was stationed by the sideboard for when Mr. Desmond would nod, but he only poured himself another Jack Daniels. He was smiling and very flushed as though he were enjoying Mr. Willinger being sharp to Ms. Tunet.

"You read Gaelic?" Ms. Winifred asked Ms. Tunet, surprised, "Gaelic poetry?" Then it came out what Ms. Tunet does for a living, interpreting at diplomats' meetings and Common Market delegates' sessions and such, but not much money in it. She loves it. She's all about words, languages. She can skip around like hopscotch in words and languages.

I got the signal then from Mr. Desmond, and I went to the kitchen. But I heard Ms. Winifred say, "Genes, it's all in the genes! They've made tests. Languages are natural to some folks. That's a scientific truth! You can check it out on the Internet."

I have to go now. Take good care of yourself, Hannah. It will be all right. I know it.

Rose sighed and wrote, "Your loving sister," and signed her name.

Hannah was the youngest child, then herself, then the three older brothers who lived in Cork. She and Hannah had always been close, so close.

Rose picked up the pen and added a postscript: "That garda sergeant, Jimmy Bryson, who likes you? I talked to him on the telephone this afternoon. About a yellow car, a Saab that someone had left parked on the road. Up near the break in the hedge. Ms. Winifred almost ran into it. Jimmy said he'd go see. He asked after you."

10

A cloud drifted across the moon and the dark bulk of the stables merged with the woods. Desmond Moore stumbled and said, "Bloody Christ!" and turned on his flashlight. "Mind the muck."

"Right," Luke said. He wished gloomily that he were in bed. It was already midnight, but after dinner Desmond Moore had wanted to sketch out a couple of landscaping ideas in the library. Desmond was a little drunk, which didn't stop him from downing two more sizeable whiskeys. Then he had insisted on Luke seeing his new horse, "A bay mare I got at a sale in Wexford, a beauty, Darlin' Pie. You've got to see her. Bought her this morning. Had them bring her this afternoon. . . . Brian!" he called suddenly into the darkness.

A light went on in a casement window above the end stable, a minute later there was the clatter of feet on stairs; from a horse stall came a neighing and a stamping of hooves. A slight figure appeared and crossed the stable yard. "Mr. Desmond?"

"Brian Coffey, my know-it-all: trainer, groomer, manager." Moore made the introduction with a drunkenly wide sweep of a hand. They stood in the light of a glaring bulb above the stable door. Brian Coffey was a thin young man, red hair rumpled from sleep. He wore well-slept-in striped boxer shorts and a beige T-shirt. He squinted at them as though the light hurt his eyes. His white, freckled face looked drugged with sleep.

"Brian's an expert on horseflesh; took him with me this morning to the horse sale. He went over Darlin' Pie like a blind guy feeling a new girlfriend's body. Perfect little mare. Let's have a look, Brian."

Smell of fresh hay, clean concrete paving, water troughs, tack neatly hung beside each stall; neighing, rustling, snorting. The end stall. Luke gazed at the gentle-eyed little mare who nickered softly. Darlin' Pie. He didn't care if Darlin' Pie went up in a puff of smoke. He didn't care that this morning Desmond Moore had gone and bought a bay mare. He was still jet-lagged. Sleep was what he cared about. And he was chilled by the night air, though he wore a heavy wool oatmeal cardigan of Desmond Moore's. He'd come to Ireland to do a landscaping job. That was all.

In the stall, Darlin' Pie stamped a hoof, arched her neck, and shook her head.

"Look at that!" Desmond Moore said softly, "Noble, her bloodline! I've got her papers, her whole lineage! Her . . . genealogy." He gazed at the mare for a long moment, then turned away. "Let's go. It's frigging cold out here."

Leaving the stable yard, Luke glanced back. Brian Coffey was standing in the stable doorway under the light, looking after them. Then the light went out.

11

At four o'clock Torrey arrived back at Castle Moore, changed into jeans and loafers, and went for a walk in the woods. She'd had no particular destination; she'd simply wanted to enjoy the woods. She walked pleasurably through a shady glen and came to a bridle path. Through the trees she glimpsed a run-down cottage, old-looking, somehow sadly romantic. She walked on along the bridle path through sun and shadow, hearing birds singing and the rustle of small animals in the brush and smelling honeysuckle and pine. Then, drawn by the shadiness, she walked deeper into the woods. She had gone on hardly ten minutes when the ground fell away and began to feel spongy under her feet. She smelled the rank odor of rotting vegetation. Bogs. Better to turn back, find dry, higher ground, fresh piny scents.

She turned to skirt a bog and saw something puzzling, something that, of course, could not be, but . . . She went closer.

A hand. On the brown, decayed surface of the bog, it looked oddly like an exotic, pinkish tan flower growing out of the waterlogged, spongy ground. A hand.

It couldn't be. It was. Torrey went closer, squinting, placing her loafer-clad feet carefully on the marshy ground. She knew it was a bog. Bog, from the Gaelic *bogach* meaning "soft ground." It would be swampy with rotted vegetation. She might sink in.

Two feet away, she leaned forward. A man's hand. On his hairy, half-submerged wrist, a wristwatch. It was only when Torrey saw the watch that she believed what she was looking at. It meant that below the swampy ground would be a man's body.

She backed away, appalled. The stench from the bog rose to her nostrils. Under there, a body. Maybe the man had gotten drunk and lost his way and fallen into the bog; maybe because of the rain it had been dangerously swampy and he had been too drunk to save himself. She shuddered. She must race back to Castle Moore and have them call the gardai, report this horrifying—"Yes, Officer . . . Around four o'clock I returned from my day in Dublin and was taking a stroll through the woods when I came upon . . ."

But for a moment, Torrey felt too sickened to move, too filled with pity and horror. She just stood staring at the man's hand, the sun glinting on the wristwatch.

A voice behind her said, "What's so fascinating in a bog, Torrey, when I've got six hundred acres of mountain and meadow, lakes and pools and glens . . . some of the most stunning views in county Wicklow?"

She turned. But Desmond Moore was no longer looking at her. His gaze had gone beyond her. He was staring into the bog. "What the hell?"

He went closer until he stood at her shoulder, looking at the pink-tan flower that was not a flower. Then he whistled. "My, God! I'd better call Ballynagh. Inspector O'Hare."

12

At 4:45, Insp. Egan O'Hare and Sgt. Jimmy Bryson of Ballynagh, tugged and heaved until they had dragged the man from the bog and flopped him over onto firm ground. An ugly sight, the man's sodden, corpulent body in a weedy tangle of brownish yellow vegetation.

Silent watchers stood all around: Desmond Moore and the American woman who'd found the body; Moore's cousin Winifred, who kept muttering, "Poor bastard!" and Winifred's English friend with the pasty face and a handkerchief to her mouth. Desmond Moore's other guest, a gangling American with a pencil behind his ear, stood biting the inside of his cheek and frowning.

Inspector O'Hare, a heavyset, keen-eyed man in his fifties, knelt and gently wiped muck from the dead man's face. A blunt-featured face, open eyes bulging, a man possibly in his sixties. His sodden hair was discernibly gray. He wore an open-throated, short-sleeved, navy knit shirt, tan pants, leather loafers.

"Anybody know this man?" O'Hare looked around. A negative shaking of heads. A wind stirred leaves in the trees. Otherwise, silence.

"Anyone seen him about?"

No luck there either. O'Hare frowned at the man's bulging eyes, then squatted down and wiped muck from the thick neck.

He tipped up the man's head and studied his neck. Then O'Hare stood up and unsnapped the cellular phone he wore at his waist.

"What's going on?" Desmond Moore asked, shifting impatiently.

"Just routine." O'Hare tapped in the number of headquarters of the *Garda Siochana,* the Irish police, at Dublin Castle, Phoenix Park. In a moment he spoke to a sergeant. Would they send a van with the technical staff and their equipment. "A quarter mile west of Castle Moore, village of Ballynagh. . . . No. Undetermined." He clicked off the phone. He looked around and said politely, "No need to wait."

He watched them trail off toward Castle Moore, then stood with arms folded, looking down at the dead man.

"What d'you think?" Sergeant Bryson said.

"Strangled," O'Hare said. "That's my off-the-record guess. Those purple marks on his throat . . ." He ran a hand over his chin. "That yellow Saab on the road could be his. Check it out and have it towed to Kelly's garage."

"Yes, Inspector."

Alone, O'Hare waited. By five-thirty, the van with the *Garda Siochana* technical staff and their equipment arrived from Dublin. Carefully, efficiently, they inched over the ground and took the photographs. By six-thirty, they were through. They lifted the bundle of the dead body onto a gurney and carried it through the woods to the van, which they'd had to park in the castle drive.

At 6:45 Inspector O'Hare arrived back at the Ballynagh garda station. Sgt. Jimmy Bryson was waiting, excited, face flushed.

"The yellow Saab," he said, when O'Hare wearily sat down at his desk, "a car-for-hire."

Tea mug in hand, Bryson stood at the inspector's shoulder looking down at the car-hire contract he'd placed on the desk. "Hired from Murray's Europcar. No keys in the car. The boot was unlocked but nothing in it, just the emergency equipment.

This Murray's contract was in the glove compartment. And their complimentary map. That's all."

Sergeant Bryson sipped tea, happy for a bit of a mystery. He felt competent and pleased with himself, the sunny weather, and his job. He was twenty-one, narrowly built, and wore his dark blue uniform with style, his stomach held in to do the uniform justice. He loved his life.

The Ballynagh police station was a glass-fronted room, twenty feet wide. It was on Bishop Street, the main street of the village, and across from O'Malley's Pub. When the wind blew from the east, it smelled of beer.

"Petrol?" O'Hare asked.

"Near empty. Could've made it to Dublin. Just."

Inspector O'Hare ran a guiding finger on the car-for-hire contract. "Lars Kasvi, 19 Vuorikatu, Helsinki, Finland. A Saab, automatic shift. Rented at the airport in Dublin, so he might've come by way of England. Heathrow. He got Murray's 10-percent discount for drivers over fifty-five."

The phone rang. It was Chief Superintendent O'Reilly of the Murder Squad at Dublin Castle. "Strangled," O'Reilly said. "Wallet was in his pants pocket. Lars Kasvi, fifty-eight, Finnish. Married, invalid wife, children, grandchildren, he —"

"Kasvi." Just as O'Hare had suspected. "Lars Kasvi left a yellow Saab from Murray's on the access road near Castle Moore yesterday morning. We just had it hauled in."

"That right? A minute, O'Hare."

O'Hare waited. He could hear Chief Superintendent O'Reilly talking to someone, a murmur of voices. Then O'Reilly came back on the wire.

"O'Hare? We've got his business notebook with names and addresses. Buyer of woolen goods for Stockmann's in Helsinki. Stockmann's is the biggest department store in Finland; fills an entire block. Mr. Kasvi was on a buying trip. We'll check his sources in Cork, Limerick, Wicklow, and so on; might turn up something. He visited six counties."

"Any theory? Though it's still too early —"

"Right. But his wallet was empty. Only a couple of pounds

in a pants pocket. Robbery a possible motive. So many teen-agers lately getting high on Ecstasy, other drugs, needing money. Aside from that, I've been in touch with Helsinki. Kasvi was a heavy drinker. Also, in Helsinki, given to picking up women in Sibelius Park. Has a snow white polar dog, his companion. Change that to past tense."

"Strangled," O'Hare said. "So it would have to have been a man? The killer?"

"Or a woman. Mr. Kasvi had such a high level of alcohol in his system, he couldn't have fought off a mosquito. Or let's say a woman of average strength. Maybe no bigger than the young woman who found the body. That American woman."

"Miss Tunet. Miss Torrey Tunet."

"Yes, Superintendent." O'Hare nodded into the phone. He would, of course, check Miss Tunet's background. Routine.

At seven-thirty, Inspector O'Hare telephoned the news of the dead man's identity, and the confirmation that he had been murdered. By dinnertime at Castle Moore, when Rose brought the bucket of ice into the library for the before-dinner drinks, they all knew.

"God! *Murder!*" Winifred Moore said, grinning. She raised her drink, which was vodka, and looked around the library at the others. "Here's to civilization on planet Earth . . . I'm starved; it's almost eight o'clock. I could eat a cow. Or a sheep." From her place near the library fireplace, she glanced at Luke, who was drinking a Coke with a twist. "You an al-coholic?"

"Yup." He never hid it. Let people make of it what they would. In the bull's-eye mirror above the library fireplace he eyed Torrey Tunet. She looked tired and sober. It irritated him that tiredness became her, softened something in her. She wore wide-cut, black satin slacks and a red silk knitted sweater that clung to her delicately curved body. He thought of his enraged throwing of the stone through the windshield years ago in North Hawk. She knew it had been him because the next morning he had found the stone in a box, ribbon-tied, at his front door.

"That damned Finn!" Desmond Moore burst out angrily. Desmond was on his second drink. His cousin Winifred and her poetry editor friend Sheila were finishing their first.

"That damned Finn!" Desmond repeated. "It'll get about that there was a murder on my property. It'll militate against people coming to visit my projected gardens."

"Quite the opposite, you fool!" Winifred said scornfully. "People *love* blood and gore."

"A fool, am I?" Desmond gave his cousin a baleful look. His eyes were bloodshot, had been bloodshot all day. He stared at Winifred with hatred. Then he smiled at her, a cold, mirthless drawing back of his teeth. "But I'm a rich fool, Winnie, keep that in mind. A fool who might even . . . marry." He wet his lips, half-turned and smiled at Torrey, then looked back at Winifred, "So, Winnie, my dear cousin, don't have any great expectations."

Winifred Moore took a gulp of her vodka. Luke saw her face redden, her usual good humor abruptly eclipsed like a light going out. Something like misery took its place — then, rage. He saw Sheila Flaxton quickly put a restraining hand on Winifred's arm and shake her head in warning; but Winifred yanked her arm free.

"I'd like to go to the airport," Winifred said between gritted teeth, "and hire a small plane and fly it over all of Dublin County, trailing smoke that spelled out 'Desmond Moore is an asshole.' "

"Ahh," Desmond said, still smiling. "Indeed?"

"Indeed," Winifred said, and threw her drink in Desmond's face.

Desmond wiped drops of vodka from his chin. For a half minute he stood gazing at Winifred. Then he turned and walked with deliberate steps to the Florentine desk. He pressed an inlaid corner of the desk; there was a click, and he pulled open a narrow drawer. He took out an oblong maroon leather case and opened it to reveal a diamond necklace on a black velvet cushion. He held up the glittering necklace with a single emerald pendant.

"Heavens!" An awed gasp from Sheila.

Desmond turned to Torrey Tunet. "I've noticed a couple of times how much you admired the portrait of my grandmother wearing this necklace, the portrait on the staircase. The necklace is a family heirloom. I'd like you to wear it during dinner this evening. It would suit what you're wearing. In fact, it suits you." He went smiling to Torrey, stepped behind her, and clasped the necklace around her neck; his fingers lingered an instant longer on her nape, then slid away, caressingly, down her back.

"But . . . *No!*" Torrey said. She looked stunned. And — Luke had to give her that — stunning. Lightly tanned throat sparkling with diamonds down the V-necked red silk sweater, the emerald pendant between her breasts. He felt a sexual stirring; in helpless anger he warred against it.

A small cough from the doorway. Rose, white-aproned, eyes downcast, announcing dinner.

13

The hell with her!" Desmond poured a Bordeaux into the Baccarat glasses. He felt excited, almost feverish. The green emerald between Torrey Tunet's breasts caught the candlelight in the centerpiece of the dining table. They were sitting down to a dinner of grilled salmon with leek sauce and potatoes mashed with spring onions. There were just the three of them: he and Torrey Tunet and Luke Willinger. His cousin Winifred had strode from the castle snorting like a dragon, followed by her acolyte, Sheila Flaxton. They'd climbed into the Jeep and torn off to Dublin for dinner with "civilized creatures," as Winifred had flung at him hoarsely in parting.

"Gone to some leather-jacketed dyke hang-out, for Christ's sake," Desmond had said to Luke and Torrey.

He felt the expensive weight of the Baccarat glass in his hand. He looked at the exquisite cut on the crystal. It signaled more than richness, more than luxury. It signaled authority. Power. He felt it almost as a sexual ecstasy. For those hundreds of years, the English aristocracy in Ireland, in their great mansions and castles, had wielded a cruel power throughout Ireland. But that was the time of his forebears. The power had shifted. Things political had changed, would change more. But he was not one for Sinn Fein. Not one for the IRA. Never, for him, to band together with anyone. Always, as if in some twilight place, he got revenge his own way. Power, through riches, was his. *His!* Not any longer for a Moore to be a stable boy under the lash of English lords. Arrogant lords. The Comerfords. He gave a sudden shudder.

"Why is it so hot!" Torrey Tunet was looking at him, questioningly.

At her words, he saw the wine glass in his hand, felt the warmth of the evening, and then — another shudder; it was always, *always* as though he himself were a stable boy of that cruel time, feeling the searing whiplash. He could feel the red welts rising, the scream in his throat.

"*Why* is it suddenly so *hot?*" Torrey appealed to him. Beads of perspiration were on her upper lip. She blew a breath upward and reached for her glass of water; ice tinkled.

Desmond forced himself from that strange miasma of the past that so often overtook him. He blinked his eyes; he became aware of the humid warmth of the evening. He watched Torrey lift the glass to her lips. Did she know what the shape of her lower lip did to men? He had plans for this young lady.

"Kasvi," Luke Willinger said, "Lars Kasvi. Poor fellow. And his family in Finland. Makes me think how in *The Virgin Spring*, that Swedish movie of Ingmar Bergman's, the thieves who raped and murdered the girl stole her robe. That bit of thievery gave them away." He half-turned away from Torrey on his right. He looked through the great arched dining gallery windows to where beyond the long sweep of cropped lawn lay the woods. It was barely dark and the sky was a wash of lilac and magenta, darkening to purple; the woods looked black. "Kasvi," he said, "Lars Kasvi driving along a country road in Ireland was possibly —"

"Plant," Torrey Tunet said, sounding absentminded.

"What?" Luke looked at her.

"In Finnish. *Kasvi* means 'plant' in Finnish."

"Oh." Was there any language that Torrey Tunet didn't dance around in? The air had grown thick and humid. Tendrils of dark curls, dampened by perspiration, clung in flat, Matisse-like clusters to her brow; they looked varnished on. Luke wanted to shed his jacket; he could feel a trickle of perspiration sliding down his rib cage under his shirt.

"Weird, this heat," Desmond said. "It happens sometimes. We're at fifty-two to sixty-eight Fahrenheit in July in this part of Wicklow, then — bang! — humidity comes in thick as a fog. It rolls up to the castle from the lake beyond the southwest fields a quarter of a mile away. The lake itself is like a cold drink."

"Ummm," Torrey Tunet said. There was dew on her upper lip. "Sounds delicious."

Desmond, looking at her, ran a finger along the rim of his wine glass. "I've a bathhouse at the lake. Stock of towels and the like. A case of lager. Swimsuits for the chaste or modest." He leaned toward Torrey. "Why not? After dinner, why not cool off the way God meant us to?"

"Yes," Torrey said. "Why not?"

14

They left right after dinner, pushing back their chairs and going out through the great hall.

It was a ten-minute walk on a grassy path. Tree branches above the path were dark against the magenta; there was a vestigal moon, still white. There was no breeze; here and there a firefly's momenary flicker.

Desmond led the way, talking over his shoulder about the Moore estate, but feverishly conscious of Torrey walking behind him at Luke Willinger's side. In his mind's eye, he saw her legs moving against her loose, black pants, saw the swell of her breasts with the emerald blazing between them, saw the small brown mole on her neck beneath her left ear, the diamond necklace sparkling on her throat. He had planted a seed; what would she do with it? Very soon he would know. He swallowed, tickled at the possibilities. Either way, she would lose.

"Southwest," Luke Willinger said, "Dublin's to the northeast, right?"

"Yes . . . I've six hundred acres," Desmond said. "Toward the northeast are the mountains, very wild; below are ancient sheep meadows; then the woods that harbor deer and small animals. The bridle path that meets the road goes through those northeast woods."

"That's where I found Lars Kasvi's body," Torrey said.

"East of the bridle path is a mess of swamp and bogs. Farther on, toward the access road to Dublin, are three or four scummy pools. Nearby only an old groundsman's cottage is still livable. The woman who bakes the bread we had tonight lives there."

"Romantic," Torrey said, "Old cottages, thatched roofs. And now, cars for hire, flights into Ireland on a dozen airlines, the Irish police force: the garda — or gardai if it's plural — officially the *Garda Siochana*, that's Gaelic."

"Meaning what?" Luke Willinger asked.

"Protector of the Peace," Torrey said. She looked up through the trees; the white moon was now almost gold. Between herself and Luke Willinger there could never be peace. Luke Willinger, a man with style and humor and with a touch of genius in his work, owed it to himself to despise her. Death had created a chasm between them. A death she had caused. And now, ironically, here he was at Castle Moore.

"There's the lake," Desmond said.

Through the trees ahead, she glimpsed the flat silver of the lake; a fragment of fog like a piece of cotton lay over it.

15

At Pizzaland Pizzeria at Saint Stephen's Green, Winifred and Sheila were eating deep-dish pizza because Winifred had been too angry to settle down to a calm, normal dinner in a Dublin restaurant, despite Sheila's expense account.

"God! How I hate him!" Winifred said bitterly, "Not to mention that I got cheated. Desmond, that arrogant pig, inherited it all. Even though my father and Desmond's father were brothers."

"You never did say why he got it. Do you know?"

"Of course I know. My poor father, Danny Moore! Officially, he died under a wagon in Dun Laoghaire, but actually he died of maudlin self-pity helped along by booze. My father was brother to Desmond's father, Sean. When pa was twenty, he visited Ireland and fell in love with a shipfitter's daughter named Sarah O'Shea from Dun Laoghaire. He got her pregnant and married her, though the Moores raised holy hell.

"She wouldn't leave her family in Dun Laoghaire, so pa stayed and went to work clerking in a ship's chandler's shop . . . to the shame of the Moores in America. They'd maybe have forgiven him, but ma died in childbirth when I was born. In some crazy heartbroken way, pa blamed the family, as though they were some vengeful, spiteful power who'd done it to punish him and my mother. He swore he'd take nothing from them, ever. And he never did."

"So *that's* how you grew up in Ireland. You never wanted to say."

"Yes . . . Grew up in Dun Laoghaire, with the piers reaching out to the sea, the harbor with the mail boats leaving every day taking emigrants from Ireland to seek their fortune in London. I ached with longing, a dirty-faced kid whose father wept in pubs. I grew up scribbling, then cleaning rooms in a guest house and taking the bus to Dublin to study lit at Trinity. Then the bus back to Dun Laoghaire, where I'd stand at the harbor watching the boats move off, whistles tooting. A month after my father was killed, I bought my boat ticket. It cost all the money I had. I was nineteen."

"So your father was a ship's chandler's clerk? If the Moores were so pissed—so angry at your father—how come you're in line to inherit Castle Moore?"

"Moores for the Moores. It was in Sean's will that the Moore property devolve on the Moores. So if Desmond died and left no wife or progeny, the property would go to Danny or his progeny. That's me, darlin'." She dropped her pizza crust on the table. "*Damn* Desmond! I could have done with a decent dinner and a bottle of Desmond's vintage wine. And Rose said there was a rhubarb pie and some special bread a woman bakes for Desmond. *Damn* him! And tonight. Just trying to torture me!" She glared at her pizza crust. "Sometimes I'd like to kill Desmond."

16

In the wooden changing cubicle beside the lake, Torrey pulled off the silk knitted sweater. She got out of her flat black sandals and slipped down her pants and panties. The swimsuits were in a big woven basket. They were all bikinis. She chose a dark blue that looked a fairly decent fit and put it on.

She unclasped the diamond necklace and laid it on top of her clothes on the folding canvas stool. She stood still, looking down at it. She was aware of a faint rustle of leaves; a small breeze had come up. She heard voices outside, Desmond Moore and Luke Willinger making their way down to the lake. Their voices became fainter. She heard splashing; they were already swimming about.

She turned from the necklace. Don't think. *Don't think.* There was a basket of Japanese rubber sandals near the little swing door. She chose a pair and put them on.

She opened the door to leave. For a moment she stood there, looking out. In the moonlight she saw that the two swimmers were already a couple of hundred feet from the edge of the lake.

She turned back. She picked up the diamond necklace and clasped it around her neck. She ran out and down to the lake. She waded, gasping, into the icy water, then dived into the blackness.

17

In the stables, the bay mare, Darlin' Pie, neighed and stamped.
" 'Tis the moonlight," Brian Coffey mumbled, turning in his
bed. His rooms were a former gardener's quarters at one end
of the U-shaped stable, right over the mare's stall. He'd put
Darlin' Pie in box number three because he liked to keep an
eye on a new-bought mare, "tune in to her," was the way he
put it.

He sat up. Eyes half-closed, he got out of bed and went
sleepily to the bathroom. When he came back he sat down on
the edge of the bed, head hanging, elbows on knees, pushing
his fingers through his red hair, rubbing his scalp.

Outside the stables, voices. Brian lifted his head, listening.
Mr. Desmond's voice, a woman's, and that landscape man's,
the American's. They'd be coming from the lake. Three people.
Usually it was just Mr. Desmond and a woman. Once it was
an English society girl; another time a student from Trinity
College; once, a village girl, just a kid. All kinds.

Brian pulled the sheet back over him, shut his eyes, and
burrowed his face in the pillow. Some things he didn't want
to know about.

18

I don't *know!*" Torrey Tunet said, flinging out her hands. "I forgot I was wearing it! Then when I came out of the water, it was gone! *Gone.* Oh, *God!*"

By Luke's estimate, this was the sixth time Torrey Tunet had repeated those words since they'd left the lake and started up the path in the moonlit dark. She was walking ahead with Desmond, who had a comforting arm around her shoulders and kept nodding his head.

"In the morning, we'll get a diver," Desmond said, also for the sixth time ... or was it the seventh? "Though frankly, I doubt we'll find it. Muddy bottom. You could sink the Eiffel Tower in that lake and never find it. Though maybe, on the shore ..." and he shrugged.

"I'm so terribly sorry," Torrey said. "Your family heirloom! Your grandmother's necklace! Was it insured?"

"Not for nearly its worth," Desmond said, "unfortunately."

Luke was treading on their shadows in the moonlight, the shadow of the little thief and Desmond Moore ... only this time, was she innocent? There was no place on her body that she could have hidden the necklace. She didn't even wear a bra under that thin silk sweater, that was easy to see. She had on just the black sandals, possibly skimpy panties, and those loose, thin black pants over her neatly rounded buttocks.

"You might really have dropped it in the dressing cubicle,"

Desmond said reassuringly for maybe the eleventh time. But the three of them had fruitlessly searched the dressing cubicle, inching over it, in case Torrey had absentmindedly taken off the necklace and dropped it somewhere before going out to swim.

Luke frowned. Something bothered him, something peculiar about Desmond Moore's reaction when Torrey had discovered the loss of the necklace and cried out in dismay. Puzzled, he gazed at the dark bulk of Desmond Moore with his arm around Torrey Tunet. He could have sworn that Desmond had been pleased at the loss of the necklace. But how was that possible? Unless the necklace was actually overinsured?

They were passing the stables when a suspicion about Torrey, the little thief, surfaced again in Luke's mind: a possibility. To his surprise, he found himself edgily trying to brush it away; it was as though he wanted to believe her innocent. Was she?

Three A.M. In black jeans, navy turtleneck, and sneakers, she went softly down the stone steps and out by the smaller side door of the west wing to the path that led to the lake. The moon was still high, but anyway she'd brought the pencil flashlight that she never traveled without.

Dead still at the lake; a duplicate moon lay on the lake's surface. At the pebbled fringe of the lake she shone the flashlight back and forth on the pebbles until she located the bigger gray stone. It was the size of her fist. She counted four stones to the right of the gray stone, and there, indeed, was the broad, flat piece of shale. She knelt and put down the pencil flashlight.

She lifted the piece of shale and drew out the diamond necklace.

He ducked into the bushes beside the path just in time. A whiff of perfume reached him as she went past. Something shone on her cheeks, as though the moonlight had turned her face to marble.

So! As he'd suspected! Still a thief. Was there some moral blindness in her mind, some inability to understand what her crooked actions did to people? This time there was no suicide and heartbreak and no tragic accident that destroyed a life. But in North Hawk, Massachusetts, she had destroyed more than one life; because what about the younger girl, her friend, now spending her life in a wheelchair?

He plucked a leaf from the bush and chewed it. Bitter. But this time the tragedy was not to someone else. This time the tragedy was the corruption of Torrey Tunet's own decency, her morale. It was a rape of what she had since — supposedly — tried to become. Don't! *Don't do it!* he wanted to cry out to her. But she had already done it.

So bitter, that leaf in his mouth, so greenly bitter. What ailed him? Strange, to be so disappointed in Torrey Tunet, whom he hated and despised. Weird to be so angry at her for thieving again. Or —

It hit him like a shock. Not so weird after all. Torrey Tunet and *him?* Impossible!

And what was worse, he was going to turn her in.

19

In the bedroom she slid the necklace into the top drawer of the dressing table. She shed the black jeans, turtleneck, and sneakers; sat down at the dressing table; and creamed off her makeup, looking into her eyes in the mirror. She knew what she was going to do. Could she go through with it? She had to. But what was the extreme of temptation? She needed the forty-thousand-dollar miracle that lay in the dressing table drawer.

The phone buzzed.

"Torrey?" It was Myra Schwartz, Interpreters International, Inc., in New York. "Torrey? Lucky you gave me that bedroom phone number. Some fancy castle! Anyway—I know it's four A.M. in Ireland, but I thought you'd want to know. Good news! I've got an assignment for you. Right up your alley. In Turkey, Ankara, with the French, some brouhaha about a boycott. You'll be there three weeks. Tell me you're pleased."

"Myra, that's great. Thanks." It would be money in the thousands, maybe several thousand dollars. But not enough. She suppressed a wild desire to laugh.

"When?"

"Middle of August. In six weeks."

"Count on me," Torrey said, "and *teşekkur.*"

"What's that?"

" 'Thanks,' in Turkish."

"Oh, God," Myra said, "I barely speak basic English."

20

Two hours before dawn, Rose, in her loose pink cotton night-gown, sat at the little desk scribbling a hasty note to Hannah in London. The note was more like a postscript to yesterday's letter. But remembering what a naïve child Hannah was, Rose, sleepless, had gotten out of bed and at the desk was sending these few more words, "About Sgt. Jimmy Bryson — When you come back to Ireland, if you go out with him and it would be nice if you would, you always liked Jimmy Bryson — *you don't have to tell him everything.* Some secrets are better kept."

Rose sealed the note and addressed it. Better not to tell Hannah about the murdered Finnish man; a murderer loose in the vicinity of Castle Moore would only set Hannah's mind to worrying about Rose.

Back in bed to keep warm, she saw the light of dawn, heard birds chirping. She had slept badly, she had been so upset and embarrassed — Ms. Winifred throwing her drink, vodka it was, in her cousin Desmond's face. Not that she could rightly blame Ms. Winifred, her so poor and Mr. Desmond so rich, and him taunting her that way, clasping the necklace around Ms. Tunet's neck.

Ms. Tunet! If only Hannah, so soft and trusting, were more like Ms. Tunet! Ms. Tunet wasn't easy to fool. Ms. Tunet had given what they called a skeptical look at Mr. Desmond, such big gray eyes she had! A skeptical look. She'd known somehow that Mr. Desmond had only been using her to torture Ms. Winifred, clasping that necklace around her neck and saying, "Wear it during dinner." He was like a bullfighter waving a red flag before a bull, maddening it. Ms. Winifred wasn't a bull; she was a poet. Still . . .

21

At eight o'clock in the morning, Fergus Callaghan arrived on his motorbike at Castle Moore to pursue his genealogical research. Rose brought him a morning cup of tea in the library and told him about a dead man found in a bog west of the castle. "Strangled!" Rose said, eyes wide with horror. "Murdered!"

Fergus Callaghan stiffened with alarm. A murderer roving about! And those bogs were near to Maureen Devlin's cottage. Maureen could be in danger. Maybe it was a madman, a serial killer. And Finola played in the woods. She, too, was a possible victim. This past Tuesday, when Maureen had given him a cup of tea and a sandwich for lunch, Finola hadn't showed up by the time he'd left. Then, on the way back to Castle Moore from Maureen's cottage, he'd glimpsed Finola in the woods. She must've been playing "buried treasure." He'd watched, smiling, as she dug a hole beneath a bramble bush and buried something she took from a bag she'd brought. And it was such an oddly secret, listening way she'd hunched her shoulders and kept turning her head! He'd chuckled, remembering his boyhood when he was about Finola's age. When she'd gone, he'd noticed something glittering among the brambles, something Finola must have dropped. He picked it up. A doll's shoe, black patent leather, with a pink rosette; a tiny fake diamond centered in the rosette, it was the glitter of the glass diamond that had caught his eye. He was surprised. An expensive shoe like this belonged to an expensive doll. Yet, would Maureen spend such money on a doll? Still, Finola might have saved the money for it herself, selling the blackberries she picked.

Carefully, he wrapped the little shoe in his handkerchief, then scooped away a few handfuls of dirt above Finola's buried treasure and laid the little shoe in the hole and covered it over, tamping down the earth and smiling to himself. Would Finola, later coming to dig up her treasure, think a leprechaun had found the shoe she'd dropped, and put it there for her all wrapped up? Leprechauns, in Irish folklore, were believed to reveal the hiding place of treasure if you caught them.

But now he shuddered, thinking of the dead man found in the bog. He had only a couple of hour's work to finish up in the library at Castle Moore, then back to Dublin. He wished he could protect Maureen and Finola in some way. If he could only think how.

22

The clock was striking ten when Torrey came briskly down the great staircase. She wore her navy suit and a beige silk shirt. She had brushed her nape-length hair sleekly back behind her ears. A small purse swung from her shoulder. She carried her briefcase. She wouldn't even have a cup of tea. She'd have a bun and coffee at the Shelbourne. "Foreign" in Hungarian was *kulfoldi*, "expire" was *lejar*, "document" was *okmany*. Hungarian was easy.

But before she left —

At the foot of the stairs, she paused an instant, smiling. This morning she would have smiled at the devil himself.

She went into the cavernous kitchen. Rose was standing at the long table putting rolls into a basket lined with a blue-checked napkin. A hanging brass lamp shed yellow light down onto the table. It was a gray, cloudy morning; no sun came through the windows. "Morning, Rose. Is Mr. Moore down yet?"

"Yes," Rose told her. "Mr. Desmond's been out touring the grounds with Mr. Willinger since eight o'clock. He's in the library now. With Mr. Callaghan, the genealogy man." Rose tucked the napkin farther around the breakfast rolls, which smelled of cinnamon. Torrey couldn't resist. The roll was warm; it had raisins and tasted heavenly.

From behind her, came Winifred's voice. "Ah, yes, the genealogy!" She reached past Torrey and took a roll from the basket. "There's something in my cousin's head that rides him like a witch!" Winifred gave her booming laugh. "Delicious rolls! I've already had breakfast — sausages, scrambled eggs, tea, two kinds of breads. I'm omniverous." She chewed the roll. "You're off to your labors, Ms. Tunet?"

"A witch?" Torrey asked, but glanced at her watch.

"Well, not *literally* a witch, Ms. Tunet. Allow me a little poetic license, if you please. But something does ride Desmond, and my poetic side assures me that he's trying to prove . . . what? Unfortunately, my poetic side doesn't tell me precisely what."

Torrey smiled at Winifred and licked a bit of cinnamon from a finger. "See you later."

She walked quickly through the great hall with its gilt-edged portraits and into the library. "Good morning, Desmond."

He was bending over a mahogany desk clear of anything but an immense chart. Genealogy, she saw. He was alone. From the open window came the sound of a motorbike starting. Mr. Callaghan departing.

"Torrey." Desmond faced her, smiling. He slouched, somehow a rich man's indolent slouch, hands in the pockets of his designer jeans. He wore a yellow cashmere sweater, thick and rich, over his bare skin. His smile was a shark's smile. "I hope you didn't stay awake worrying about my grandmother's necklace. I —"

"I didn't."

He went on as if he hadn't heard. "I'm not going to have divers search the lake for the necklace. Waste of time." His cold green-yellow eyes were clear, his voice vibrant. An air of self-satisfaction emanated from him, irritating her. He was eying every inch of her; he was so sexually aware of her that she felt it like an invasion.

"Divers? Yes. Definitely a waste of time, Desmond." She smiled back at him, feeling good, feeling fine, happy with herself. She drew something from the pocket of her navy jacket and tossed it onto the mahogany desk.

"What the—!" His voice broke off.

It lay there, sparkling, the heirloom diamond necklace with its single, pear-shaped emerald.

Desmond looked up from the necklace. He stared at her. "So you had it all the time." His voice was soft, his eyes calculating. "You could have conned me and gotten away with it."

"Could I have? In a way, yes." She eyed him, her lips quirked. "What kind of a serpent was it, Desmond?"

"What serpent?"

"The one that tempted Eve."

A silence. A vacuum cleaner went on in an adjoining room. For a full minute Desmond Moore stood silent, slouching against the desk.

Then he laughed. "You guessed I was trying it on? I've never met a woman, rich or poor, who was above temptation. A little temptation, a little guilt—you would have owed me. You're the kind of woman who would pay the debt. It would have been interesting in bed. How could I have known you're smart enough to have guessed." His voice was admiring.

She shrank into herself. He was uncannily right about her: she would have paid for the necklace, paid in the coin he wanted.

"Not that I would have lost anything, anyway." Desmond drummed his fingers on the desk, eyeing her. "Did I mention the necklace is insured for forty-five thousand dollars?"

"Did you? I don't remember."

Desmond gazed at her. He smiled. He licked his lower lip, then bit it, holding it between his teeth.

An instant ago, she had been in control. Now he was making her nervous.

Desmond picked up the necklace. He held it, swinging it back and forth, watching her. "You've turned out to be so honorable. What if I were to say that you could have the necklace?"

"What?" Puzzled, she stared.

He came close to her. An inch away, he took one of her

hands and clasped her fingers around the necklace. It was a rough gesture, so rough she winced. Her fingers felt bruised. But of course it was not intentional cruelty . . . or was it?

". . . on account," he added softly.

"On account?" She stared at him.

"Keep it until tomorrow. *Then* make up your mind if you want to keep it for good." His jaw had a brutish look; his greenish eyes were cold and avid. He licked his lips, clearly thinking of lustful favors, plenty of them of various sorts. Over a period of time. His home was in Brookline, in Massachusetts.

Forty-five thousand dollars. If this was the miracle she needed, it was a punishing one. That many dollars' worth of bedding with the lickerish Desmond Moore. Months of it. She felt sick. She felt sick, too, that he would give away his grandmother's necklace for his sexual kicks. Incomprehensible. But she'd bet anything that he'd collect his forty-five thousand from the insurance company, claiming the necklace had been lost in the lake. He'd even had a witness: Luke Willinger.

He was leaning toward her. He gripped her hair at the crown, pulling back her head. His mouth came down, but not on her mouth; it came down on the tiny mole on the side of her neck, below her ear, his tongue flicking out, licking the little mole over and over, his breath quickening. She felt almost overcome with nausea.

The phone rang. Desmond pulled away, his breathing heavy. He picked up the phone; his hand was unsteady. "Hello?"

Estate business, as it turned out. She felt too shaken to move. He put down the phone. "I have to leave." He nodded toward the necklace that she still unconsciously clutched. "Take your time. Take . . . until you get back from your conference tomorrow in Dublin." She hated the way he looked at her.

When he was gone she opened her cramped hand that clutched the necklace. She looked at the red bruises on her fingers. There was a cut on her forefinger, blood oozed. What a sick bastard he was!

She thought of Desmond Moore's hands on her, and she almost gagged. And he'd make her pay cruelly in bed for having trumped him. She shuddered to think how.

But if she had the money! Massachusetts General Hospital, the surgeon from Texas, the physical therapy, the wheelchair become an artifact. Her mind formed the dazzling pictures be-cause . . . *because it could happen.* Finally.

She took a deep breath. She closed her fingers and slipped the necklace into her pocket. She was no longer a thief. Could she become a whore?

Leaving the library, she felt numb. In a way, she almost had to laugh. She had wished for a miracle to bring her the money she needed. And this, at last, was the miracle. A miracle almost too bitter to bear.

23

In Dublin, shortly before twelve noon, Thursday, Luke Willinger strode purposefully across Saint Stephen's Green toward the Shelbourne. The sun shone, the flowers in the formal gardens tossed in the light breeze. Noontime picnickers on benches were unpacking lunches; children raced about. A breeze snapped the flag above the hotel.

The elegant lobby was quiet, gracious, soothing. Luke's eyes still ached after a sleepless night and two strong cups of morning coffee. Pacing the planned landscaping acreage at eight o'clock this morning with Desmond Moore, he'd been unable to concentrate on landscaping possibilities. Desmond, in high spirits, hadn't seemed to notice. He'd something up his sleeve and was tickled about it. He'd worn jeans and a yellow cashmere sweater over bare skin. His brassy hair had gleamed.

In the Shelbourne, Luke approached the reception desk. "Good morning. The Hungarian-Belgian Conference. Can you find out what time they have a lunch break?"

"Hungarian-Belgian, sir? I'll inquire." The clerk tapped on a computer then picked up the phone. "Conference Room Six." As he did so, the elevator doors opened and Torrey Tunet emerged. She was alone. She looked crisp and fresh in a businesslike dark suit and beige silk shirt. She carried a briefcase. Even from the reception desk, Luke could see an excitement in her, a wide-awake look of satisfaction, something accomplished. Did she love her work that much? He felt a surge of pleasure at her business triumph—and immediately thought, *What the hell am I thinking?* In five minutes he was going to nail this miserable little thief. That's why he was here. She'd cough up that heirloom necklace. Or else. For an instant he seemed to smell her perfume as she'd gone past him where he'd hid, coming from the lake in the moonlight.

Torrey Tunet, a skinny Romanian-American kid back in North Hawk, Massachusetts. Luke was eighteen when Torrey committed her first crime, the crime that had changed his life. He'd been at Harvard that autumn, a junior. He was going to be a doctor like his psychoanalyst father. A solid future. He'd felt privileged; he was the son of one of the richest and most highly respected men in North Hawk. Then his world exploded. Because of the Romanian kid—Torrey Tunet.

"So cough it up," Luke said. "You can pretend you found it later on the shore."

"And if I don't?" She leaned back in the captain's chair. She stared back at him across the table. The pub smelled of fries. It was around the corner from the Shelbourne. It was five minutes to twelve and still empty, except for a lone customer at the bar. Outside, it had darkened. Rain spattered against the plateglass window. Another few minutes and the lunchtime crowd would begin surging in.

There was a plate of chips on the table. They both had poured tea from a teapot; it was steaming in their cups.

"Or I tell Desmond." He felt coldly implacable.

"Why didn't you tell him before?" She was studying him, a look of curiosity.

Why hadn't he? He hesitated; something had puzzled him. "To give you a break. A chance to make up a story. Maybe that you'd gone down to the lake, searching, and had found the necklace on the shore."

"Give me a break, why? You hate me."

He knew abruptly what had held him back. It was that he

always had to understand things. He did not understand why she had stolen the necklace when Desmond had implied she might become his wife. Did she have an uncontrollable desire to steal? Like a kleptomaniac? He doubted it.

She sipped tea. "So . . . why?"

"I thought you might be interested in marrying Desmond. In that case . . ."

"In that case, why steal from him? I see." She was eyeing him over the rim of the teacup. "I would never marry Desmond Moore."

"Oh, no?"

"Neither would he marry me. He was only implying it to torture his cousin Winifred."

So she was a realist. And acute. He was chagrined that she'd made a shrewder assessment of Desmond than he; because now that she'd said it, he recognized it was true about Desmond torturing his cousin. Added to that, he felt annoyed that he had not assessed Torrey accurately either . . . his assumption that she would have married Desmond.

"Excuse me, I've a phone call to make." She got up. He watched her get change from the bartender and go to the phone on the wall. She still had that jaunty walk he remembered.

That unforgettable jaunty walk. As a boy, he'd seen her around North Hawk, seen her growing up. A gangling kid, tall, thin, with dark curvy hair and eyes like a gray storm. Not pretty but passionately alive. Her father, the Romanian, had married into the town, had arrived in North Hawk one day, darkly handsome, wiry, with a warm handshake, a heavy accent, and a watchmaker's knowledge. He'd fallen in love and married quiet, soft-spoken Abigail Hapgood Torrey who had no family and worked in the bank. But Vlad Tunet had a head full of dreams of adventure — expeditions in Alaska, explorations in Peru, mountain peaks in Tibet, treasure under the seas fringing New Zealand. A watchmaker's shop in a New England town could not hold him. He'd gone off exploring half a dozen times before he'd finally departed North Hawk for good, leaving a quietly heartbroken Abigail Hapgood Torrey Tunet and her young daughter.

"Have you got eight pence?" Torrey was at his elbow. "I need more change for the phone. The bartender's gone in the back."

He felt in his pocket and gave her a handful of pence.

"Thanks." She went back to the phone. He heard the chimes as she dropped in the coins.

She'd been eleven when her father had left North Hawk forever, her romantic father. She had adored him. Once, he'd brought her back a present, a bandanna, orange, with a design of blue peacocks. A Chinese-looking thing. Even after her father was gone for good, she'd worn the bandanna around town like a headband, peacocks on her forehead. Incongruous, what with the jeans resting on her skinny hips. Yet the whole of it somehow exotic.

Like him, she was a reader. Luke, four years older, and a frequenter of the North Hawk Library, would see her there with a stack of books. She read devouringly. Winter nights, the library closed at nine. She would sit until late at one of the little reading tables, the radiator hissing underneath; it was an old building with hot water heat. She wore woolen socks, and her bare knees were red and cracked from coming in from the cold. "Hi, Torrey," he would say, with kindly superiority, going past, his books under his arm. She would look up, bemused, her stormy, black-fringed gray eyes hardly aware of him, "Hi," and go back to her reading. She could speak Romanian. Other languages came easily to her. When she was twelve, there'd been a piece about her in the *North Hawk Weekly*. She'd won a prize of twenty-five dollars for translating for little grammar school kids from Spanish-speaking countries who spoke no English. She had learned Spanish from tapes borrowed from the library. Why? "I don't know," she'd told the *North Hawk Weekly* reporter.

The pub door opened, a spatter of rain swept in on a wind, and two men in caps came in, took off dripping raincoats, and hung them on an antlered mahogany rack. The bartender, cutting lemons into a dish, nodded a greeting.

"Lord save us, that's a lovely girl," the skinnier of the two men said. He was looking at Torrey Tunet. She was standing on one leg, rubbing the back of her calf with her other foot while she talked on the phone. Her short dark hair was damp from the rain, one wing-shaped lock curved on her cheek.

"I would sell my pasture to buy her a pint," the skinny man said.

"She's taken, Seamus," the other man said — and to Luke, "Excuse my friend, mister. We've been celebrating. His wife just had her sixth. Weighs in at seven pounds."

"That's all right." Luke lifted his cup of tea to the skinnier man. "Congratulations."

Her briefcase, so close he could touch it, lay on the pub chair beside him. He glanced at it; then again . . . and again. In it would be papers relating to the conference. What else? The stolen necklace? Did she keep it with her, not daring to leave it in her bedroom at Castle Moore?

When had her thievery started?

She'd had few friends in North Hawk after her father went off adventuring. Abigail Hapgood Torrey was a poor manager. She and her daughter moved into a run-down tenement. The town proved to be social snobs.

But Torry had a worshipper. She had faithful little Donna Lefebvre from a poor French-Canadian family, her father a postal worker. Donna, two years younger, idolized Torrey and did whatever Torrey said.

So Torrey, passionately alive and with the spark of her adventurous father in her, was the ringleader of a gang of one — Donna, fair-haired, innocent, willing, pudgy. Poor little Donna. As it turned out, tragic little Donna.

Luke gazed, frowning, at the black briefcase. Thievery, thievery.

Torrey, the instigator. Donna, her acolyte, following the dazzling pinwheel that was Torrey, the mischief, the excitement, the incredible fun. Luke remembered one autumn day seeing them, aged thirteen and eleven, Charlie Chaplins, each twirling a cane, with burnt-cork mustaches and in baggy pants and old top hats, strolling down Main Street at 5:00 P.M. And it wasn't even Halloween.

It was the following year that Torrey began to baby-sit. She baby-sat for Luke's little brother, Joshua.

In the pub, Luke closed his eyes but he could not block out the horror he was seeing in his mind.

When Torrey returned from the pay phone and sat down, he said immediately, sharply, "That's it. Make your choice. Return the necklace or I tell Desmond you stole it."

She laughed. Or rather, it was a giggle. Then, suddenly sober, she gave him a straight look. "You want the truth? Desmond was playing a nasty little sex game. He wanted me to swipe the necklace. I obliged. Anyway, in the morning I gave him back the necklace. And—surprise! Desmond then gave it to me. For good."

Luke stared at her. "Jesus! What kind of jackass d'you think I am—to believe Desmond gave you a family heirloom worth more than twenty thousand pounds!" He leaned toward her over the table. "You stole the damned thing! *Stole* it! You could—"

"Listen," she began, "I—"

"*Stole* it! You could go to prison," he said, and found he was shaking with bitter anger, "not like that first time."

24

Torrey flinched. Hopeless to make Luke Willinger believe her.

"Well, then . . ." She stood up. At the bar she got change for a pound note. She came back and dropped the pence she'd borrowed from Luke onto the table. "Go ahead! Tell Desmond I stole his heirloom necklace. Go on, tell him!"

"I'll do that." Tight-lipped, Luke glared at her. She shrugged and walked out of the pub. It was drizzling; she put up her folding umbrella.

Back at the Shelbourne, she learned that the fussy Hungarian delegate had had a stomach upset; the afternoon meeting was cancelled. She came out again into the drizzle. She'd had no lunch, only tea at the pub. But she knew she wouldn't be able to eat. All she could think of was the necklace in her briefcase. What was it worth? Twenty thousand pounds? More? Thirty? Enough, certainly, for the surgery that would release Donna from the wheelchair. Yet the thought of being in bed with Desmond Moore sickened her.

In the rain, she wandered blindly through Dublin, gazing unseeingly into shop windows, staring from the bridge into the sluggishly moving Liffey, biting a fingernail, unable to make up her mind. She was not a cat with nine lives; she had only this one. "Tantalus," she said, aloud. She was tantalizing herself, an agony of indecision. Pawn or sell the necklace and have money for Donna's surgery? Or return the necklace to Desmond and be free of him? The drizzle stopped; she was hardly aware of it.

Grafton Street. Ahead, across the street, she saw Weir's. It was one of the most prestigious jewelry shops in Dublin. Torrey hesitated. Then she crossed the street.

"Good afternoon." She placed her leather briefcase on the plateglass counter. An air-conditioner hummed. There was a smell of lemon oil–polished mahogany and a feeling of quiet elegance. Several clocks on a counter delicately chimed the quarter hour: 4:45. She'd run it close; most shops in Dublin closed at five.

"Good afternoon." The clerk smiled courteously. He was clean-shaven, in a dark suit, impeccable. At a counter nearby, an elderly woman clerk, polishing a silver urn, smiled at Torrey. Three or four customers browsed.

"My necklace." She had wrapped it in a tissue and put it in a business envelope. She snapped open the brass clips of the briefcase, took out the envelope, and unwrapped the necklace. "Perhaps you can help me. I'm told it's quite valuable. But I don't know. It was left to me by an aunt. I thought you might be able to tell me . . ." Or perhaps Weir's itself might be interested in buying the necklace.

"Left to you by your aunt, was it?" The clerk nodded encouragingly.

Torrey held up the necklace. The diamonds glittered; the pear-shaped emerald at the V shot green fire.

The clerk shifted the black velvet pad on the counter but did not touch the necklace. " 'Tis its worth you're interested in?"

"Yes."

"We have a department for —"

"Mr. Colby? Can you help me a moment?" The elderly clerk at the next counter was beckoning.

"Excuse me, please."

Waiting, she dropped the necklace onto the velvet pad. She

pushed it around, gazing at the glittering stones. She didn't really like diamonds, couldn't see what the fuss was all about; it was just that they were valuable. She preferred a burst of fireworks. Or what was that tangerine-colored bird? It would be the male; the male always had the plumage, brilliant colors like the male peacocks on the bandanna from her father.

She glanced over at the next counter. Mr. Colby was not there. She had been waiting almost ten minutes. Ah, here he came, skirting another counter at her left.

"I'm sorry to've kept you waiting." He looked down at the necklace on the black velvet. He was perspiring. He looked up at her, then he looked past her shoulder and gave a great sigh.

She turned. Two gardai in blue uniforms were coming toward her.

"But it is *my* necklace!" Torrey said, frightened and angry.

No one looked at her. The elderly woman clerk was repeating to Detective Inspector O'Gorman, who had just arrived from the *Garda Síochana*, what she had told the two gardai minutes before. "I recognized it as the Moore necklace from the photo in *The Sunday World* about the diamond exhibit last year, the V of diamonds with the emerald at the base. And having heard about the murder on the radio—"

"What has my diamond necklace got to do with the murder of Mr. Kasvi?" Torrey looked in bewilderment from the two gardai to Detective Inspector O'Gorman.

"Not Mr. Kasvi," Detective Inspector O'Gorman said, "the murder of Desmond Moore."

25

Inspector O'Hare wanted to retch. That would have made two of them because Moore's new stable lad, a seventeen-year-old, was throwing up onto a bale of hay beside Darlin' Pie's box. Brian Coffey, Moore's skinny red-haired trainer, in jeans and a faded maroon jersey, was standing, mute, his white, freckled face contorted; he was shaking his head back and forth, his eyes denying the ugliness he stared at.

Desmond Moore's knife-slashed, bloody body lay just outside box four; but the horse, Black Pride, was gone, the stall door splintered. The scent of blood in the stable had stirred the other three horses in their boxes. There was a frightening cacophony of shrill whinnies, stamping, and neighing. Darlin' Pie, in box three, reared and screamed.

O'Hare swallowed saliva. Two murders in Ballynagh within a week. As though a serial killer was on the loose. He looked down at Desmond Moore, who lay face up.

"My!" Sergeant Bryson squatted down beside Moore's body. Bryson's young face looked appalled. "Oh, my!"

A knife must have been driven into Moore's stomach and yanked upward between his ribs to his breastbone. His yellow cashmere sweater was red-black with the blood that must have spurted, maybe even jetted out like a fountain. One hand was clenched at his breast, as though in reflex to stem the flow.

"He would've died at once, I hope," Bryson said pleadingly,

as though asking someone indeterminate for confirmation. He reached out a hand as if to close Desmond Moore's staring eyes, but —

"Don't touch him," O'Hare said. "You know better, Sergeant!"

From the police car in the stable yard, O'Hare called the Murder Squad at headquarters in Dublin. The van with the technical crew would arrive shortly; Castle Moore was only twenty-five minutes from Dublin.

Back again in the stable, O'Hare scanned the floor, the murder weapon — a bloody knife, surely, by the look of Desmond Moore's slashed body — could be lying somewhere here. But it wasn't. Had the murderer taken it with him?

"See if there's a knife in that bale of hay or along the stalls," he said to Sergeant Bryson, "But don't touch it; wait for the gardai from Dublin."

He looked around for Brian Coffey, who still stood mute and staring. Coffey and the new lad, Kevin Keating, had found Desmond Moore's body only a few minutes ago, when they had returned from Flaherty's Harness Shop in Ballynagh and entered the stables. Minutes later, an incoherent Brian Coffey had rung up Inspector O'Hare. The poor fellow still looked in shock, eyes wide, face white. The lad, Kevin, had ridden off in search of Black Pride. In the stable yard, Janet Slocum and Rose stood hugging their arms and looking around in fear and excitement.

"I was at that card table," Brian Coffey said to Inspector O'Hare, jerking his head toward the rickety table in the stable office. "About two o'clock it was, just before I went to Ballynagh to meet Kevin at Flaherty's. I was making out the list, the tack we needed to buy. And I heard voices. Mr. Desmond talking with somebody in the stable."

Inspector O'Hare stood over Brian Coffey, who was sitting forward on the edge of a faded, overstuffed tartan couch, elbows on knees, hands clasped. The room was small, not much bigger than a horse box. The walls had glossy photographs of horses and racing events tacked up. There was a calendar from a feed company. The card table served as the office desk. Sweaters and a duffle coat hung on a rack in one corner. Beneath the rack were a couple of pairs of worn boots. A wood floor had been crudely laid down.

"And . . . ?"

"Yes, well—" Brian Coffey's red hair was wet with sweat; nervous sweat it had to be; the room was not that warm—"so I was making out the list."

Brian Coffey moved his hands up his skinny white arms, shoving up the sleeves of the faded maroon jersey, rubbing his arms as though they were cold. He hunched his shoulders and licked dry lips. "Mr. Desmond had this store room made into an office last month, temporarylike. He had plans for a yard of a dozen horses, to start. He'd be buying at auctions. He wanted to—"

"Yes," O'Hare said, trying to be patient, his jaw aching with the strain. Sergeant Bryson sat at the card table, making notes with a ballpoint pen. "So it was two o'clock?"

"Yes, about two. A few minutes after two, anyway. I'd had Kevin sort out some old boxes of harness—a sad lot, rust and corrosion—we'd get rid of it. Mr. Desmond said to charge the new harness at Flaherty's. T'was a big list. The stables had been let go. Even paint for the stables had—"

"Yes," Inspector O'Hare interrupted. He clicked his thumbnail. *Get on with it.* "So you heard Mr. Moore talking with someone . . . ?"

"Near box number four, they were, Black Pride's stall. I heard Mr. Desmond's voice go up, high like, the way it sometimes gets when he's angry, but most people's goes down low when they—"

"Any words? Did you understand what they—"

Brian Coffey shook his red head. "No . . . But angry! Mr. Desmond and the other one. But none of my—And not worrisome. Mr. Desmond often gets angry, like with jobs not done right, wrong stuff delivered, things like that. So I just finished making out the list." Brian Coffey looked down.

Something wrong. O'Hare sensed it. Since he'd been a kid, he could always tell: a silence across the supper table between his mom and dad, his mom's quick look down at the plate, a bruise glimpsed on her arm, the half-heard crash of a dish in the night.

"Go on." O'Hare leaned forward, trying to look into Brian Coffey's brown eyes. Coffey had the kind of thin white face that to O'Hare meant working-class Irish. They worked in shops, tilled fields, drove with their carpenters' tools in the back of their van, hopefully strummed guitars, their minds whirling with movie star and television dreams. Some went to Trinity; some had Ireland's love of horses and became jockeys, groomers, trainers. They worked or rode for rich owners or breeders. Some knew the inside of prisons; most knew the inside of pubs. Brian Coffey, with a boy's thin frame, was still unmarried at thirty-five, like a third of the Irishmen of his upbringing—never marrying because, as iconoclastic O'Hare saw it, between no birth control and the economy, they did not quite dare.

"And then?" O'Hare said.

Brian Coffey gulped. "Flaherty closes up at three. And it wasn't my place to—So I went out behind, where I keep my motorbike, and I went off to Flaherty's." Brian shook his head. "We'd've been back sooner, but coming out of Flaherty's we met Mr. Callaghan and—"

"Who? Who's Mr. Callaghan?"

"Mr. Fergus Callaghan, a man who traces your ancestors. He—"

"A genealogist, you mean?"

"That's right. One of those. He's been tracing back for Mr. Desmond, the Moores' history and where they—"

"Yes, yes, all right, Brian. So in Ballynagh, coming out of Flaherty's . . ."

"Yes, well we talked a minute, Mr. Callaghan wishing Kevin well on the job at the Moore stables. He thought he knew Kevin's family, but it turned out to be other Keatings. He—"

O'Hare, impatient, cut him off. "Yes, well—At the stable—

You didn't glimpse the other person? You only heard their voice?"

"Who?" Coffey blinked, his white face strained, his voice exhausted.

"The killer"—O'Hare said patiently—"who killed Mr. Moore."

"Oh," Brian Coffey said. "Yes. Just his voice."

26

At 6:30 P.M., Thursday, Winifred Moore, at a table in Keenen's Pub on Parliament Street in Dublin, shouted wildly from a corner table. "Sheila! Over here! Sheila!"

Sheila, red-faced with embarrassment, threaded her way through the throng around the bar and plumped down. "Really, Winifred! You don't have to *scream*. Anyone'd think you'd been brought up in a barn."

"Desmond's been murdered. *Knifed!* In the stable at Castle Moore." Winifred's square-jawed face was burningly alive. Her voice was thick with excitement. Her eyes glittered. "It was on a news flash on television. Torrey Tunet killed Desmond! She stole that ugly Moore diamond necklace and tried to peddle it in Dublin. They caught her."

Sheila made an exasperated hissing sound between her teeth. "I don't look at television, as you well know. Are you drunk? You *promised*—"

"Oh, stop it! I'm not drunk. Or hallucinating. It *happened*. There—" Winifred jerked her head toward the television set above the bar. A news flash had come on; the newscaster was saying Desmond's name. Then something about Torrey Tunet.

In the noisy bar, Winifred watched Sheila's jaw drop as she distinguished the newscaster's words. There was a momentary shot of a jewelry clerk at Weir's on Grafton Street being interviewed.

"I can't *believe* it!" Sheila's eyes were wide with shock. "Something's wrong. Winifred, Torrey Tunet's too smart. If she killed Desmond, she wouldn't be stupid enough to try to sell the necklace in Dublin right after. She'd hide it and take it to America to a . . . you know . . . a—"

"A fence," Winifred said. "But I'm glad Ms. Tunet *was* that stupid. Otherwise, you know what the gardai would think?" She watched Sheila's face turn pale and nodded with grim satisfaction. "Otherwise they'd think *I* killed Desmond. After all, I'll inherit. And I don't have an alibi."

"Alibi? Where *were* you this afternoon, Winifred?"

"Ah," said Winifred, "hanging about the piers in Dun Laoghaire, holding the poetry medal in my pocket in case I ran into my dead pa, so's I could show him. As though he'd done right . . ." Her voice had begun to quiver. She bit her lips, gave her shoulders a shake, and stood up. "Come on! I already paid, but I had to wait for you. It must be merry hell at the castle."

27

In here, sir, Ms. Tunet's room."

Janet Slocum, the long-faced, bony maid senior over Rose, the other maid, opened the door to the bedroom and Inspector O'Hare stepped inside, followed by Sgt. Jimmy Bryson.

It was seven o'clock, two hours after Ms. Torrey Tunet had been arrested at Weir's in Dublin. The evening sun shone golden through the wide bedroom windows.

Inspector O'Hare surveyed the bedroom, thinking how his wife would have loved it. There was a queen-sized canopy bed and a marble fireplace full of silk flowers, and a thick rug with scrolly designs. There was a rose-colored lounging chair, a pair of soft chairs, and a scattering of small tables with Moore family photographs and bits of decorative things on them — porcelain cherubs and the like, naked little reclining figures with wings. The kind of thing his wife particularly liked.

The *Garda Siochana* in Dublin was holding Ms. Tunet for theft, and possibly for murder. The gardai had impounded the Moore diamond necklace, which had been variously reported on the RTE, the Irish National Television News, to be worth ten thousand pounds, twenty thousand, thirty thousand, and even a half-million. On RTE, Torrey Tunet had rated a full thirty seconds of vehement denial. She had not murdered Desmond Moore. She had not stolen the Moore necklace. Mr. Moore had given her the necklace. Undeniably attractive she was, with that swag of satiny dark hair and the style of her and that uplifted chin, despite her grim situation.

"Anything special, sir?" Janet Slocum asked from the bedroom doorway, "that you'll be wanting?"

Inspector O'Hare shook his head. He narrowed his eyes at a scattering of books, writing paper, and letters on a lady's desk near a window. "Just having a look round." *Maybe to draw the noose securely.* Murder was not on his list of approved activities. "Sergeant," he said to Jimmy Bryson, "check out this room and the bathroom. You're looking for a knife. If no luck, we'll try her car; it's still parked in Dublin."

"Yes, sir."

At the little inlaid writing table, O'Hare searched the drawers: stamps, pencils, paperclips. No knife. O'Hare stood over the desk, frowning, pulling at his nose. A book lay on the blotter, *The Loom of Language,* Subtitled: *An Approach to the Mastery of Many Languages.* Inspector O'Hare flipped it open and read: "An example which illustrates how to make associations for memorizing words of Romance origin is 'hospitable.' The Oxford Dictionary tells us that this comes from the Latin verb *hospitare* (to entertain). The related word *hospite* meant either 'guest' or 'host,' and it has survived as the latter. Another related Latin word is *hospitale,* a place for 'guests,' later for 'travelers.' This was the original meaning of 'hospital,' and survives as such in *Knights Hospitallers.*"

"What's that?" Jimmy Bryson was beside him, rummaging in a wastebasket.

"Hmmm?" Inspector O'Hare read on. "In Old French it appears shortened to *hostel,* which exists in English. In modern French *s* before *t* or *p* has often disappeared. That it was once there is indicated by a circumflex accent over the preceding vowel, as in 'hotel.' "

"Inspector?"

"Yes, Sergeant?" Unwillingly, he looked up. Bryson was holding out a paper. "This letter. It was on the floor. Must've fallen off the desk." He handed it to the inspector.

"Dear Donna," the letter began. Inspector O'Hare scanned

it. It said only that Torrey Tunet would be returning to North Hawk in a week and that she was excited about the possibilities, and that *"You're not to worry about the money. I will manage it somehow."*

"Donna," O'Hare said. He looked over the letter at Bryson. "That would be Donna Lefebvre. Her fellow thief. The one mentioned in the fax."

The fax from the North Hawk police in Massachusetts, in answer to O'Hare's routine inquiry, already lay on his desk at Ballynagh. Reading it, O'Hare had said, "Mother of God!" under his breath. He'd been struck with the pity of it, the pity that the young Torrey Tunet's half-mischievous thievery had ended by destroying the Willinger family and putting Torrey's younger friend in a wheelchair for the rest of her life. Terrible. Yet O'Hare found himself helplessly awash with sympathy for the perpetrator, Torrey Tunet. But now Miss Tunet was an adult and there was murder involved.

Inspector O'Hare carefully folded the letter and slid it into an envelope he found on the desk. He glanced down at *The Loom of Language* and shook his head sorrowfully. "Miss Tunet reads interesting books. But she could well be convicted of murdering Desmond Moore. Prison is as good a place as any to pass the time with books."

"Yes," said Sergeant Bryson, "well she might! Did she think we'd believe that Desmond Moore would give a thirty-thousand-pound necklace to a young lady he'd known for less than a week? She must take us for looneys."

"Yes," Inspector O'Hare said.

"And no alibi," Jimmy Bryson said, incredulously. "Just strolling around Dublin! Eating a Chinese takeout in Saint Stephen's Green! Walking along the Liffey. Come, now!"

"Weak," O'Hare had to concur. Miss Tunet, with the jaunty walk and the low, husky voice, a voice with a lilt that was almost Irish. A wave of sadness again washed over Inspector O'Hare. Thievery was one thing. But Desmond Moore's slashed body lying among bits of hay in the Castle Moore stable was another.

O'Hare shook his head; he would have to phone Chief Superintendent O'Reilly at the *Garða Siochana* headquarters in Dublin and tell him about the fax from America.

He gave a last lingering glance toward the naked, winged cherubs on a nearby table. They looked to be made of marble. His wife's birthday was coming up; maybe he'd find one at a shop in Dublin. "Come along, Jimmy." He went toward the door.

"Right." But Jimmy Bryson, drawing out the single word like a sigh, sounded as far away as county Cork. Inspector O'Hare glanced back. The sergeant was looking at Janet Slocum, who had not left the bedroom. She had been so still, the inspector hadn't realized she was still there, bony, thin-lipped, eyes like gimlets. "Is Rose around?" Jimmy Bryson said to Janet Slocum, "Rose Burns?"

"Ah, no she isn't, sergeant. Gone to London last night on the ferry from Dun Leoghaire. Went to spend a couple of days with her sister, Hannah. Hannah's been seeing the sights in London, the Tower and such."

"Ahhh . . . vacationing, is it?" Sergeant Bryson cleared his throat. "And Hannah, how is she enjoying London? Does Rose say?"

Janet's long face took on an odd look, almost wary. She thrust her hands into the pockets of her bibbed white apron and rocked a little on her feet. Inspector O'Hare noticed for the first time small pockmarks on Janet's flat cheeks; she had missed out for looks. Her hoarse voice didn't help.

"And why wouldn't she be enjoying it, a big, exciting city like London?"

"They'll be coming back soon, will they? Rose and . . . and Hannah?"

"Oh, yes, Sergeant. That they will."

O'Hare, always sensitive to undertones in a voice, regarded Janet for an instant while Sgt. Jimmy Bryson heaved up a sigh from somewhere around his booted toes. It seemed to O'Hare that Janet Slocum was speaking on two levels, an upper one open, a lower one veiled.

28

At six o'clock Friday morning, Luke Willinger, numb and incredulous, drove to Dublin. Last night, around five o'clock, the gardai had arrested Torrey Tunet in connection with the murder of Desmond Moore.

On Moleston Street, Luke sat through the hour-long AA meeting in the community house behind Saint Anne's. He didn't hear a word anybody said.

The meeting over, he stopped at a coffee shop around the corner. Someone had left a copy of the morning's *Irish Independent* on the counter. Luke glanced at the lead story and promptly scalded himself on his cup of coffee.

"Jesus!" On the front page, favored position, right side, was an account of the sensational tragedy in North Hawk, Massachusetts, sixteen years earlier. It was accompanied by a photograph of the young Torrey Tunet at that long-ago court hearing. There she was, skinny, in a real dress instead of jeans, but with that peacock bandana around her dark hair.

An enterprising journalist on *The Irish Independent* had somehow obtained the North Hawk information from Superintendent Inspector O'Reilly's office at the *Garda Siochana* Murder Squad headquarters in Phoenix Park.

So! Torrey Tunet's past in North Hawk was exposed! The exposure seemed to Luke to justify his years of grievance against her for the destruction of his family and his having to drop out of school. *"The wages of sin,"* he thought grimly, rattling the newspaper. Not to mention pigeons coming home to roost.

He reread the *Independent* piece, mentally corroborating every fact supplied by the police records in North Hawk. It even gave the calibre of the Smith & Wesson gun that had killed his stepfather. It was a weird feeling.

Then he simply sat there on the plastic stool, feeling strange. Something was wrong. He had always thought of himself as honest with himself, cleanly honest in fact. And fair. And decent. Not a paragon, for God's sake! But certainly a man of character; if not a Socrates, at least a worthy disciple of such a philosopher. And certainly not a person prey to emotions to the point of blind rage, to an arbitrary desire for revenge. Yet for sixteen lousy years —

Jesus Christ, he thought, *she was only fourteen!*

He sat there, stunned, as though the fact that Torrey had been a kid of fourteen was news to him. My, God! He'd never given a thought to the fact that she was a fourteen-year-old. Why not? Because he was an emotional eighteen-year-old at the time, swearing eternal hatred of Torrey Tunet for his father's suicide. He'd locked himself into that grievance.

Meanwhile, Torrey Tunet had been growing up and becoming a person with qualities unknown to him. She wasn't locked into being a thief. That was only in his head. Who was she? What was she?

For the third time, he read the paragraphs in *The Irish Independent.* Torrey claimed that Desmond Moore had given her the necklace.

He sat back. He suddenly wanted desperately to believe it. But she'd stolen the necklace. He knew it. In the moonlight at the lake, spying on her, he had seen her take the necklace from beneath a piece of shale.

Yet . . . in the pub near the Shelbourne, Torrey leaning across the table saying, *"Desmond was playing a nasty little sex game. He wanted me to swipe the necklace. I obliged. . . . in the morning*

I gave him back the necklace ... and then Desmond gave it back to me. For good."

Had she been telling him the truth? Or was she still a thief ... and now a murderer?

"If you're through with that paper? They're all out of the *Independent*." The woman's voice at his shoulder had the hoarseness of a long-time drinker. She sat down on the plastic stool next to him, a skinny woman with a long-boned face, dun-colored bun of hair, pockmarks on her cheeks. She'd been in the row of folding chairs at his left at the AA meeting. He handed her the paper. "It's all yours," and added, "I'm Luke." Just as they did back home, in Ireland AA members gave only their first names.

"I know," the woman said, "I recognized you. From Castle Moore. I'm Janet, the senior maid. Senior above Rose. There's just the two of us right now. Mr. Desmond wasn't free with money for service." She glanced down at the item about Torrey Tunet. "I saw all that on this morning's television. What a laugh!"

"A laugh?"

"Ah, for sure!" Her tone was ironic. "Who was that king who sold his kingdom for a mess of pottage? No, in the Bible. That boy. Sold his soul."

"His birthright."

"Right, his birthright. Anyway, so did *she*, this American, Ms. Tunet. Except it was her body she was selling, but same thing."

"How you mean, a mess of pottage?"

"Just a minute, I want some coffee and a bun. The coffee at this morning's meeting was swill." She ordered coffee and a sugared raspberry bun. When they came, she took a long draught of the coffee. "Got to get my blood stirring before getting back to Castle Moore."

Then, eating the bun and sipping the hot coffee, she told him about the mess of pottage.

29

In the small, square room at Pearse Street Garda Station, Torrey looked in amazement at the aluminum tray with the breakfast the female garda placed before her: orange juice, a bowl of hot porridge, a plate of scrambled eggs with three plump sausages, thick-sliced bacon, and broiled tomato. There was a basket of brown bread and white toast, a slab of butter, and a pot of hot coffee.

"An Irish breakfast!" She looked questioningly at the garda. "How come?"

The garda folded her arms. "And if you don't like it, you can order from outside. We're wanting no more complaints from prisoners about being too ill-fed to think straight under arraignment."

Torrey laughed. She couldn't help it. Besides, she was hungry, even ravenous. She dug into the breakfast, meanwhile concentrating on the incredible facts: the murder of Desmond Moore and herself suspected of killing him.

Unbelievable. And unbelievable to awaken here. Her navy suit was crumpled; she'd slept in it. The Dublin Metropolitan area comprised Dublin city and the greater part of the county and portions of county Kildare and Wicklow. Castle Moore was in that portion of Wicklow, so here she was, detained at the Pearse Street Garda Station in Dublin. Detained.

"Detained." From Middle English, *deteynen*. From Middle

French, *detenir.* The Latin? She couldn't remember. Anyway, meaning "hold." *Tenir.* Held in custody.

"You want to see the paper?" The garda held out *The Irish Independent,* folded so that Torrey could see her picture on the front page. There she was, aged fourteen, in the North Hawk courtroom, blue dress, short hair combed smooth. And there sat her mother, so vulnerable, so shamed, in one of the varnished courtroom chairs. Torrey had ached so for her mother.

"No, thanks, I don't need to see it. I was there, after all." She couldn't help the spurt of zany humor; she'd never been able to be wholly serious. Even with the awfulness of her situation here in Dublin, some inner laughter, okay, a despairing laughter, bubbled up. Or was it hysteria?

The garda gone, Torrey sipped coffee and tried to ward off despair. She wondered how Oscar Wilde had felt in prison, though now she couldn't remember where he'd been imprisoned—oh, yes, Reading Gaol, that would be England, not Ireland, though he was Irish; *gaol* was the British variation of the American "jail," but what was it called in Ireland? *Gaol,* too? Likely. Old French was *jaiole,* from "cage"; then all the way back to Late Latin, *caveola,* equivalent to Latin *cave,* "an enclosure."

She bit her lips. She knew what she was doing by playing with words: escaping from remembering. Her whole life, since North Hawk, had become words. Words were her refuge.

North Hawk, population 3,040. The nearest big town was Keene, New Hampshire, eight miles away across the state line. There was the North Hawk post office, the two pharmacies, the health food store, the small supermarket. A handful of North Hawk business people commuted to Boston and Keene. Most houses were substantial, Victorian, not suburban; there were tree-shaded streets with sidewalks where children roller-skated or drew pictures with colored chalk or played hopscotch. There were enough handymen and carpenters with pick-up trucks; there were plenty of gardeners so people didn't always have to clip their own hedges. The town had everything it needed, including two dentists and two internists. And one highly respected psychoanalyst. Dr. James Willinger.

Thursday afternoon, September 12, 1980. "Mrs. Willinger wants to know if you can baby-sit Joshua on Saturday night," Torrey's mother asked her when she got home from school. "Two dollars an hour. It's bound to be four or five hours — they're going to Keene, Dr. Willinger's receiving some kind of award."

Saturday night, six-thirty, sweet smell of honeysuckle, soft evening air. Torrey brought her game of Monopoly in her shoulder bag. And she brought twelve-year-old Donna. "I'll pay you fifty cents an hour, we'll play Monopoly and have fun," she told Donna. After, Dr. Willinger would drop Donna off when he brought Torrey home. And Mrs. Willinger was leaving ice cream and cookies. Both chocolate. Their favorite.

Joshua Willinger was seven, angelic, and slept like a rag doll. "He's played out from playing," pretty Mrs. Willinger giggled. "He won't wake up, you lucky girls." She was all dressed up. She had shoulder-length blonde hair and didn't look old enough to be the mother of Luke Willinger, who was off at college. Dr. Willinger was shorter than his wife, but handsome in a keen-eyed, unsmiling way that chilled Torrey a little.

She and Donna got bored with Monopoly after an hour. They wandered around, looking at the furniture, the pictures on the walls, turning over books. In the kitchen they got the chocolate ice cream from the freezer and ate it with the cookies at the kitchen table.

They wandered finally into the Willingers' bedroom. Torrey opened a closet door and looked at Mrs. Willinger's dresses and shorts and jeans. "Boring." She made a face and closed the closet door. She pulled open Dr. Willinger's closet door.

That's how it started.

That's when Torrey said, "Dress up! Let's!" Mischievous, laughing, daring, she pulled a pair of Dr. Willinger's pants off a hanger. She was tall for a fourteen-year-old, already five feet six. Dr. Willinger was not much taller. Dressed in Dr. Willinger's well-cut charcoal gray suit and striped tie, Torrey strutted around the room. Donna, in the doctor's rolled-up trousers, fell down laughing. They pulled out vests and pants and ties and dressed and undressed, laughing and posturing. They reached up and yanked boxes of the doctor's winter clothes down from the closet shelves and, finally, the suitcase.

The suitcase.

They sat on the floor, staring at the money.

"What do you mean, scared? Don't be a baby, Donna!"

"Oh, my!" Awed. "Where'd he get all that money, Torrey?"

"Stole it, silly. That's why he hid it in the closet."

"*Stole* it? Why would he do that? How can you say he stole it, Torrey?"

Torrey said, "There must be a billion dollars here. Or at least a million. Anyway, *thousands.*" The money was all jumbled up, fifty-dollar bills, and tens and twenties in bunches with rubber bands around them, just thrown into the suitcase. They counted the money; it took an hour. Two hundred and twenty thousand dollars. They stared at each other.

"Maybe it's *her* money," Donna said, "Mrs. Willinger's. Maybe *she* stole it."

"No, because people pay him. Patients. You're supposed to give a share to the government, that's taxes. Like that dentist in Keene didn't do last year? He went to jail."

"Jail . . . ," breathed Donna, eyes wide. "Dr. Willinger!"

Torrey picked up an inch-thick bundle of bills. "If this were ours, we could hire a limousine and go to Boston and maybe hear the Grateful Dead."

". . . and I could have a big birthday party with a cake from Miss Pringle's . . ."

". . . buy Golo boots . . . And Wrangler jeans. Oshkosh overalls."

"Take an airplane to New York and go to Radio City . . ."

"Just *some* of this money could buy you that set of drums in Robbins's Music Store window. You'll never learn on those dumb old drums the Smiths threw out. You *deserve* some good ones. You *deserve* them. Do you hear me?"

"Oh, Torrey!" Donna's voice quavered; she clasped her hands and gazed at the bundles of money in the suitcase. "But we can't take any; it's not ours."

"It's not his either! It isn't *his* money. He's cheating the government. He *deserves* to have us take it! A little of it, anyway. We could take just a little."

"Torrey!"

"Well? . . . Besides, we could give some to the government. Send it anonymously. Maybe a thousand dollars. Or ten thousand. To help cancer. And ten thousand to help polio. All kinds of diseases. Things like that." She yanked at her ragged short hair that she'd cut herself. "I'd have my hair cut at Grace's Salon. And a real manicure."

"Torrey!"

"If we took just a little, like a couple of bundles, Dr. Willinger wouldn't even notice. It's such a *mess.*" Torrey looked at Donna's frightened, yearning face. Donna's bangs, skimpy and blonde and damp with perspiration, were falling into her eyes. Torrey suddenly pulled two twenty-dollar bills from a bundle. She shoved them into the pocket of Donna's old, worn shirt that had been passed down from her brother. "You have to get the *feel* of being rich. Don't you dare spend this. Just get the *feel* of it. There's a whole thing about how you feel about things, that if you *feel* rich you *are* rich. Some minister said that. It was in a sermon."

Donna covered her pocket with a trembling hand. "We can always put it back, can't we? . . . Next time you baby-sit Josh?"

"Of course." Torrey eyed the money in the suitcase; then abruptly she reached out and delicately twitched a hundred-dollar bill from under a rubber band. "I'll just take this. Just because." She didn't herself know why. She was not going to spend it, after all, not even to have Grace give her an expensive haircut. But it was something she somehow had to do, to be equally involved, to be fair to Donna.

"Because what?"

Torrey shrugged. "Anyway, we don't have to decide what to do right now. And we don't have to take tons of money now. The suitcase can be our bank. We can come to it when we need money. Like for emergencies."

Before they left the Willingers' bedroom, they carefully hung up Dr. Willinger's clothes and put everything to rights. For the rest of the evening they sat on the living room couch, talking excitedly and shivering a little though the hall thermostat was set at seventy-five and the evening was warm.

It was Mrs. Sam Olmstead, shopping for cassettes in Robbins's Music Store, who was responsible for the exposure of Dr. James Willinger. All that the elderly Carl Robbins did was question Donna Lefebvre in puzzlement when she tried to buy the set of snare drums in the window for forty dollars down and a promise of the other six hundred the following month, and Donna had abruptly collapsed into a pool of hysterical tears, hiccuping and finally babbling about a suitcase of hundreds of thousands of dollars in Dr. James Willinger's closet.

Mrs. Sam Olmstead's son, Horace, was one of the two reporters on the *North Hawk Weekly*. Mrs. Olmstead telephoned Horace at the paper and told him what she'd overheard in Robbins's Music Store.

Horace was young, eager, ambitious, thorough. It was he who circumspectly learned from one of Dr. Willinger's patients that Dr. Willinger, as part of his therapy approach, insisted on his patients paying him in cash, telling them not to be afraid of touching money; money was not dirty. He even, the patient told Horace, "made me take the cash out of the envelope and hand him the bills, touch them, not be ashamed of loving money: 'It is all right to love money.' "

It was Horace who did all the groundwork: He spent an hour with Torrey Tunet, sitting in his car in front of her house and talking with her, and it was Horace to whom she finally gave the hundred-dollar bill she had taken from Dr. Willinger's suitcase. Yes, she and Donna had counted the cache of money.

The amount? Torrey sighed. "Two hundred and twenty thousand dollars." Horace's eyebrows went up.

An hour later, Horace, back at his desk at the *North Hawk Weekly* office, made a phone call to the IRS. Then, having leaked his information to where it counted, he roughed out a sensational scoop for the *Weekly*, meanwhile keeping an eye on the Willinger household.

That same week, on Thursday, Dr. James Willinger was named as a potential director of the prestigious American Psychoanalytic Association, the "esteemed national organization," as it was described. Dr. Willinger was consequently photographed for the *Weekly*, standing smiling with his wife and two sons, Joshua, aged eight, and Luke, aged eighteen; Luke was home from Harvard for the weekend.

The two government men who arrived at the Willinger front door at ten o'clock on Tuesday three weeks later, departed at ten-thirty with the suitcase, leaving Mrs. Willinger ashen-faced, in shock. Horace Olmstead, who got out of his car as the dark-suited government men departed the Willinger home, was turned away at the door by the daily maid. But before he left, he heard Mrs. Willinger on the hall phone speaking to her husband's office.

Dr. Willinger never returned home from his office.

No one knew where he got the gun. It was a Smith & Wesson .38, a snub-nosed little revolver. The *Weekly* speculated later that Dr. Willinger kept the gun in case of attempted robbery or the like. Or even for protection against a disturbed patient.

In any event, after receiving the telephone call from his wife, Dr. Willinger took the gun from the drawer, put it to his temple, and squeezed the trigger. In Horace Olmstead's opinion, Dr. Willinger had a suppressed desire for drama. Surely a psychoanalyst could have prescribed himself a lethal drug, could have chosen a less messy demise? " 'Ours not to wonder why,' " Horace quoted Kipling to his mother, " 'Ours but to do and die.' "

But the worst had been Donna.

It was as though when they'd opened the suitcase, a swarm of evil snakes had crawled out and entangled them.

Dr. Willinger's death had not been enough. Nor his widow's nervous collapse. Nor little Joshua being shunned for his father's crime. And not even Luke Willinger having to leave Harvard and go to work for Hinkler Sons Landscaping to support his mother and Josh.

No. The worst was Donna Lefebvre, aged twelve.

30

At Castle Moore, at eleven o'clock that Friday morning, Winifred sprawled luxuriously in a tapestry chair in the library. She wore a white shirt and a khaki skirt, but she felt like royalty. It was *her* tapestry chair now, as was Castle Moore and all its attendant riches. On the Aubusson carpet at her feet lay the scattered newspapers. She and Sheila were watching the RTE television news in case of further reports on Desmond's murder. Sheila was sitting on a fringed hassock.

"You never can tell what *lurks* in people," Sheila said. "I'd never have guessed. Torrey Tunet seemed a perfectly nice young woman."

"Oh, *nice!* So was Henry the Eighth nice, except when he was beheading his wives." Winifred gave a huge laugh. She hugged her arms, her color was high, her eyes bright. "Besides, Torrey wasn't nice. She had too much guts for *nice.*"

"Quibble, quibble, quibble," Sheila said.

Winifred didn't answer. All night she had walked the rooms of the castle, excitedly planning, breaking into sudden disbelieving laughter, and shaking her head. Sheila in her wake kept saying in a shocked tone, "How *can* you, Winifred? So callous! With Desmond murdered . . . *murdered!*"

Winifred, with a shrug of her big shoulders, had sardonically paraphrased *Hamlet*, with " 'T'was an obliteration devoutly to be wished,' " and at Sheila's horrified gasp had qualified, grudgingly, "at least by a person who had a rage against him — somebody with something screamingly unbearable in his or her head."

In the tapestry chair, Winifred flexed her big fingers, then relaxed them. It was a habit she'd had since childhood that somehow relieved her tension. As a child, growing up in Dun Laoghaire, wretchedly poor, she had been tense with embarrassment and shame at her torn stockings, cheap dresses, and the margarine sandwiches she'd brought to school for lunch. Rage ruled her heart. Being motherless was one thing. Having a feckless drunkard for a father was worse. That her father, Sean, was one of the rich Moores in America, neglected by them, was an injustice that in childhood made her clench her dirty little fists. She'd raged with the knowledge, somehow gained, that her favored cousin Desmond in America had a pony and went to expensive schools. Envy had tortured her. *If I were only Desmond,* she would think, sitting on the curb outside McCarthy's Pub, flexing her fingers, or standing on the pier watching the ships depart with immigrants for England . . . and as, years later, in London, when Desmond inherited Castle Moore, she would say to Sheila in half-humorous despair, "Why *him?* Why not *me?*" Last year, at the time of the Dublin Horse Show, departing Castle Moore after their three-day visit from London, she had said broodingly to Sheila as they drove away, "There's a thing or two I suspect about Desmond. Unsavory. None of my business. But if it's true, I can feel a *little* sorry for him, rotten as he is."

" 'Rotten?' " Sheila had said. "You're just envious of Desmond. You'd do better to expend your energies on your poetry, Winifred. You've almost enough for a small volume. It could go for eight pounds. Maybe more. English pounds."

But Winifred had shaken her head. "I said 'rotten,' Sheila, and I meant rotten. I don't toy with language." She'd made a wry face and added, "I hope to God that being a shit isn't genetic."

Now, in the library, Sheila picked up the television remote

and fiddled with it, watching the screen. "That psychiatrist's coming on again in a minute."

"Dear, God! Another asinine know-it-all with a half-assed theory about why Ms. Tunet killed Desmond."

Sheila spotted Luke Willinger in a duffle coat going past the library door. "Luke! Hello!" She turned down the sound on the television.

Luke paused. "Morning." He glanced in at the newspapers scattered on the floor at Winifred's feet. "Can't stay. I've got to—"

"Please!" Winifred called out quickly. "Come in! Just for a minute. Please! We missed you at breakfast. Rose said you'd gone to Dublin."

"Right." He came in. He stood with his hands in the pockets of the duffle coat; the shoulders were spotted with rain. He looked from Winifred to the television screen, then back at Winifred. Their eyes locked. Luke shrugged. "Go ahead."

"Yes." Winifred eyed him. "I read this morning's *Irish Independent*. It's delivered. That North Hawk story about Torrey Tunet . . . You read the *Independent?*"

"Yes."

"That psychoanalyst in North Hawk who shot himself—that was your father?"

"Stepfather."

"What the *Independent* says—that's what happened?"

"Just about." He dropped into one of the red leather chairs beside the fireplace, stuck out his legs, and waited. The collar of the duffle coat was rucked up in back.

"I'm sorry," Winifred said. She'd read the story twice. There was poetry there, a dirge, an epic, a saga; yet it was really only a sketchy little event in a small American town.

Sheila was nervously fiddling with the television remote. The sound suddenly blasted, an interviewer's voice booming, "In your opinion, Doctor?" and a man in rimless glasses screamed back, "Guilt! Her enormous guilt made her do anything, *anything* to get money to pay for the young woman, Donna Lefevbre's surgery. Even . . . *murder.*"

"Turn that thing *down*, dammit!" Winifred yelled. Sheila fumbled wildly. The volume rose to deafening; the psychiatrist's voice thundered, "She wanted the Moore diamond necklace at any cost, even murder. Why? To expiate her former crimes—thievery, Dr. Willinger's suicide, and paralysis of the younger girl, Donna Lefebvre."

"Sheila! For God's—" The television screen went blank. Sheila, pressing buttons frantically, had turned it off.

They sat. Sheila said, finally, appalled, "Paralysis? What paralysis? The paper didn't—And we must have missed it on the TV. . . . Oh, Winifred!"

"For God's sake, Sheila," Winifred said, "don't start that. You sound like a soap opera." She looked at Luke in the red leather armchair. "What's that idiot psychiatrist talking about? What paralysis?"

Luke rubbed a hand over his face, pulled his nose, coughed, then shrugged. "When it happened—the thievery, my stepfather's suicide, all the publicity—Donna's parents were devastated. They were in shock. George Lefebvre, Donna's father, was a postal worker at the North Hawk post office. When the story broke, he found himself a public spectacle. Half the people in North Hawk suddenly needed rolls of stamps and a dozen other post office services. Poor George! The Lefebvres, with three younger kids, all boys, were a decent French-Canadian family, plenty like them in Massachusetts.

"Anyway—two days after my stepfather's suicide, Donna's mother found her packing some clothes in an old overnight bag. It was just before supper. She was terrified that Donna was so ashamed that she'd try to run away. So after supper, she and George Lefebvre sent Donna upstairs to bed and locked her in. They planned to consult their priest in the morning."

Luke Willinger stopped. He gazed at the pattern on the library rug. He looked from Winifred to Sheila. He took a breath.

"Late that night, an ambulance brought Donna to the North Hawk Mercy Hospital. She was unconscious. They said later that she was claustrophobic. Locked in the bedroom, she was like a terrified bird, wild to escape. She jumped out of the second-story bedroom window. It did something to her spine. She couldn't move her legs. She was paralyzed. For life."

Neither Winifred nor Sheila moved. Then Sheila, hand at her throat, whispered, "For life . . . Oh, that poor . . . that poor—Winifred, I need a drink. I know it's morning, Winifred, but I *need* it."

"Not when you're upset," Winifred said impatiently. "It'll make you sick," and to Luke, "An appalling tale. What's it got to do with Torrey Tunet stealing the Moore necklace?"

"Surgery. There's a new disc operation, possible for Donna's kind of spinal injury. Very delicate surgery. The tab, what with the hospital, therapy, medication, the works, has got to run forty, fifty thousand dollars. Maybe more."

"So that's what that jackass psychiatrist meant? Why Torrey Tunet stole the necklace? That, about guilt? Torrey wanted the money to pay for the operation?"

"Right."

"God! It must have broken Torrey's heart. Donna's being paralyzed. She would've blamed herself."

"Not to mention," Sheila said, "that everybody in North Hawk would have blamed her, too. And for the suicide. They'd've treated her like a pariah."

Winifred eyed Luke. "You, included, of course."

He met her speculative gaze. "Naturally."

"Balls!" Winifred's voice crackled with outrage. She rose like a thundercloud from the tapestry chair. Her square-jawed face with its high color was furious. "Balls! For God's sake! A daring, mischievous fourteen-year-old finds an illegal cache of money—and a twelve-year-old kid wants some drums! Where do you keep your head, Mr. Willinger? In a box buried underground?"

A voice from the doorway, tired but amused, said, "What a lot of noise in here! Sounds like the overture to Wilhelm Tell."

They turned. Torrey Tunet, in her rumpled navy business

suit, stood in the doorway, briefcase in hand. Her face was pale, she looked exhausted; but she wore lipstick that looked freshly, carefully applied.

"You're here?" Winifred stared. "I thought you were being held by the *Garda Siochana*. The paper said —"

"They let me out. On bail."

"Bail? Where did you find the money for bail?"

"I didn't."

"Then who posted bail for you?"

Luke, in the red leather armchair, cleared his throat. "I did."

31

In the rose marble shower with its fragrant soap, Torrey scrubbed off the linoleum-and-disinfectant smell of imprisonment, the echoing police corridors, the clang of metal doors. She slid her fingers at last through the clean silkiness of her dark hair and with her palms sleeked water from her breasts, down her waist and flanks.

"Ms. Tunet?" A knock on the bathroom door.

"Just a minute." She stepped from the shower and snugged a towel around her breasts. In the bedroom she found Janet, the senior maid, waiting.

"Mr. Willinger wants to know if could you meet him at twelve o'clock, before lunch, at the five-bar gate. That's just past the stables."

"Tell him yes. Thanks, Janet."

She was still stunned that Luke Willinger had showed up at her arraignment at the Pearse Street Garda Station and posted bail for her. Then, when she'd been in the toilet, he'd disappeared.

Bewildering. He despised her. And he believed she'd stolen the necklace. Cock-and-bull, he'd thought, when she'd tried to tell him the truth in the pub. Cock-and-bull. They *all* believed she'd stolen that damned necklace — the gardai, the Irish newspapers, the radio and television commentators, and the population of Ireland. And Luke Willinger. So what was he up to? Laying some kind of trap for her?

In the bedroom she sat down at the dressing table and began to put on her makeup. Behind her, Janet Slocum said, "D'you want this cleaned?" She was holding up Torrey's dirty, crumpled navy suit. "There's a place in Ballynagh that can do it in one day, if I ask."

"Yes, please. And thanks." In the mirror, she glanced at Janet, an angular woman in a pale blue uniform with a white bibbed apron. Janet had a long-jawed face and small, brown, monkeylike eyes. She was in her thirties and wore her brown hair in a bun. Something about her made Torry think she had lived hard.

Dressed in a gray flannel shirt, pink belt, dark pants, and comfortable walking boots, Torrey picked up her navy wool sweater. At the bedroom door, she turned back to Janet. "I thought Rose took care of this wing of the castle. Is she all right?"

"Oh, yes, ma'am. But Rose is away. She's off in London for a couple of days' holiday. She'll be back tonight."

Something in Janet's voice made Torrey look searchingly at her. Their eyes met. Torrey had a feeling that Janet knew what was what in a world larger than that of Ballynagh.

32

That mare's to be sold," Janet said to Brian Coffey in the stable yard. Brian Coffey had just trotted Darlin' Pie back into the yard after a half-hour's exercise.

"What! Says who?" Brian slid down from the mare's back, ran a caressing finger down her nose, then gave her a slap on her glossy neck and handed the reins to Kevin, the new lad. Brian's tan cotton jersey was wet with sweat, his red hair damp, with strands sticking to his pale, freckled forehead.

"Who says so? Ms. Winifred Moore, the new owner of Castle Moore. That's who says so."

"Ah, no! Ms. Winifred won't be having the stables then?" Brian's voice was stricken. He looked unhappily after the mare that Kevin was leading into the stables. "I'll be out of a job again! Kevin, too. Not so bad for a young lad like him. But I'm thirty-two! And fellows lining up for my kind of job." He looked miserably into Janet's small, monkeylike eyes. "What about you? You and Rose?"

"Ms. Winifred's keeping me on. Rose, too."

Brian turned away. "I never have the luck." His voice quavered.

Janet said, suddenly gentle, "Maybe Ms. Winifred'll change her mind about the stables. She's still bouncing around on the griddle. Rags to riches."

But Brian only shook his head and turned away, shoulders sagging.

33

In the library, now that Torrey Tunet had gone upstairs to shower and Luke Willinger had gone off somewhere, Winifred and Sheila were alone. Sheila, sitting on a fringed hassock, looked at Winifred in the tapestry chair. "Heavens, Winifred! Mr. Willinger is ridiculously naïve. Bailing Torrey Tunet out of jail! Can he actually believe that Desmond *gave* her the necklace?"

"Why not?"

"Oh, Winifred! Of course Torrey stole it. She wanted money for Donna Lefebvre's surgery. Commendable, I'm sure. Nevertheless, theft and murder." Sheila shuddered. "And may I remind you, Winifred, that the necklace is rightfully yours, as part of your inheritance."

"Rightfully? Desmond just might have given it to Ms. Tunet. She's not beautiful, but she's got something different, special. Poetic, you might say. Anyone could see Desmond was tomcatting after her. He might've given her the necklace. For future sexual favors."

"Sexual favors? Ridiculous!" Sheila yanked at the fringe of the hassock. "Desmond was rich and attractive. He could get all the sexual favors he wanted. He wouldn't need to bribe a woman with expensive gifts. He'd only to say a flattering word and crook his little finger."

Winifred gave a bark of a laugh. "Desmond despised

women! Seducing a woman with a necklace, buying her, in effect, gave him license to do whatever he wanted with her. Or rather . . ." She shrugged.

"Or rather, what?"

" — Or rather, *to* her. To Desmond, women were contemptible flesh to be used. Knowing Desmond, I'd say used sadistically."

"Oh, Winifred!" Sheila pulled nervously at the fringe of the hassock.

"As for Torrey," Winifred said, "there's something pristine and courageous about her. He'd have the added pleasure of turning her into a slut. He'd gloat."

"That's disgusting. You can't really believe your cousin Desmond would — "

"You're ruining that fringe, Sheila . . . *my* fringe, now."

" — really believe Desmond was that . . . that perverted. You've no foundation. You just arbitrarily think such awful things."

Winifred shrugged. Still, she was positive that there was more to it than the months of punishing sex-on-demand, sex of every variety Desmond might have demanded from Torrey Tunet, or even the vicious pleasure of turning Torrey into a slut. Slut wasn't quite right. Victim was closer.

"You make things up out of thin air," Sheila said.

"Maybe so." But there it was: her suspicion that a certain kind of ugliness in her cousin Desmond had started years ago, such long, sad years ago.

34

Fergus Callaghan, with an aching sense of foreboding, knocked and almost stumbled into Maureen Devlin's cottage, barely waiting for her to call out to him to come in.

"Good afternoon, Mrs. Devlin."

He stood just inside the cottage door, holding the can of green paint he'd brought and seeing Maureen spottily because of the bright sunlight he'd come in from and the dimness of the room. Maureen Devlin had done what she could with this old deserted gamekeeper's cottage, but she couldn't punch out windows and let in the sunlight.

"I had my kitchen painted," he said, distractedly, "and I had this green left over, almost half a can. I thought maybe for your front door." He tried to quell his feeling of apprehension. No, more than apprehension: fear. "I could paint it for you." His voice shook. Green paint. Pitiful excuse for coming to the cottage.

"Paint?" Maureen's voice was dull. Fergus felt an even sharper unease. Maureen was at the stove, moving pots around in an aimless, distracted way. She was in her long, black skirt and a gray blouse with the sleeves rolled up. Her curly, burnished-looking hair, tinged with gray, was held back from her forehead by small, curved combs on each side, above her ears.

Now that Fergus could see better, he saw fearfully that

Maureen's face was pale and strained. And when she glanced toward him, there was not the usual mischief in her eyes as though she was teasing him, laughing at his awkward shyness with her. She seemed, in fact, not even to see him. *Finola*, he thought. *Does she know about Finola?* He felt a choking in his throat. He managed, "I thought . . . maybe if you don't want green, I have some white left over from the trim. I'd only have to throw it away if I didn't give it to you." What did she know about Finola? Where was Finola? The door to the bedroom where she and Finola slept was closed.

"I've no time for painting." She didn't even thank him; she just stood rubbing her arms and looking into space as if he weren't there.

He felt dizzy with a kind of panic. He said, "I could paint it for you . . . the front door. I could use the brush the painter used for my kitchen."

Maureen didn't answer. She uncovered a big bowl on the table, punched down a batch of dough, and covered the bowl again with the towel.

A kitchen timer pinged. Maureen put on mitten pot holders and took a pan of bread from the oven. "Finola put these in for me. They're just ready." She put the loaves on a wooden rack on the table, six fragrant loaves. The delicious smell of fresh-baked bread filled the room.

Maureen stood very still for a moment, her back to him; then she turned. "The papers say that the American young woman, Torrey Tunet, killed Desmond Moore. What will they do to her? The police?"

Fergus said, "I don't know."

Only now did Maureen meet his gaze. The anguish in her eyes was like a blow. He felt such a rush of pity and love and horror and terror that he might have screamed or fallen to the floor. But he only stood there holding the can of green paint, the wire handle cutting into his fingers.

Maureen said, "Leave the paint. And thank you . . . Did you come to order bread? You can have one of these loaves if you like."

He lowered the can of paint to the floor.

"I'll make holes in the bag because the bread's still hot; it mustn't get soggy." Maureen put a loaf into a brown paper bag. She pierced the bag several times with a fork. Fergus put down his pounds and pence and picked up the bag. He could feel the heat of the bread rising from it.

Outside, going toward his motorbike, Fergus felt dizzily at war with himself, as though he were two people. All his life he had been a man of honor.

So this was agony. Agony because of the patent leather doll's shoe that he'd seen on Desmond's desk in the library at Castle Moore on Thursday morning. He had been putting his brief-case of genealogy papers on the library table when it had caught his eye. A doll's shoe, black patent leather, with a pink rosette, a tiny fake diamond centered in the rosette. Staring at the little shoe, he had felt sick. But could a maid have found the shoe and put it on the desk? He had to know. *He had to know.* He had then searched through Desmond's desk, searched through his personal papers, found his Visa statements, and run a trembling finger down lists of purchases. And stopped at one. The doll had not been bought in Dublin, but in another city. And with reason: Careful, ugly planning. That kind of reason. And its fruition. A child's fear and guilt. But then something had gone wrong for the molester, and Finola had put the doll in a plastic bag and buried it in the woods.

But even then he had not been able to believe it. *Was it really so?* He had left the library and in the woods where he had seen Finola bury her treasure by the bramble bush, he had brushed away the dirt and uncovered the little doll's shoe still wrapped in his handkerchief. It was the mate to the doll's shoe that was now in his pocket. Or was it really the mate?

For a moment, he just knelt there. Then he dug deeper.

The doll was in a plastic bag. He could see pink and blue through the plastic.

He'd pulled off the plastic and gazed at the doll. Expensive. Golden-brown hair, a delicately painted ceramic face, the glass eyes with their curly lashes, the silk dress, and the crocheted socks; the socks had each a tiny rosebud. But the shoes were missing. Of course. One had been wrapped in his handkerchief, the other in his pocket.

It was the rosebuds on the socks that somehow filled Fergus with horror, as though they made him realize the actuality of the doll being there, having been buried and now in his hands.

He'd carefully put the doll back in the plastic bag and gone back to his motorbike beside the bridle path. He'd slid the bag into the carrier on the motorbike.

He had not returned to Castle Moore. All the way back to Dublin, he was sick with rage. In his kitchen on Boylston Street, he sat for a long time with his head in his hands.

Now, this terrible Friday morning, holding the bag of bread, Fergus stumbled away from the cottage. He was filled with fear and pity for Maureen. That fearful anguish in her eyes, anguish because she knew. Maureen at the stove moving pots around in an aimless, distracted way, her face pale and strained. The way she seemed not even to see him. Maureen of the lovely white feet, of the delicious bread, the droll humor, the love for her little girl. Maureen, Maureen, Maureen . . .

But if Inspector O'Hare learned of the molestation of Finola and its perpetrator, the owner of Castle Moore, he would train his sights on the dangerously wild-hearted Maureen Devlin. He loved Maureen Devlin. Above all, he loved Maureen. The arrest of Torrey Tunet as a suspect in the murder of Desmond Moore had stunned him. He had blindly assumed that Desmond's murder would forever remain a mystery. What now was he to do?

When Fergus Callaghan was gone, Maureen folded her arms and shivered. She stood gazing unseeingly at the fresh-baked loaves on the rack. Hours crawling with horror, the night a waking nightmare. A chestnut horse with a red-and-black plaid blanket; she had known in shock who it was when Finola had said it.

"Who is 'he'?" she had asked Finola. In her apron pocket

she had clutched the car keys she'd found under the cottage window, the keys on a key chain that said Volvo . . . so the man from Helsinki had stopped his rented yellow car only a hundred yards from the cottage . . . he had come through the hedge to the cottage . . . he had looked in the window and seen something so secret and ugly that he had to be killed. The pediatrician in Dublin had confirmed what Maureen had suspected in horror about her child so strangely quiet and lethargic.

"Who?" Maureen had repeated to Finola's bent head, flushed cheek.

"I don't know. A man. One time he came on a horse. A chestnut. It had a red-and-black plaid blanket. He brought me a doll."

"One time?" Her heart lurched. "He came more than once?"

"Three times. He hurt me. But he brought me that doll. When he'd leave, he'd take the doll back. He said each time that next time he'd give it to me for good. This last time, he . . . he . . . something happened. And he forgot the doll. So now it's mine. It—I buried it, I was afraid."

"Something—What happened?"

Finola's eyes went wide and strangely blank. Her voice was a whisper. "Someone came."

35

At six-thirty, Dennis O'Curry, trembling, locked the door of his butcher shop and pulled the green shade halfway down, as usual. Everyone in Ballynagh knew that meant he'd closed up.

His heart thumping, he went to the butcher block and picked up the wire brush. He scraped it back and forth on the wood, cleaning it, a rhythmic motion he always found calming.

But this time it couldn't soothe the knot of anxiety in his chest. Was he going crazy? He used to have dizzy spells, maybe a half-dozen in all, up to five or six years ago. But after his wife had made him go to the doctor and stop eating the leftover ends of cold cuts, the dizziness had stopped.

So what was this . . . a new craziness? He'd gone across to O'Malley's Pub for his usual lager at four o'clock. Everybody in Ballynagh knew it was his siesta time, just like in Spain and maybe Portugal; it was his four o'clock fifteen-minute siesta.

And when he'd come back, there it was. Beside the butcher block, as usual. Where it belonged. The knife. His good butcher knife that had been missing since yesterday. He'd picked it up and stared at it. Here it was. And he'd been blaming Maureen Devlin for mislaying it. Yesterday he'd wanted to telephone Maureen to ask where she might have put it, but it was her day off and she didn't have a telephone. Not that she'd even remember! Absentminded, Maureen was, these last few days, going stock-still, staring blankly across the marble counter at this or that customer as though she was in a trance. Like this morning when he'd asked about the knife, just a blank look. A week ago he'd considered raising her by four pounds a week. She was worth it, he'd thought, so he'd always bent a little, like allowing her an hour off last Tuesday morning because she'd said she had "personal business." She'd always been closemouthed. None of his affair anyway—a good-looking widow, what she did and with what man in her bed, was up to her. He'd even been planning to lace into her about being careless, about putting things in their proper place. Knives, especially. So he wasn't going to give her that raise. Not yet, anyway.

Someone was knocking on the glass. Old Mrs. Reardon. She had bent down and was peering under the green shade. He shook his head. Closed meant closed.

At the butcher block he stood thinking, anxious, bewildered. He looked again at the knife. Those dizzy spells. Could it be that the knife had fallen on the floor and later he'd picked it up without thinking and automatically put it in its proper place beside the butcher block?

Best to say nothing. Not to his wife, not to anybody over at O'Malley's, not to anyone . . . or before you knew it, they'd be carting him off to a bedlam place.

36

The five-bar gate was two hundred years old and made of hickory, most of the bark long gone. Torrey reached the gate and found Luke Willinger waiting, one foot on the bottom railing of the gate, gazing across a meadow where sheep grazed.

Suspicious, still stunned that he had posted her bail, she said with deliberate coldness, "Hello, Luke," and when he turned and saw her, "Why'd you post bail for me? It isn't as though I'm your favorite person."

He took his foot from the gate and faced her, wearing jeans and a tan jacket over a black T-shirt. Torrey expected to see the tension come back to his jaw that was there whenever they met. But this time, it wasn't. He was simply looking at her. She was startled, unnerved. "Well?" She pushed a fingernail under a piece of bark on the gate and chipped it off. "Naturally, I'm confused."

"Naturally," Luke said. "I'm a little confused myself. You might say that I posted bail for you because this morning I started remembering the kinds of pranks you played as a kid in North Hawk. So—"

"You *what?*"

"Wednesday night at the lake, you were having Desmond on, weren't you? Carrying on like a banshee about losing the necklace. You must've guessed what he was up to with you. Tempting you. Did you? Guess?"

She stared at him. "Yes, I guessed."

"Then sneaking down to the lake, getting the necklace from under the rock — you had me fooled. When'd you give it back to him?"

"Next morning. In the library." She was stunned, then bewildered. "But why, then, in Dublin, in that pub —? You threatened me! Threatened to tell Desmond I'd stolen —"

"Yes. At first, I thought — So I would've turned you in for stealing the necklace. As I warned you in the pub."

"You're leaving me far behind," Torrey said. "What are you telling me?"

"I'm saying that I didn't twig it until later. Until early this morning in fact." He gave her a straight look. "Now I'm asking you: Did you give the necklace back to Desmond the next morning?"

"Yes."

"Right," Luke said. "And then Desmond gave you back the necklace for good. Buying you into bed."

She felt her face go red. Anger? Shame? "And now I suppose you believe I was peddling the necklace at Weir's? That I'd decided to become Desmond's whore?"

"Of course! Damn it! Desmond must've expected something in return! He wasn't a philanthropist. You were making a deal with him!" His voice shook with anger as he glared at her.

She folded her arms and stared at him. Why was he so angry?

"Obviously it was a deal: you and Desmond."

Bewildered, she said, "What are you up to, Luke Willinger? What game? I'm not a fool, Luke." And when he only looked back at her, she said slowly, the thought forming as she said it, "You've got a reason! *For some reason* you believe Desmond later on really did give me the necklace. That's why you posted bail for me."

She felt, as she said it, that a breeze, cool and fresh, had swept across the meadow, taking her confusion with it. She said, "What is it? What's the reason?"

Then she waited, somehow relaxed. She felt she had an infinity of time, the meadow, the hills and mountains in a hazy distance, the grasshoppers humming, the sun warm on her head. She could see that Luke Willinger's forehead was getting sunburned. Likely, hers, too; neither of them had thought to wear a hat. She put her hand to her forehead. Hot. And now, relaxed, waiting, because in this particular chess game it could only be his move. She even smiled at Luke Willinger.

He said, "You're pretty damned acute. I've a good reason." He eyed her. "It won't be the sweetest thing to your ears."

"Try me. I'm a big, brave girl. Woman."

"Good. Because in Dublin early this morning in a coffee shop, I met someone who confided to me something about Desmond and the necklace. I can't tell you who that person was or how they knew. I had to swear to keep her out of it. But here's what I learned."

He paused, seeing himself at seven o'clock this morning in the coffee shop, Janet Slocum on the plastic stool beside him, her pockmarked face serious, telling him between bites of the sweet bun what she'd long since discovered. . . . Janet Slocum saying, "If Ms. Tunet killed Desmond Moore, he had it coming. It was justice. A crazy kind of justice! If she really stole the necklace and killed Desmond Moore, as the police say she did, she stole a necklace worth only five pounds!" And when Luke looked at her in disbelief, " 'Tis true! He had a cache of those paste necklaces that he palmed off on young girls who he then used sexually." Janet laughed scornfully. "Had a whole box of them in his bedroom, he did! I know a girl, only sixteen, who tried to pawn one of those necklaces. Poor thing! She was pregnant and needed an abortion. But abortion's illegal in Ireland, so she went to London. When she tried to pawn the necklace to pay for the abortion, she was offered only five pounds."

"So that's it." Luke folded his arms. "Desmond gave you a necklace worth peanuts." He expected to see Torrey's face stricken, outraged. Instead, she only went a little pale. Then she looked off and gave a little laugh. "Would I have sold my pure white body in exchange for the necklace? As Desmond expected? For a minute there, in Weir's jewelry shop, I almost thought yes. But I'll never know. If I'd given in, if I'd played Desmond's game, I suppose he'd have used me a time or two in bed before I tried to sell the necklace and discovered it was a fake." She shuddered, then frowned. "I'm sorry for those other women."

"Girls, not women. He used young ones . . . I was told. But there was something particular about you."

She cast him a quick glance. "Variety, maybe. I'm going to demand that the gardai have the necklace appraised. When they discover it's worthless, they'll have to admit that Desmond Moore might have given it to me . . . that although he wouldn't have given me a necklace worth maybe twenty thousand pounds, he'd certainly give me one worth five pounds."

He regarded her uneasily, hating to point out her still precarious situation; nevertheless, he said, "But the gardai may suggest that you believed the necklace was worth twenty thousand pounds and so you stole it."

"Oh, damn it, of course! Where's my head."

"Better to wait, not tell the gardai anything, not insist on having the necklace appraised. It's too weak a defense. So far. But if we —"

"We?"

He said impatiently, "Why not? Waste of years, waste of emotions, that snare I trapped myself in in North Hawk. And trapped you in. You caught it from me, like a virus, that hatred. Yes, 'we.' I'll help you . . . if that's all right with you? I've already got an idea or two." He flashed an encouraging look at her. Unfortunately, he was lying; he had no ideas. But he'd work at it. His glance slid past Torrey's shoulder, down to the left where the meadow ended and the long bulk of the stables lay. There, on the scrubbed concrete floor outside Black Pride's stall, Desmond Moore's blood was now a pale pink stain.

They left the five-bar gate and walked the two miles to Ballynagh. Luke had earlier told Janet that they would not be having lunch at Castle Moore. "Too much for us to talk privately about," he'd said to Torrey, "and Sheila Flaxton has a dozen ears and besides she thinks you're guilty as hell. Makes for a lousy appetite."

So at O'Malley's Pub in Ballynagh, noisy with its lunch crowd of regulars, they ate plates of eggs and ham, hunks of bread slathered with sweet butter, and drank steaming hot black tea from ten-ounce mugs. They ate as hungrily as though they were soldiers stoking up for the battle of their lives, which, as Torrey pointed out, was grimly true for her. Luke, over a second mug of tea, said, "In North Hawk — What happened to the peacock bandanna? Blue peacocks on it? I used to see you walking on Main Street when you were a kid, looking like a pirate with that bandanna around your head. And little Donna Lefebvre trotting beside you. The pair of you, off on your adventures, your excitements. Later, when I had to hate you, I'd get flashes of you in that peacock bandanna. It made hating you more difficult."

"My father's gift, that bandanna, before he went away for good. I heard five years ago, from my mother — she's married again and living in California — that my father had died in New Zealand. The flu. Overnight. He'd been captaining a tourist cruise boat. White uniform, spic-and-span, with a captain's gold-braided cap that said HARMONY CRUISES. Perhaps that shamed him; it wasn't the high adventure he'd gone to find."

"Every person hungers," Luke said. "All kinds of restless, confused appetites. My stepfather's, for instance. I've sometimes wondered, did something make his tax evasion 'all right' in his mind? Justify it? A highly respected psychoanalyst. Yet hiding suitcases of money."

"Like Desmond Moore and his sexual avidity," Torrey agreed. "All unleashed. No boundaries. As though he had a right, had found a reason to justify—" She shuddered. "But that's just my feeling."

Luke said nothing. Torrey, sensing something held back, looked at him. "What is it?"

Luke frowned. He shook his head. "I'm thinking of something that affected Desmond. But I don't want to make a peach pie without peaches."

"Try," Torrey said. "The peaches may appear."

Luke said, "The night before Desmond was murdered, he got drunk and told me a tragic tale. In the castle library, did you notice that portrait over the fireplace?"

"The jolly looking gentleman in whiskers and flowered waistcoat, with a gold-knobbed cane? Looked eighteenth century."

" 'Jolly'? Oh yes, with a jolly gold-knobbed cane."

"What about him?"

"Albert, the Duke of Comerford. Castle Moore was Castle Comerford before the Moores owned it. The Comerfords were Anglo-Irish. The Anglo-Irish—they were really English—became the great Irish landowners in Ireland after England conquered Ireland. Anglo-Irish means a different religion, a different nationality, a different class from the Irish. Really English and Protestant landowners. They held despotic power over the conquered Irish. Perhaps you know?"

"I know Irish history, yes."

"Desmond kept that portrait of the Duke of Comerford over the fireplace to remind him. 'To look at it and remember,' he told me."

"Remember what?"

"Albert, the Duke of Comerford, had once beaten an Irish stable boy to death. A stable boy of sixteen. The boy had neglected to feed one of the Duke's breeding horses."

Torrey clattered down her mug of tea. "Oh, no! I can't—! Was he imprisoned for it? The duke?"

"Not even fined. Not even hushed up. All an accident. Had lost his temper. Gave the stable boy's family ten pounds. Desmond said the boy was put in the ground, the priest said his words, and the grave digger threw in the dirt. Catherine Comerford, the wife of Albert, sent a wreath of roses to the burial. It was said that the same week, Albert, Duke of Comerford, entertained the mayor of Dublin at dinner at Castle Comerford."

"God! Do you believe it actually happened? The stable boy beaten to death?"

"More to the point, Desmond did. In fact, he knew. It was Moore family history."

"How? Are you telling me . . ."

"Yes. The stable boy was Terence Moore, Desmond's great-great-grandfather's young brother."

They sat. Torrey said, "That's quite some peach pie you've dished up. What's your point?"

"I'm not sure. Desmond's personality—or maybe character. Why, for instance, would he keep Duke Albert's portrait before him, a red flag, reminding him? Any healthy-minded person would have had the portrait carted away, or sold or burned. But Desmond kept it there above the fireplace, facing his desk. Something weird about that, as though he were using it in some way. He even had a spotlight shining down on the portrait. On the jolly Duke of Comerford."

"Yes. Weird."

They took a short cut back to Castle Moore, crossed a meadow, and skirted the low, white stables where a blowy west wind raised a swirl of dust in the stable yard. In the chill of the wind, Torrey shivered. She gazed at the stables where the stable boy had been beaten and died. A red-haired young man in suspenders, jodhpurs, and ankle boots was crossing the stable yard with a bucket, probably oats for the horses. She recognized Brian Coffey and remembered that Coffey had ridden with Desmond Moore to a horse auction in Wexford the morning that the man from Helsinki, Mr. Kasvi, had been strangled in the woods. Desmond Moore had planned to develop a Castle Moore stable, with Brian Coffey as the stable manager. She felt sorry for Brian Coffey, who would now likely be out of a job. So would the new lad, Kevin, hired to help Brian Coffey. A pity.

The lad, Kevin, came into the tack room carrying a broken pitchfork. The fork had come loose from the handle because the handle was rotting. It would have to be cut down. "I was tossing and tidying the straw bed around Big Shot," he said to Brian Coffey, who was putting down an empty bucket, "and it just came off. It—"

"Let's have a look."

Kevin handed over the pieces. He was glad of the warmth of the tack room, which was heated by the stove whose dry warmth protected leather from mildew and dried the dampness out of the horse rugs.

Kevin gazed around with satisfaction; he liked the neatness, the warmth, the horse smell. Mr. Coffey had put him to work cleaning up this neglected tack room first thing when he'd hired him a month ago. The saddles and bridles were now neatly ranged, the brushes on shelves, the straps hung on hooks.

Over on the left, the three-pronged harness hook still held the bridle that Mr. Desmond had last used when he rode the chestnut, Black Pride, the day that he and Mr. Coffey had ridden to Wexford and bought Darlin' Pie. The red-and-black plaid rug that went under Black Pride's saddle was still on a line near the stove; Mr. Coffey had told Kevin to put the rug there to dry out the dampness.

"It can be fixed, Kevin." Mr. Coffey handed him back the fork and handle. "Meantime, you'll find another fork in box number four. Four is storage, for now."

"Yes, Mr. Coffey."

Taking down the other pitchfork, Kevin wondered if he and Mr. Coffey would be out of a job. They said in the kitchen that Winifred Moore, the new owner, didn't plan to keep a stable. Mr. Coffey had a long face on him about it. Troubled, he was. Gloomy. And a bit jumpy.

37

It rained all weekend. The mountains around Ballynagh disappeared, hidden by drifting rags of fog. Hazy yellow lights shone from O'Malley's Pub and the few shops. The fruit on Stevens' outdoor stand was wet; people sloshed with hunched shoulders; the bus splashed its way on the main street, north to Dublin, south to Cork. Sergeant Bryson had Saturday afternoon off; he was in his garage at home, working on his bicycle.

In the Ballynagh garda station Saturday afternoon, Inspector O'Hare sat absorbed over an open account book on his desk. Strange and revealing this account book. In some way that he couldn't understand, it gave Inspector O'Hare a sense of poetry. Yet there was no poetry on the pen and ink pages. It was, simply, a small account book he had taken from Miss Tunet's bedroom at Castle Moore.

Miss Tunet earned money erratically: Greece, Portugal, Spain, Belgium. Jobs that paid decent amounts of money. She spent it confusingly. She lived as frugally as the Little Match Girl. She drove a ten-year-old car. She'd bought no clothes during the past year except a winter coat from a thrift shop in Boston, thirty dollars. She'd sent away to a mail-order house for a six-dollar gadget for cutting her own hair. Yet she was making sizeable monthly payments for an expensive van with special handicap controls. The van had undoubtedly been bought for Donna Lefebvre, the paralyzed victim of Miss Tunet's first thievery. A guilt purchase. So Miss Tunet at least felt guilt or remorse about her friend. Maybe she had two sides: good and evil.

Inspector O'Hare sat back. Miss Tunet's career, her interpreting jobs, took her to countries all over Europe and Eastern Europe. A beautiful cover-up for stealing. O'Hare pulled thoughtfully at his nose. Miss Tunet had an oddly lovely face beneath that satiny swatch of dark hair that fell across her brow; she could get away with a lot with a man, make a dupe of him until too late. Maybe she gloried in it. Maybe she kept double books and had an account book of a strangely different nature secreted somewhere.

The phone rang. It was Chief Superintendent O'Reilly in Dublin. "The Desmond Moore investigation, Inspector," came O'Reilly's deep voice. "Ms. Winifred Moore, of London, will inherit Castle Moore and other assets of her late cousin. So I presume — "

"Yes, Superintendent," O'Hare said quickly, "I'm aware that Miss Moore has had considerable enmity toward her cousin — her parents having been cut out of the Moore fortune thirty-five years ago and it no doubt rankling. I have an appointment to question Miss Moore on Monday as to her whereabouts at the time of Desmond Moore's death." O'Hare felt an enormous relief to be able to report his appointment with Winifred Moore to Chief Superintenent O'Reilly. He had, always, a chilling fear that he would overlook a simple, obvious bit of routine investigation; he had nightmares of his superiors at the *Garda Siochana* headquarters in Dublin regarding his dereliction with surprise, scorn, contempt. Or worse: laughter. He added, now, "The bits and pieces are falling well into place." When Superintendent O'Reilly had hung up, O'Hare thought, *Waste of time questioning Winifred Moore.* He looked down at the account book on his desk. Yes. Pointless to interrogate Winifred Moore.

38

On Sunday afternoon, in the unseasonably cold and drizzling weather, Rose arrived back at Castle Moore from her trip to London. She was so exhausted that she was trembling. She dropped her overnight case on the chair in her room in the west wing, pulled off her wet raincoat, and collapsed onto the bed. The crossing from England to Dun Leoghaire on the Sealink ferry had been rough; a lot of passengers had been seasick, though Rose had only felt queasy and had eaten nothing on the ferry. Then there had been the bus trip to Dublin, changing to the bus that went through Ballynagh, and walking along the hedged road and up the winding drive to Castle Moore beneath a lowering sky in the raw, bone-chilling drizzle. She yearned for a cup of hot tea and some crackers and jam. Later, when she got up the energy, she'd undress, put on her flannel bathrobe, and fill her electric teapot at the bathroom faucet. The jam and the box of crackers were on the closet shelf.

"So you're back." Janet stood in the doorway, tying on a starched, freshly ironed white apron. Her small eyes, so monkeylike, looked searchingly at Rose. "How is Hannah? Did she come back with you?"

Rose smiled at Janet, grateful for the concern in Janet's whiskey-hoarse voice. It was no secret to Rose that Janet Slocum went often to Dublin to sit at AA meetings in church basements and community houses, going off even on rain-swept days or on cold winter nights, taking the bus to Dublin and back. The knowing had somehow made a closer friendship between them; they shared confidences.

"Hannah's fine, but she's staying in London two more days. The ferry trip would have been too rough for her, considering . . ."

They looked at each other. Rose settled back and closed her eyes. "In two weeks, Hannah will be seventeen."

39

On Sunday afternoon, Luke crossed the immense, lofty hall of Castle Moore, his footsteps echoing on the polished flagstones. He went into the library, walking now on priceless Aubusson carpets. The library was gloomy, the long windows rain darkened; it had been raining all day. Luke pressed a switch on the left of the carved doorway. A half-dozen lamps on chests, tables, and breakfronts immediately lit the library with soft lights.

Luke crossed to the broad mahogany table. He would collect his sketches for the landscaping project. Desmond's tax-saving landscaped gardens were a vanished dream. Good-bye to his twenty-thousand-dollar fee. And good-bye to poor Desmond, most foully murdered.

He glanced at the gilt-framed painting of the duke of Comerford. Ruddy-faced Albert, Duke of Comerford, in his flowered waistcoat, one well-kept hand on his gold-knobbed cane. Had Duke Alfred beaten the stable boy with that gold-knobbed cane? Or had he snatched up a horse whip and whipped the boy? Rage and power spinning out of control.

Luke turned from the portrait. Four of his six rolled-up sketches were on the mahogany table. He saw the other two behind Desmond's leather chair at the Florentine desk, propped against the bookcase whose bottom shelf held a row of videos.

He picked up his sketches, glancing at the titles on the video sleeves. Then he looked more closely, surprised. *Landscaping of Traditional Gardens* and *Irish Gardens, Twentieth Century*. The sleeves of those two videos looked well-handled, the corners worn.

Luke's eyebrows rose. Had he underrated Desmond Moore's aesthetic interest in landscaping? Had Desmond had a stronger interest in Irish gardens than Luke had suspected?

The video player was on an ornate, polished table beside the fireplace. Luke loaded the *Irish Gardens, Twentieth Century* video into the player, turned on the power, set the channel, and pressed the play button. The video came on.

Five minutes later, sickened, he turned it off. He removed the cassette and put it back in the bookcase, next to the other well-handled *Landscaping of Traditional Gardens*, which he could only presume would be as obscene, as lascivious, as perverted as the cassette he had viewed.

Then he stood whistling between his teeth, eyes narrowed, thinking. What he was thinking was far-fetched. But . . . worth pursuing?

He left the library.

40

In her bedroom, Torrey wearily put down the list she'd made of words that were the latest slang with Hungarian teenagers. The newest slang in Budapest could pop up at the conference, even from that fussy Hungarian who had recovered from his upset stomach but had now lost his voice. Laryngitis.

All this rainy weekend, she'd worked on her translations. Luckily, she hadn't been fired from the Hungarian-Belgium job. She guessed that the Hungarians and the French-speaking Belgians didn't look at Ireland's RTE television or read *The Irish Independent*. Or maybe they'd felt they couldn't easily shift horses in midstream? She was their original horse.

Meantime, until little Mr. Fusspot got his voice back, which might be in a day or even a week, she was on reduced pay. So—She shivered. She had time to worry, to sweat, to drive herself half-mad trying to figure out how to save herself from an indictment for murder and theft.

She pushed aside the list of Hungarian slang and got up. She was in her gray slacks and black turtleneck. It was already six-thirty; she should shower and change for dinner. Winifred had invited her and Luke to remain at Castle Moore as her guests during the investigation.

A gust of wind, a spatter of rain; curtains billowed at one of the long windows. She crossed to close it. At the window she gazed out a moment at the gray veil of rain over the hills and craggy mountains; somehow beautiful. She leaned out and looked down to the left. She could see one end of the stables. There, on the cement walkway, Brian Coffey and Kevin had come upon Desmond Moore's body.

Brian Coffey. And Kevin, the new lad.

Torrey drew back inside. She pulled the window closed and latched it. Brian Coffey. And Kevin.

She stood by the window a moment longer, thinking.

Tomorrow morning after breakfast she would drop in at the stables.

41

Monday morning at eight o'clock, the air was brisk and sunny; fat white clouds floated in a brilliant blue sky.

In the stable yard, Brian Coffey said apologetically to Torrey, pushing a hand through his red hair, "No, ma'am, sorry ma'am, not the chestnut, not Black Pride, he's too big and strong willed. Only Mr. Desmond rode Black Pride."

"Oh . . . ? I just thought he was beautiful. Any horse will do then," Torrey lied. She smiled innocently at Brian Coffey and twitched her nostrils as though she might smell out a whiff of a clue to Desmond Moore's murderer.

She had awakened at six. She didn't have jodhpurs or breeches and boots, but wore blue jeans and sneakers, a white pullover, and a khaki waterproof shell. She'd had a buttered roll and a cup of coffee standing up in the kitchen, too tense to eat anything more.

"Well, what horse then?" If she had to ride some damned horse to justify her coming to the stables, she'd do it. Covertly, she studied Brian Coffey. He had a thin, worried-looking face, an unhappy face. And pale. As though his freckled skin might never have been touched by the sun; it was not a skin that tanned.

"The brown mare, then," Brian Coffey said. "You can have Walk Baby. She hasn't yet had her morning exercise."

"Fine." She followed Brian Coffey into the stables, close on his heels. She looked around at the stalls with their half doors. The hay-strewn cement walkway smelled of horse and fresh hay. Kevin stood before a stall, filling a red aluminum pail with a hose; he ducked his head at Torrey. He looked as innocent as a gosling. "Ma'am," he said, as they passed.

In their stalls, two horses jerked their heads at her. One lifted a quivering lip, showing yellow teeth, and stamped its feet. A rusty pail of currycombs sat on a low wooden bench.

In front of box four, Torrey saw an open carton filled with shiny new steel hasps. The door of the stall itself was a splintered mess of rotten wood.

"That's where . . . ?" Torrey stopped and folded her arms. *Come on, Brian, let's chat, let's talk. Tell me about it, Brian. I'm a friend, Brian, right? Finding Mr. Desmond's body must have been a horror, right, Brian?* She toed a bunched bit of damp hay.

"Yes, that's it." Brian's voice was toneless as he gazed at the splintered door. "That was Black Pride's stall. That day . . . the murder . . . When it happened, the loud noise terrified Black Pride; he went wild. Burst right through that old, rotting wood." Brian blew out a breath; Torrey smelled stale beer. Loud noise? Did he mean voices? More than voices?

"All the stalls needed new doors," Brian went on in that odd, dead tone. "Mr. Desmond had already ordered the wood and hardware, new hasps and such. But now . . ." Brian kicked the carton of hardware. His shoulders had a defeated look.

"Loud noise?" Torrey's heart beat hard. She said, deliberately scornful, "Voices aren't that loud! And horses are used to barking dogs. So you can't tell me — "

"The shot!" The words burst defensively from Brian Coffey. Then he gasped and jerked his head up. The look he gave her was as startled and confused as though the words had not come from him. "No, I mean their voices were loud . . . like shooting anger at each other, like shots. That's it . . . That's what I meant."

Torrey felt a wild, dizzying excitement. Got you, Brian! Desmond had been viciously knifed to death. But . . . a shot?

Could there have been a gunshot that Brian Coffey hadn't reported to Inspector O'Hare? Brian Coffey must know more than he'd told. She'd find out what it was. But don't rush it. Brian had hunched up his shoulders as though he'd ducked back into a shell.

Now, damn it, she'd have to ride that mare, Walk Baby, or Brian might get the wind up.

Two miles from Castle Moore, she reined in the mare. This was surely a bridle path she had come across; there were distinct hoofprints in the soft earth and broken branches on one side. Possibly it was the bridle path that Desmond Moore and Brian Coffey had taken two days before Desmond was murdered, the day the man from Helsinki was strangled. She looked around at the woods. It hummed with crickets; birds sang; small creatures scurried in the underbrush.

A branch snapped. She turned in the saddle. Nothing. Nobody. But somewhere out there was Desmond Moore's murderer. She imagined a still, watching figure, a masked face, the murderer's head in a black, knitted balaclava. Under the mask, he was smiling. He wanted her to pay for his evil deed, while he went free.

He was out there, somewhere. But she was on a track. She would keep Brian Coffey in her sights.

42

At eight o'clock Monday morning, Luke Willinger walked quickly through the upper hallway and down a half-dozen stone steps. He made a right turn and was in the south wing of the castle.

His head ached. Appalling nightmares of men and children, outgrowths of Desmond's *Irish Gardens, Twentieth Century* video, had awakened him during the night, leaving him feeling as if he was gasping on some rocky shore, only to drift asleep again and be borne back into a poisoned tide.

Then, abruptly awake, he'd suddenly remembered something Janet Slocum had told him at their second encounter at the coffee shop in Dublin. Janet Slocum, an odd one, with bits of conjecture that she dropped at odd moments. Janet Slocum . . . finger tapping significantly at her temple. He'd have a look right now.

He'd dressed quickly in corduroy pants, white shirt, and black V-necked sweater. Whatever hell people made on earth, it was a glorious morning, the air a drink of fresh cold water through his open windows.

He strode along a corridor through a series of dark-stained, polished arches and equally dark wainscotting, with royal blue walls. At the end of the hallway on the left was a wide, ridged door with a filigreed bronze knob. Luke turned the knob and opened the door to the late Desmond Moore's bedroom.

For the next five minutes he stood leaning back against the wrought-iron footboard of Desmond Moore's bed, arms folded, staring at the gilt-framed oil painting on the Regency-striped red-and-gold wall. So this was the painting that Janet Slocum had told him about. "Shows he wasn't right, upstairs" — tapping her temple — "or why'd he have *that?*"

It was a portrait of a lady in silks and satins. She was seated on a stone bench in a garden. She had two children at her knee, a boy and a girl, exquisitely dressed, and three lean hounds lying nearby. The little boy was about three, the girl about eight or nine.

The gold plaque on ornate frame said *CATHERINE, DUCHESS OF COMERFORD AND HER CHILDREN,* 1790.

Luke finally stirred. Downstairs, he came into the raftered kitchen with its cavernous fireplace, heavy cupboards, and the big, modern iron range.

Rose was there, alone. She was at one of the marble counters, cutting bread, singing under her breath

"Morning, Rose . . . Is Janet about?" There would be corners of Janet's mind, that, stirred up, would bring something important to the surface that he could grasp. He had the damndest feeling that if he could discover the machinations of the mind of the late Desmond Moore, he might save the very alive Torrey Tunet.

Rose shook her head. "Janet's gone to Dublin. Has one of those — " she stopped, almost biting her tongue. She went red. *One of those meetings,* Luke guessed. An AA meeting. A meeting for drunks. Like me.

Rose cut herself a thick slice of bread. The crust crackled under the knife. "Would you like a slice, Mr. Willinger?"

"No, thanks, Rose."

"You're sure? 'Tis bread from heaven, that tasty! Still warm from Mrs. Devlin's oven. I must ask Ms. Winifred, does she want to keep on having the bread delivered. T'was Mr. Desmond who'd always insisted on it."

"Yes?" He was restlessly wandering the kitchen, thinking of

the portrait in Desmond Moore's bedroom; Dublin was a half-hour away. If Janet Slocum had gone to the eight o'clock meeting at Saint Anne's she might be back at Castle Moore by nine-thirty.

"This here's the heel," Rose said. "It's the best part, and with a dab of butter on it. Chewy." Rose buttered the heel and put it on a plate. "Go ahead . . . This past week, Maureen Devlin's been delivering it herself. A hardship, it must be, what with her having to get to O'Curry's in Ballynagh at six."

"Who? What?" He picked up the buttered heel and bit into it.

"Where she works. Mrs. Devlin. O'Curry's butcher shop. Till last week, the little girl delivered the bread. Half-asleep she'd be, flaxen hair, hardly combed, lids halfway down over her eyes. Just slits of the bluest blue showing. Shy, she was. Sometimes I'd be up and have the kitchen door open and she'd hand me in the bread. A pretty little thing, the child. Finola, her name is. About eight. You'd see her playing in the woods."

"A pretty little thing," Luke repeated. He was staring at Rose. "Finola. Playing in the woods."

For some ten minutes after leaving the kitchen, Luke sat in his rented car before the castle. The sun reflected on the hood of the car; birds sang in the bushes, a squirrel hopped onto the broad stone steps of the castle, held a bit of something between its paws, nibbled and nibbled it, then whisked off.

Luke started the car. He would go to the village. Exactly why he was going to Ballynagh, he could not pin down. Finola was only a name. Yet he had a peculiar sense of foreknowledge. It had happened to him before, more than once, in dealing with landscaping clients—as though he were glimpsing a fully completed project when, amazingly, he had barely started the conception.

In Ballynagh, he drove slowly up the main street. Likely the butcher shop, O'Curry's, would be somewhere along here.

There was almost no traffic on the cobbled street. The sun struck the cobbles and reflected upward; the morning was warm and breezy. Three or four women were getting on a bus marked DUBLIN; the bus driver was chatting out the bus window with a man in shirtsleeves and a greasy vest. A horse and cart stood before O'Malley's Pub. A couple of men in shirtsleeves touched their caps to Luke as he drove past. Across from O'Malley's Pub he saw a shop with gold lettering on the window: O' CURRY'S MEATS.

He parked a few feet past the butcher shop and sat for a minute.

"Which way to Dublin, mister?" A couple of teenagers on motorbikes, Canadian emblems on their caps, and gunning their motors, stopped beside him on the cobbled street. "Lost our map."

"Straight ahead, two miles up. You'll see the road signs." He watched them out of sight.

Rose in the kitchen, the bread crackling under the knife, *"A pretty little thing, the child. Finola."*

He got out of the car, pulled open the door of O'Curry's, and went in.

A couple of customers, stocky housewives with shopping bags, were at the counter, trading laughter and remarks with a heavyset, red-faced man in a white apron, who was cutting meat at the butcher block. The shop smelled of smoked meat and spices. Behind the counter, next to the cash register, a dark-haired woman, also in a big white apron, stood with bent head, wrapping a package of meat in shiny butcher paper.

"And what's the little one doing here, Mrs. Devlin?" one of the woman customers said and jerked her head toward the back of the shop. Luke turned.

The child sat on a chair, legs folded under her. She looked to be about eight years old. She wore a navy cotton jumper over a white T-shirt and was reading a book, her finger moving slowly over the page, her lips moving soundlessly. Her silky pale hair fell across her cheeks.

"She's come to learn the butcher business!" the red-faced Mr. O'Curry said, with a jolly sounding laugh.

"No," the dark-haired woman said, head still bent. She was

tying string around the wrapped package of meat; she had a low-toned voice, music in it, to Luke's mind. "School opens in another week. I want her doing her reading instead of going off berry picking." And in a lower voice, "You know how children are."

"That I do" — said the woman customer — "having five of my own! You leave them alone for a minute and — Mother of God! — who knows what they'll get into!"

Maureen Devlin lifted her bent head to hand the package of meat across the counter to the customer and for the first time Luke saw her face . . . the very blue eyes, the glossy brown hair in curls and ringlets, untidy and mixed with gray strands, the shape of the woman's face.

And stood dumbfounded.

It was a face he had seen barely an hour before in the portrait in Desmond Moore's bedroom. The face of the duchess of Comerford.

43

Luke drove back to Castle Moore. He found Winifred on the weedy tennis court smashing balls across the net, practicing her serve. When she saw Luke, she came off the court and mopped her sweaty, sunburned face with a towel.

"If I weren't a poet, I'd be on the tennis circuit," she greeted him. "Inspector O'Hare wants to see me for questioning. Maybe I did away with Desmond is the idea."

"That genealogist," Luke said, "the fellow who was researching the Moore family background for Desmond?"

"Fergus Callaghan. What about him?"

"What happened to Callaghan's research? His genealogical research for Desmond? What did he find out? About the Moores?"

Winifred grinned. "God knows! Probably nothing. Mr. Callaghan quit on Desmond. Couldn't stand my bastard cousin, no doubt. I couldn't even find a bill from Callaghan. If I know Desmond, he wanted this Callaghan to fudge up exalted phony stuff about our family."

"I always thought genealogists delivered phony stuff," Luke said, "if they figured that's what you were paying them for."

"Did you, now?" Winifred draped the towel around her sweaty neck and gave him a derisive look. "Not this Fergus Callaghan. He's a special breed of Irishman. More interested in Irish history than in a pint of Guinness. He's deep into Irish tradition; writes little essays in Gaelic for the Gaelic press. I've a friend with similar interests; he reads Callaghan's stuff. That's how I know. Can you imagine Desmond trying to subvert a man like that? Not that I can prove it. Not that I even care to." She looked shrewdly at Luke. "What's this about?"

"I'm in a forest," Luke said, smiling at her, "following a trail of bread crumbs."

"You mean," Winifred said, "you're falling in love with her."

44

In the late Desmond Moore's bedroom, Rose turned the key and locked the door. She went to the gold-leaf Chinese cabinet. She slid open the drawer and lifted out a box. She opened the box and took out one of the diamond necklaces. She held it up. The diamonds glittered, the emerald sparkled. There were at least six or eight of them left. Mr. Desmond had always kept one in a red leather jewelry case in the Florentine desk in the library. Rose imagined Mr. Desmond in the library lifting a necklace from the velvet in the red leather case, a girl's eyes widening, the girl giving a gasp. *Come into my parlor.* The world was stocked with girls transfixed like rabbits at the sight of a diamond. And offered to them by the rich and handsome Desmond Moore. Rose dropped the necklace back in the box, returned the box to the drawer, and closed the cabinet.

"Swoon first, weep later," Janet said, when they'd found out about it, though too late, too late. . . . Rose could feel her face squinch up. She shouldn't cry; she'd look a mess, serving lunch. Janet said she should stop coming in here and brooding about it; she was just driving needles under her fingernails.

Now Janet had told Mr. Willinger about the necklaces and how Mr. Desmond did it. "I wouldn't have told him anything, except that he's, you know, one of . . . one of . . ."

"Yes," Rose had said. Janet meant because Mr. Willinger was AA, like her; the AAs had some kind of understood thing among them, a communion like, like they were all Catholics or something.

Rose dug her handkerchief from her pocket and blew her nose. Hannah was all right now; their mother didn't know a thing. "It's like nothing ever happened," Janet had comforted her when she'd got back from London yesterday. They'd had a biscuit and tea in Rose's room, Rose still shivering in spite of her warm flannel robe.

Rose had managed a smile over her biscuit. She truly loved Janet; Janet was her best friend. It was good to be back at Castle Moore in her cozy room, comforting somehow, and always good things to eat down in the big kitchen.

45

The house at Fourteen Boylston Street was Georgian, of white stone. It was tall and narrow and had a paneled front door with a fanlight.

It was three o'clock in the afternoon. The leafy street was quiet. Luke had driven to Dublin directly after lunch; Winifred had gone back to the tennis court; Sheila was chasing balls for her. Torrey had not appeared for lunch. He'd felt a sharp disappointment. Where was she? Doing what? Meantime —

There were two polished brass nameplates beside the door. Luke pressed the bell of the upper one. Because he was expected, there was the immediate sound of a buzzer. He pushed upon the door and went up a curving staircase that had a white banister with mahogany trim. Another door. He knocked.

"Ah," Fergus Callaghan said, opening the door, "Mr. Willinger." He wore tan corduroy pants and over a blue shirt, the kind of shapeless beige cardigan that made Luke think of Rex Harrison as Professor Higgins in *My Fair Lady*. Fergus Callaghan was short, thick in the waist, and balding; but to Luke there was somehow a romantic quality to the man, perhaps because Winifred Moore had told him of Fergus Callaghan's interest in Irish history. Luke thought of old Irish folktales and romances, wars and famine, Gaelic songs, ruined old towers, Vikings, Norman adventurers, and Cromwell.

Yet as he came into Callaghan's airy, spotless study, he saw that the long table beneath the bow window held the newest model of a fax-computer-printer machine. It was expensive state-of-the-art equipment. It was, in fact, the same equipment that Luke himself owned. So this genealogist, Fergus Callaghan, wasn't kidding around.

"Well, then," Callaghan said, "sit down, Mr. Willinger." He waved toward a green leather armchair and himself settled on a similar chair facing it, hands clasped between his knees, face patiently inquiring.

"Thanks . . . Interesting photographs." Luke glanced around. On the walls were black-and-white photographs of manor houses and castles, thatched-roof cottages, and even a blacksmith shop. Over a bookcase of thick reference books was a three-foot-long color photograph of heraldry, perhaps twenty-five to thirty coats of arms.

"Yes . . . some clients bring photographs."

Luke said, "I'll get right to it. I've become a partisan of Ms. Tunet in this investigation about the murder of Desmond Moore. You probably know I posted bail for her?"

"Yes. It was in the *Independent*."

"Now I seem to've become an amateur detective. I've taken a bite out of the apple and I like the taste."

Fergus Callaghan gave a kind of inquiring laugh, more of a cough.

"In relation to the murder," Luke said, "I've become curious about the Comerfords, the Anglo-Irish family to whom the English king — Charles the Second, was it? — gave the castle and its six hundred acres. And it remained Castle Comerford until about twenty-five years ago when the Moore family came into possession. Isn't that right?"

"Quite. Quite accurate." Fergus Callaghan's brow was furrowed; he looked puzzled.

"A cause for deep satisfaction in the Moore family, no doubt," Luke said, "though possibly tinged with bitterness."

"Bitterness? Because of Ireland's history, you mean? The suffering under English rule? Possibly. Still, all in the past, what with the Irish republic. One can't keep blaming —"

Luke leaned forward. "Ideally, yes, Mr. Callaghan. But I can imagine someone, for whatever reason, putting on a hair shirt of . . . of remembrance, let's say. Wounds of the past. Rubbing in the salt. Thinking about their family's bloodshed. And how often they died of starvation while the great Anglo-Irish landlords in Ireland, landlords like the Comerfords, for instance, ate beef and drank cream."

"I don't see, Mr. Willinger—" Fergus Callaghan stood up, his face a little pale; his hands in the pockets of the cardigan dragged down the sweater. "You have a respectable knowledge of Irish history. As for the Comerfords and any relationship to Desmond Moore's family, I have not made a psychological study of—I hardly—that is not precisely my field." His voice shook with distress. "So there is really nothing—"

Luke said, "I was in Desmond Moore's bedroom at Castle Moore. On the wall there is a portrait of Catherine, Duchess of Comerford, and her children, 1790."

Fergus Callaghan looked bewildered. "That is rather odd. Seeing that given the bitter history of the past, one would've thought the Moores, and then finally Desmond Moore, would've gotten rid of such a portrait. There's a good market in the antiques business for such old paintings. And, of course, Sotheby's or Christie's—Still, Desmond Moore also kept a portrait of the Duke of Comerford in his library. He could have gotten rid of that, too."

"But he didn't."

"Well, as I said, odd." Callaghan shifted from one foot to the other and glanced toward his worktable as though politely waiting for Luke to get up and leave.

Instead, Luke leaned forward in the green leather armchair. "Odder still, Mr. Callaghan, is that in the portrait in Desmond Moore's bedroom, the face of Catherine, the Duchess of Comerford, is the face of Maureen Devlin of Ballynagh."

They stood in Fergus Callaghan's small kitchenette. "Cold tea is fine for me," Luke said. The pitcher of tea on the kitchen table had bits of mint floating in it. Callaghan poured two glasses.

In the workroom again, they sat down, ice tinkling in Luke's glass, the ice a concession to American tastes.

"I didn't know about the portrait in Desmond Moore's bedroom," Callaghan said. "But in Ballynagh, even the little ones know that Maureen Devlin is the last of the Comerfords. English blood. And bringing up her little girl as a Protestant, though Danny Devlin was Catholic. So Maureen Devlin is different. The Anglo-Irish think themselves Irish, but they're fooling themselves. And even nowadays plenty of Irish Catholics in the Irish republic can't forget British rule. The troubles in Belfast rub the sore spot sorer whenever it looks like getting to heal. Not that it ever will."

"So it appears." He felt like a spy, watching Fergus Callaghan's face, the tenderness in his eyes when he spoke of Maureen Devlin, the tremor in his voice. He said the name Maureen as though it were part of an ancient lyric: Maureen . . . Maureen.

Luke abruptly put down his glass of tea and got up. "Thanks for clearing up my confusion about the portrait. Maureen Devlin being a Comerford." He looked down at the balding genealogist who sat slumped in the armchair in his Rex Harrison cardigan, the glass of tea resting on his corduroy-clad thigh. "If anything occurs to you that might help the investigation, Mr. Callaghan, I'd appreciate your calling me. I'm still at Castle Moore; it seems Winifred Moore is thinking of going ahead with the landscape design."

"Yes, of course. I'd be glad . . ."

"Torrey Tunet didn't kill Desmond Moore, Mr. Callaghan. I'm positive. So even the smallest clue that might help . . ."

"You can count on me," Fergus Callaghan said.

Luke drove south through the streets of Dublin. Except for visiting the National Botanic Gardens the morning he'd arrived in Ireland, he'd seen little of the city. AA meetings at Saint Anne's hardly counted. It was already five o'clock, traffic along

O'Connell Street was noisy and heavy, cars and buses and people on bicycles and motorbikes; he had to drive slowly. The sidewalks were filled with men and women who were jamming into pubs, some in work clothes, others in business clothes and carrying briefcases. There were teenagers chatting on street corners and mothers with shopping bags and children at bus stops. The streets were sunny, the air dry; people who jostled each other kept their good nature as though it would be a pity on such a beautiful day to bother becoming angry. It was remarkable to Luke that in a half hour he'd be driving along the hedged roads of Wicklow, in the quiet countryside of hills and mountains and glens, of isolated little villages and an occasional castle. He drove on; and, driving, he seemed to see Fergus Callaghan sunk in the chair, naked love on his face. Enviable, to feel such love.

"Watch out!" A woman jumped back from the traffic, glared at him, shook a fist; he was on Fitzwilliam Street, going too fast. Pay attention. He slowed.

Half an hour later, he turned from the access road with its high hedges and drove through the iron gates that led up the tree-lined drive to Castle Moore.

Just inside the gates, he braked to a stop. Castle Moore lay in the late afternoon sunlight. He gazed at it and thought how it was built on the stone remains of the ancient Celtic castle, and then fort, that had once stood there. It had been fought over and fought around. Men with swords and pikes and iron rakes and kitchen knives had torn and stabbed and slashed and killed other men and their women and children and babes-in-arms through the centuries. They had raped and murdered for power, for ownership, and in vengeance.

Was it still going on? Rage and hate; sexual vengeance visited on the hated Comerfords? Revenge? Or was it disguised perverted lust, masquerading as vengeance? And then, in consequence, bloody retaliation following, swift as a speeding arrow? Luke gazed at Castle Moore, but instead of the castle looming in the sunlight, he saw a woman's face. Was he off track? His imagination plunging into some wilderness of fantasy? Or was it possible, just possible, that Maureen Devlin had killed Desmond Moore? Not with a sword or a pike or an arrow, but with a knife.

He drove slowly up to the castle.

"Hello!"

He turned. Torrey Tunet was coming through the trees from the direction of the stables. White T-shirt, blue jeans, the peacock bandanna around her dark hair. Made him think of a pirate.

"You have a minute?" Luke said. And at her nod, "Come into the library."

46

Stop that damned video," Torrey said. "It's so revolting I want to cry."

Luke turned on the light on Desmond's Florentine desk and clicked the remote. The bathtub scene of the naked man and the child halted and the video of *Irish Gardens, Twentieth Century* rewound with a whirring sound.

It was just past six o'clock, dinner would be at eight; Winifred and Sheila would soon return from Dublin where they were seeing a rerun of *The Crying Game.*

"Oh, God!" Torrey rubbed her bare arms and gave a shiver. "What can you actually prove, with this?"

"Nothing, so far," Luke said. "But what I'd like to prove is that Maureen Devlin would have reason enough to murder Desmond Moore."

"Any mother would. But what are you talking about? You can't go to Inspector O'Hare with this video and a murder theory. It only proves that Desmond Moore was a pedophile. And anyway, that child isn't Finola. Surely Finola can't be the only child in the neighborhood."

"True. But I've done a bit of sleuthing. Try this on;

"Fiona is the only child who arrived at Castle Moore early every morning, delivering bread. 'A pretty little thing,' is the way Rose described her to me."

"But—"

"Finola was left alone at that cottage in the woods from before six in the morning, when her mother left to work at Curry's Meats. 'You'd see her playing in the woods,' is what else I learned from Rose. The woods close enough for Rose to look out and glimpse her. Or to be observed from the Castle Moore library, for instance. It gave me a chill."

"You're giving *me* a bit of a chill. Still, that's hardly—"

"Add to that the fact that there aren't other likely children around, not nearby. The only place anywhere near Castle Moore is a half-mile away, the Sheedy farm, hard-working farm boys, and the twins, they're girls, fourteen, local soccer champs. The other children are strictly within the village, most of them from a bit down the valley beyond Butler Street."

"You're reeling me in. But only a bit. I still—"

"And what I told you, Desmond's psychotic rage against the Comerfords, that portrait in his room: Lady Comerford, the image of Maureen Devlin. Lady Comerford, with her young children. Maureen Devlin is a Comerford. I visited Fergus Callaghan this afternoon. He confirmed it. To Desmond, it would've been a perfect excuse for his pedophilic choice of Finola."

"Reasonable, but not quite—So that's what you've been doing! Sleuthing. Even going to Dublin to see Fergus Callaghan. But we still haven't any proof that Maureen Devlin discovered Desmond was up to something with her little girl. And that she murdered him. If you went to Inspector O'Hare, you'd be putting her head on the block."

"It might save your own head."

She shivered, remembering her night at the police quarters in Dublin.

Luke shoved his hands into his pockets. "You're right about Maureen Devlin. My evidence so far is pretty damn good. But it's not quite good enough. Still, I have a feeling that—"

"Mr. Willinger?" Rose stood in the library doorway, "Brian Coffey is in the stables. He's just back from his family in Galway, his sister's wedding this afternoon. Ms. Winifred said would you please be telling him about the stables because of the plans. The landscaping? He's in the office at the stables, so if—"

"Thanks, Rose."

With Luke gone, Torrey looked at the bronze clock on the Florentine desk. She would give it fifteen minutes. Time for Luke Willinger to give the message about landscaping to Brian Coffey and leave the stables.

Since four o'clock, she had haunted the stables, waiting for Brian Coffey to return from Galway and his sister's wedding in Oughterard. He'd gone by bus this morning according to Rose, a token visit; he couldn't yet trust Kevin with the castle's horses.

Brian Coffey. It was Brian who knew something about that bloody murder in the stables. Brian. A gun shot. It was a solid lead. And now Brian was back from Galway.

She looked at the bronze clock. Ten minutes more.

The clock ticked. Five minutes.

Torrey got up. *Merde!* Her muscles ached from this morning's horseback ride. A second ride today would be torture. But it was the only excuse she could think of. She groaned. Get on with it. Brian Coffey.

In the kitchen of Castle Moore, Janet sat down at the scrubbed wood table and poured herself a cup of tea. The lamb roast was in the oven, sending up the smell of rosemary and thyme. The bread pudding was in the pan on the stove. The honeyed carrots were in the black baking dish next to the pudding. The rest would be easy, though Rose usually forgot to take the ice cream out of the freezer, so it was hard as a rock at dessert time. "Some day I'll break my arm dishing it out on account of you," Janet often said to Rose in exasperation. "Take it out at seven o'clock and put it in the refrigerator. That'll give it an hour to get creamylike."

At the range, Rose buttered a piece of toast, sprinkled it with sugar and cinnamon, and put it in a saucer and brought it to the table. She sank down and poured herself a cup of tea from the brown pot. She was frowning in thought. "Remember last summer—that dented pink celluloid pig Mr. Desmond found in the shrubbery?"

"What about it?"

"Remember he left it on his desk? When I threw it away, he yelled at me for throwing things out without his say so."

Janet nodded. "He always had a fit if anything was missing. What's his is his, and don't you dare touch it. Past tense."

"Like about that little shoe. On his desk."

"What little shoe? A paper weight was it?"

"No," Rose said, "Just a little patent leather shoe with a rosette on it. Like for a doll. He had me combing the library with a magnifying glass. But it wasn't there." She criss-crossed her cinnamon toast with a knife, cutting it into four triangles.

"Well, it's not your fault," Janet said.

"I guess," Rose said, picking up a triangle of buttery cinnamon toast. "But where did the shoe come from in the first place? And where did it go?"

47

Brian Coffey, with a thankful feeling of deliverance, said good-bye and thanks to Mr. Luke Willinger in the stable yard.

He came into the tack room. It was just past half six o'clock. The horses were out of the field and in their stalls. Watered and fed. Brian could see that in his absence Kevin had done his job right. Now the lad had scrubbed himself up in the shower, put on his good pants and sweater, and gone on his bike to see a girl in Ballynagh, pedaling off in a plastic raincoat. A light rain had begun to fall.

In the tack room the air was warm and misty and smelled of leather and hay and mold. Brian had a homey feeling of coziness to be back from his day in Oughterard for his younger sister's wedding. He loved the Moore stables. From down the walkway, he heard Black Pride nicker. Black Pride had proved his stall door no stronger than a bit of plywood that day of Mr. Desmond's murder. He'd bolted. It had taken Kevin a feverish four hours to find him and get him back to the stables before dark.

At the card table, Brian picked up the phone and dialed the number in Oughterard. He was smiling, so relieved. He had a momentary twinge of guilt that he ought to be calling collect. But this was horse business, wasn't it? In a way. So the phone call could rightly be billed to the Moore Stables.

"Eileen?" he said in Gaelic, when his married oldest sister

answered. She loved the Gaelic. Oughterard in Galway was one of the few places in Ireland where people still spoke the old tongue, a Gaeltacht area. Even the road signs were often only in Gaelic. "I'm back okay. The bus got to Dublin and I took the local. Good news!—I keep the job! Mr. Desmond's landscape man, Mr. Willinger, came to see me. He says Ms. Winifred's going ahead with the landscaping and she's keeping the stables besides!"

His sister sounded so pleased, so delighted for him. Then— "Brian, you might pay them a visit, Maureen and the little one, Finola. After all—"

That whore! No. Never. He stopped smiling. He could feel the sweat starting under his armpits. He'd sometimes wished that when he'd first come to Hennessey Stables in search of a horse-training job, they hadn't referred him to Castle Moore in Ballynagh. But that's the way the world worked. Honey came in a bitter cup.

"Brian? Are you there?"

"Maureen's a whore!" he burst out. "I know it for sure! A whore! I know of three men she's been screwing! I'll not visit her!"

"Brian!" Eileen's shocked voice.

"Why did Uncle Danny have to marry that wild one, anyway?" he said passionately. "Grandpa Seamus always said Danny could have had her without marriage vows."

At a sound in the walkway outside the office door—a footstep?—Brian looked toward the doorway. Nobody there. Probably only one of the horses stamping. Besides, he was speaking in Gaelic.

"Brian, are you there?"

"I'm here, Eileen. . . . Grandpa Seamus said Danny liked it that Maureen was a Comerford and him a carpenter. Like he was conquering the English at last."

"He loved her." Eileen's voice, so quiet, her gentle voice made the harsh Gaelic sound rich as yellow cream.

From one of the stalls, a horse whinnied and stamped, as if disturbed. Brian hardly heard. He was no longer happy, but tense, sweating, his skin gone clammy under his red cotton jersey. Dare he tell Eileen? . . . Eileen, to whom as a little kid he'd always run. . . . Eileen, who took away his bewildering hurts and lifted him from the dark, heart-pounding places into safety with her words that were like firelight warmth, soft, dry clothes, and loving arms.

"Brian?"

"Eileen! It's about Maureen and Mr. Desmond. I have to tell you!"

"Brian, what ails you? You sound—"

But Brian was looking again toward the stable office door. "Hello?" His voice quavered, cracked. A figure appeared. The American young woman. So he *had* heard a footfall. How long had she been out there?

Into the phone, in Gaelic, he managed, to Eileen, "Someone has come in and is standing as good as nailed to the floor. I'll call you back tonight at nine o'clock when the little ones are asleep. I'll tell you then. I won't have to pay for the call; it goes on the Moores' bill—stable expenses."

He hung up, the sweat cold on his back, and turned to the American woman in the doorway.

48

"Hello, Brian." Torrey smiled at Brian Coffey from the doorway of the stable office. She felt she would choke with concealed excitement. Someone named Eileen. Nine o'clock tonight. *"Maureen's a whore!"*

"Evening, ma'am."

Torrey felt a rush of pity. Brian's voice that she'd just overheard on the phone speaking in Gaelic had sounded violently angry and excited, yet somehow like a child crying out in fear of the dark. Now his pale blue eyes looked at her almost unseeingly. She sensed that Brian was still caught up with that phone conversation, impassioned, cut off.

"What is it, then?" Brian Coffey said. His voice trembled.

Emotional exhaustion, Torrey guessed. Brian Coffey was sitting hunched over at the desk, one hand still resting on the phone. Such a white skin he had! *Anemic?* Torrey wondered. She met his gaze. Abruptly he snatched his hand away from the phone as though he had burned it. *Oh, my!* Torrey thought. She tried to look disinterested.

Since eight o'clock this morning, when Brian had blurted out those confused words about hearing a shot ("No — voices . . . like shots . . . that's what I meant!") she'd known she had to discover what he was hiding.

And now, unexpectedly, a jackpot? *Nine o'clock tonight.*

"I hope it's not too late for me to go riding; it's almost

seven." She smiled at Brian Coffey, hoping desperately that he'd say it was too late. Her sore muscles cried out for a hot bath. But no way she could back out now; Brian Coffey might become suspicious.

"No, ma'am, that's all right." Brian got up.

Torrey followed him into the tack room; tack hung on the walls, horse blankets were piled. Among them a beautiful black-and-red plaid caught her eye.

In the yard, she watched Brian saddle Baby Talk. Or was the mare's name Baby Face? She had a block. How come she could speak colloquial Russian and tell jokes in two Scandinavian languages but couldn't remember a horse's name? Was that, too, genetic?

"Ready, ma'am."

Astride, walking the mare from the stable yard, Torrey whistled between her teeth, a toneless whistle. It was a habit, that whistling, when things were going well for her.

A hundred yards down the access road she reined the horse to a stop. She looked at her watch. Seven o'clock. Give it twenty minutes. "A refreshing jaunt," she'd lie brightly to Brian Coffey; then she'd head for a hot bath.

She kicked the horse's side, reining it about. Then she just sat. It was as though she were seeing the beauty of Wicklow through a clear crystal. Birds sang, breezes ruffled the leaves of trees, the pungent evening smell of flowers, grasses, and loam was sharp and delicious in her nostrils.

Quarter past seven. She seemed to see Brian Coffey's pale eyes looking into her eyes as though searching for what she might have heard; at the same time, veiled, confident in his secrets.

Twenty past. Back to the stables. She was already hungry for dinner. Roast lamb, Rose had said.

"Go!" she told the horse. "Giddap!" She shook the reins and kicked the mare's sides and Baby Face — or was it Talk Baby? — trotted back down the road and up the drive to Castle Moore.

49

"Let me smile with the wise, and feed with the rich,' " Winifred quoted, grinning around at to the others at the dinner table. She forked a second helping of the juicy-looking roast lamb from the silver serving platter that Rose, at her elbow, held out. "Dr. Johnson said that. He did like a good dinner."

"Well, you can feed with the rich every meal now," Sheila said tartly, "even when you're alone." Across from her sat Torrey Tunet. Torrey's color was high. She looked . . . well, mettlesome, Sheila thought. Hardly a poetic description, but one couldn't be poetic *all* the time. She also looked rather off center. Her swatch of silky hair was a bit awry on her forehead and her gray eyes were a little wide. She was wearing brown velveteen pants and one of those black turtlenecks that ballerinas wore a lot. Torrey could get away with it, with her slender neck. As for Luke Willinger, who was slathering a parsleyed potato with butter, he had on a shirt and argyle sweater and no tie, as though he were relaxing over a comfortable dinner at home, with maybe a book propped against the sugar bowl. And Winifred! Impossible! "You might," Sheila said to Winifred in exasperation, "get a decent-looking jacket instead of wearing that moldy old jumble sale bargain."

"In due time," Winifred said. She took a last luxurious bite of the roast lamb. "I think there's ice cream for dessert. Then we'll want a cognac with the coffee. How about some poker after dinner?" She looked at the others, then glanced at her watch. "It's hardly nine o'clock. We could have a couple of hours before bed."

Torrey jumped to her feet. "Hardly *nine?* This damned watch of mine! That's the second time — Will you excuse me? I've got to . . . to get some tapes down on hard copy and send them off in the morning's mail. I'll have to skip dessert."

"Do go ahead . . ." Winifred started to say. But Torrey had already gone.

Straw tickled her nose. Darlin' Pie's tail swished past her face. She was at the wrong end of Darlin' Pie's stall, the dung end, alas. But she'd be able to hear better there. In the dark, she slid the cassette recorder from her jacket pocket. With her pencil flashlight she looked at her watch. Two minutes to nine.

The stable office must once have been a stall. The partition that had been built up above the opening between the office and Darlin' Pie's stall was flimsy fiber board, a temporary measure, Desmond Moore had had big plans.

Footsteps in the walkway, going past. A minute later, a light went on in the stable office. Torrey could see streaks of light through the ill-matching boards behind Darlin' Pie's rear.

A sigh, a mutter, a series of coughs, the sound of pacing; then a chair pushed back, the tap of numbers on a Touch-Tone phone, Brian Coffey's voice. "Eileen?"

Torrey, cross-legged in the straw, clicked on the cassette recorder.

50

To Fergus, the early morning air of Boyleston Street in Balls-bridge was surely the sweetest and freshest in Dublin. It was Tuesday morning. He sat at the kitchen table in his tan cardigan having breakfast. The casement windows were open to the back garden below. His black tea steamed in the blue china cup. He buttered his toast. This was his morning's special moment of peace.

The phone rang.

"Yes?" he said into the phone. Then, "Yes . . ." and, "Yes. Certainly not." He hung up. He could hardly breathe.

"Ten o'clock this morning, Mr. Callaghan, at the garda station in Ballynagh." Inspector O'Hare's voice on the phone had been chillingly without inflection. "I hope it will not inconvenience you." A command performance, nevertheless.

By nine o'clock, Winifred had breakfasted, jogged four miles, practiced her tennis serve, and written two poems, one a villanelle, the other a rondel. "Just to keep my hand in," she'd told Sheila. Both poems resoundingly praised Ireland's recent vote to make divorce legal. Publication of the poems in the Irish feminist press was certain.

"*Now* what?" Winifred said to Sheila, when Rose came to tell her that Inspector O'Hare of the Ballynagh garda was on the phone. She was in sweatpants and shirt at her laptop computer in the dining gallery of Castle Moore. "You take it, Sheila."

Back from the phone, Sheila said, "Ten o'clock at the Ballynagh garda station, if you don't mind. Important, he says."

"You're coming with me, Sheila. I'm sweaty. I'll have to shower again first. Read these poems, Sheila."

"Maybe it's something about the murder. Inspector O'Hare, I mean," Sheila said. "Why he called."

"Which murder?" Winifred said. "We seem to have a plethora." She went to shower.

There weren't enough chairs. Inspector O'Hare swore under his breath. It was already 9:45. "Borrow some folding chairs from across the street, the Grogan Sisters' Notions," he said to Sergeant Bryson. "They have ladies' knitting parties; they must have chairs."

"Right." Sergeant Bryson took off. The police station door clicked closed behind him.

Inspector O'Hare looked over at Miss Torrey Tunet, who was pacing the room and whistling "The Lion Sleeps Tonight" between her teeth. She looked fresh as a petunia, in white pants and a pink flannel shirt, a satiny band of dark hair falling across her forehead.

Yesterday he hadn't a single lead to the murder of Mr. Lars Kasvi. Now, though, Torrey Tunet had presented him with a surprising bit of information. Tenuous, but worth this effort.

Where was Sergeant Bryson with those chairs? O'Hara looked toward the door. He had felt it incumbent on him to request those involved to be here. The next hour would be like . . . like luring a mouse out of a hole. Miss Tunet had provided the bit of cheese.

51

"Good morning." A contralto voice, deep, melody in it. The garda station door closed behind the woman who entered. It was ten minutes to ten.

"Ahh, Mrs. Devlin," Inspector O'Hare said. "Thank you for coming."

Torrey turned, full of curiosity. Maureen Devlin, at last. She was a woman in her thirties, certainly. Not slender but full-bosomed, and with a confident lift of her chin. She wore a full-skirted black dress and a man's well-worn brown jacket. Her skin was weather-roughened. Her hair, a warm brown, worn in a knot at her nape, had crinkled strands of gray. She looked around the room at everyone, her blue eyes guarded. They came to rest on Fergus Callaghan, who had arrived five minutes earlier. Mr. Callaghan gave her back a haggard look.

"Well, now," Inspector O'Hare said, feeling that he might have a heart attack out of excitement. *Only one more person to come.* He introduced Mrs. Devlin to Miss Winifred Moore and her wispy English friend, Miss Sheila Flaxton. Then to Miss Tunet and *her* friend—or lover?—Mr. Luke Willinger, who, as far as O'Hare could see, was a totally unnecessary presence that was just using up one of the Grogan Sisters' folding chairs.

"You know Mr. Callaghan, of course."

"Yes," Maureen Devlin nodded. "How do you do, Mr. Callaghan?"

Five minutes past ten. The wall clock ticked. Ten minutes past. Inspector O'Hare sweated. *The last person. Where was he?* Inspector O'Hare took a box of stale Fig Newtons from his desk drawer and offered them round. Nobody accepted except Mr. Willinger, who took two. At the smell of the cookies, Nelson rose from his corner and padded over to Inspector O'Hare, wanting his share. "Bad for your teeth," O'Hare said, and gave Nelson a dog biscuit from the bottom drawer.

The door of the police station opened.

Brian Coffey stood in the doorway, trying to catch his breath. He was in jeans and boots and an olive, cowl-necked woolen sweater. His red hair lay close to his head in flat clumps, as though he'd wet it and brushed it flat before he left the stables. The door closed behind him. He said, breathless, to Inspector O'Hare, "The lad Kevin took sick, went giddylike, so I was out exercising Black Pride myself. Janet Slocum came waving at me, shouting that the garda station at Ballynagh telephoned, could I be here at ten o'clock. I came on my motorbike, fast as I could." He blew out a breath, hit his chest with a fist, and looked at the wall clock facing Inspector O'Hare's desk.

"It's only a quarter past," Torrey said loudly because she had an insupportable need for Brian Coffey to look at her. She wanted to feel sympathy for Brian Coffey and his secrets. He looked so skinny and vulnerable, with his pale skin and money-anxious eyes. It was hard for the Brian Coffeys in Ireland, the job market being what it was. But . . . a whiff of chicanery, a bit of deceit, a con here and there when needed. That much, she was sure, from this fellow in the cowl-necked olive sweater.

Brian Coffey met her gaze, blinked, and looked confusedly at Inspector O'Hare.

When Coffey was seated, the inspector glanced toward Miss Tunet. She was looking at the cassette recorder on his desk; her black-lashed gray eyes had an intense look.

O'Hare cleared his throat. "I have here, on cassette, an eight-minute conversation between two people. You may recognize the voice of one of the speakers. However, the tape is in Gaelic. Not all of us — I, for instance — speak or understand much Gaelic, though Gaelic is Ireland's official language and is now required study in our schools. Miss Tunet, however, adept in languages — her field — has printed out a translation that Sergeant Bryson will read aloud. Now if any Gaelic-speaking person among you would first like to hear the tape, for verification — "

"I would, Inspector!" Fergus Callaghan said loudly.

"Of course." The cheese was in the trap. O'Hare leaned forward and turned on the recorder.

52

The cassette tape stopped. Brian Coffey, his lips white, stared with incredulity at the tape recorder. Fergus Callaghan sat slumped; his face had a shattered look like a crazed piece of china.

"Now in English, Sergeant," O'Hare said.

Sergeant Bryson read the translation aloud from Miss Tunet's printed pages. Finished, he squared the pages and put them down in a neat pile on Inspector O'Hare's desk.

Dead silence. Then Sheila Flaxton said, "Oh, my!" She looked with avid interest at Maureen Devlin, who sat very still. Maureen Devlin's eyes looked frozen upon a bitter sight.

"Shut up, Sheila," Winifred Moore said. But she too looked at Maureen Devlin.

"All I said"—Brian Coffey cried out angrily, leaning forward in the folding chair—"all I told my sister Eileen on the phone was family stuff! I told her just that one little thing! About Maureen Devlin. Then we hung up. So why's all this . . . ?" And he looked aggrieved, yet frightened, at Inspector O'Hare.

"The one little thing," Inspector O'Hare said softly. "Yes, indeed."

"Yes! Only that Mr. Desmond went to screw with Maureen Devlin! He even said it that way! 'A quick screw with the widow Devlin,' and he laughed and made a dirty joke about it; then he rode off to the cottage while I waited on Bishop's Path. 'A half-hour screw,' he said."

No one spoke. There was a waiting silence, ears attuned to hear an outraged denial from Maureen Devlin. It did not come. No one looked again at her frozen face. Inspector O'Hare said, "Mrs. Devlin? If you would like to respond?" She looked at him, then gave a slight shake of her head. "No."

"And the rest about her" — Brian's voice cried out for justice — "that I knew about Mr. Callaghan always in and out the cottage, coming and going on his motorbike! And then that other man who was in bed with Maureen Devlin. That's all I told my sister Eileen about!"

"So we heard," Inspector O'Hare said. He turned to Fergus Callaghan for a fierce denial. "Mr. Callaghan?" But Mr. Callaghan, who had opened his mouth to speak, glanced toward Maureen Devlin and said, abruptly, "No. Nothing."

"See? That's all. Just to stop her nagging me to go see my Aunt Maureen and her Finola!" Brian Coffey looked bitterly at Maureen Devlin. Then, involuntarily, he cast a quick, startled glance at Inspector O'Hare.

"That's clear enough," O'Hare said agreeably. "You say you waited on Bishop's Path, the bridle path, for Mr. Desmond to return from, ah . . . visiting Mrs. Maureen Devlin?"

To the inspector's satisfaction, Brian Coffey seemed suddenly to shrink into himself; he wet his lips. "Yes, sir."

"What day was that, Mr. Coffey, that you waited on Bishop's Path for Mr. Desmond's return?"

A cough, a sigh, someone murmured, someone whispered, the clock ticked. Brian Coffey looked down at his hands clasped between his knees. He matched his thumbs together, side by side, and stared down at them.

O'Hare said, "Might it have been the day you and Mr. Desmond rode to Wexford to buy a horse?"

Brian Coffey was absorbed in his thumbs. "The day? The particular day?" He flexed his thumbs. "I don't exactly . . ."

"Take your time," O'Hare said generously. He darted a glance at Miss Tunet. She sat with her legs crossed, watching

Brian Coffey. She'd been right. Right and passionate, bursting into the station and setting the recorder smack down in front of him on the desk.

"What's this? What's this?" he'd said, angrily.

"A thread, a bloody thread," she'd answered, "or is it only the English who say 'bloody'?" She'd pressed the play button. "You might be smart enough, Inspector, to spin it into a noose."

O'Hare looked back at Brian Coffey. He waited.

"The actual day?" Brian said. "I guess so. When we bought Darlin' Pie. A mare."

Inspector O'Hare spun the thread. "That would be the day before Sergeant Bryson and I visited Castle Moore and questioned everyone in regard to their whereabouts the previous day. We hoped for any kind of information. We were concerned about an abandoned yellow Saab and the disappearance of the driver—a Finnish gentleman from Helsinki."

Inspector O'Hare leaned forward. "If I remember correctly, Mr. Coffey, you told Sergeant Bryson that you and Desmond Moore had traveled Bishop's Path together to the access road. Nothing about your waiting alone a half-hour there in the woods while Mr. Moore was at the groundsman's cottage. The bridle path is not far from the bog where . . . where later the missing man's body—"

"What're you trying—?" Brian Coffey cried out. His skinny body in the cowl-necked sweater gave a violent shudder. "Just because I didn't tell!" Another shudder. "I didn't do anything!" His white face went even paler.

"Mr. Coffey—," O'Hare began.

"No!" Brian Coffey looked with clenched fists at Maureen Devlin. "How could I tell and shame my family? Maureen Devlin being my Uncle Danny's widow!" He looked wildly around the room, then back at Inspector O'Hare. "Now *they* all know." A bitter cry. "If I'd told when you and Sergeant Bryson came to Castle Moore that morning, it'ud get about. A village like Ballynagh is all gossip."

"I guess that's so," O'Hare said. Coffey was right, God

164

knows. The gossip in Ballynagh, the sly whispering, the rumors. Every village the same.

"Well, now," O'Hare said, "I think we all understand about that. But let me get to — The important point, Mr. Coffey, is that while you were waiting in the woods, did you see anyone? Or hear anything out of the ordinary?"

"No, nothing. It was just the woods." Brian Coffey's voice had the ring of truth.

O'Hare sighed. From the street he heard the bus rumble past on the way to Dublin. In the garda station, there was only the sound of Nelson snoring in his corner. Miss Tunet and the others were looking at him, waiting.

"Well," he said. "Well . . ." Helplessness washed over him. He swallowed. This meeting, Miss Tunet's brilliant idea, wasn't so brilliant after all; it could've been a mistake, just the public ruination of Maureen Devlin. He felt sorry for Maureen Devlin, her sexual weaknesses, her desires, her passions. And there she sat, shoulders straight, her face tipped down and sidewise, her blue eyes looking into space. Admission of a lascivious half-hour's dalliance with Mr. Desmond Moore. Yet, oddly, O'Hare thought of the downbent head of the plaster Madonna above the doorway at the Ballynagh library.

O'Hare cursed inwardly. Threads into a noose? A mouse to the cheese? It was only for family shame that Brian Coffey had kept silent about that half-hour alone in the woods. O'Hare coughed. He could not look again at Maureen Devlin for the shame of her.

Momentarily at a loss, he temporized, "Well —"

"Inspector, may I ask Mr. Coffey a question?" Miss Tunet interrupted. She was not looking at him; she was gazing at Brian Coffey.

O'Hare shrugged; he waved a hand signifying yes.

Torrey said, in her lilting voice, to Brian Coffey, "I don't want to drag you back to such unpleasantness, Mr. Coffey, but" — she glanced toward Maureen Devlin — "I am thinking of your aunt's reputation and how important you say it is to you and your family. I —"

"It is that!" Brian nodded his red head. "Important! The Devlins—"

"Oh, absolutely," Ms. Tunet interrupted. "But you have told us"—here she waved a hand encompassing Winifred Moore, her friend Sheila, Fergus Callaghan, Luke Willinger, and Sergeant Bryson—"that your aunt, Maureen Devlin—a whore as you call her—slept with three men."

"So she did! So she—" Brian Coffey stopped, mouth open. His eyes widened on Ms. Tunet.

"—and I'm sure," Ms. Tunet went on, "you would not want to leave us with that impression . . . if it were not true."

"No. No, ma'am."

"There was Desmond Moore, who told you he himself was sleeping with Mrs. Devlin."

"Yes." Barely a whisper.

"The second lover—Mr. Callaghan—was that more or less a guess?"

"Let me alone!" Brian Coffey's voice shook.

"And then," Ms. Tunet said, and recrossed her legs, "you said there was a third man. Who was *he?*"

Brian Coffey said, "I'm going to be sick." One hand flew up to cover his mouth. Sergeant Bryson leaped up, grasped Coffey by the shoulder, and propelled him swiftly across the room and into the toilet.

53

They stood outside the Ballynagh garda station on the sunny street, talking and looking at their watches, waiting to go back inside. Five minutes went by. Winifred Moore, in a denim skirt and belted navy jacket, smoked a brown cigarette, holding it between thumb and forefinger; she kept looking impatiently past Sheila at the station door so as not to miss seeing Sergeant Bryson the moment he appeared to allow them back.

"Weak stomach, that chap, Coffey," she said to Luke Willinger. "Needs to suck a lemon. Or is it that 'Conscience doth make cowards of us all'? Got something up his pullover sleeve, no doubt. Can't wait to hear." She turned to Sheila, "What d'you think, *mon amie?*"

"I think you smoke too much," Sheila said. She was gazing covertly at Maureen Devlin and Fergus Callaghan, who had gone farther up the street; they were walking slowly back and forth, heads bent, talking. "She has secrets," Sheila said to no one in particular. Torrey, nearby, said, "There's Sergeant Bryson. We can go in."

Brian was back in his chair, facing Inspector O'Hare's desk. The perspiration had dried on his forehead, but his face still had a sickly pallor. He looked, thought Torrey, as though he had had devastating word from a judge and was now in the hands of the executioner.

Inspector O'Hare pressed the recorder button and the cassette began to turn. "Go ahead," he said to Brian Coffey.

"I was working in the tack room," Brian said tiredly, arms folded, head bent. "It was the day after the Finnish man's body was found. I was brushing and cleaning the tack myself. Kevin was out exercising Black Pride. I shook out Mr. Desmond's favorite horse blanket, the black-and-red plaid. Clumps of dried vegetation fell off it. Yellowish stuff. I know that yellowish color. Bogs around here in Wicklow don't have it; we have it in Oughterard. But the bog—that bog where they found the Finnish man's body—that bog has it."

Brian raised his head and looked at Inspector O'Hare. "It frightened me! I stood there holding the blanket. I felt like . . . frozen. Paralyzed. Just then, Mr. Desmond came into the tack room. He saw what I was looking at on the blanket: the yellow muck from the bog."

Brian wet his lips. "Mr. Desmond told me then that a terrible thing had happened. 'I'm confessing to you, Brian,' he said.

"Then he told me that when he'd left me on Bishop's Path and got to Maureen Devlin's cottage, he'd found Maureen in bed with another man. It was the Finn. 'He attacked me,' Mr. Desmond told me. 'He was savage, a brute. He tried to kill me. I defended myself. I tried to stop him. I got my hands around his neck. It was an accident that he died. I put him on Black Pride and took him to the bog.'"

Brian looked from Inspector O'Hare to Maureen Devlin in her black skirt and an man's old jacket. "All I could think of was *her* and us Devlins and Mr. Desmond coming to the cottage and seeing what he saw!"

The recorder gave a click. Ms. Tunet said, "Damn!" and leaned quickly forward and gave the recorder a knock with her fist; then she blew out a breath and nodded an okay to Inspector O'Hare. Brian Coffey looked at her, a dazed look, but he seemed not quite to see her. He took a breath.

"Mr. Desmond said that if Inspector O'Hare found out we weren't together for that half-hour on Bishop's Path, I'd go to jail as an accessory to murder because I hadn't told him the truth—that Mr. Desmond had left me in the woods for that half hour. And it had all been an accident! 'Only an accident,' Mr. Desmond kept saying. And he said, 'You see!—I put myself in your hands, Brian.'

"So I kept quiet. What was the good now of saying anything? It'ud been an accident that the Finn died! And my telling would've made Maureen Devlin look the whore she is. And wasn't there my little cousin Finola to think of? Her to be tarred with the mother's dirty brush?" Brian looked around for approval. "Bad enough that Finola must've been seeing nasty things her mother was doing with men. And—"

"Stop it! *Stop it!*" Fergus Callaghan was on his feet, his face congested. In an instant Sergeant Bryson was at Callaghan's side, his hand on the genealogist's shoulder. "Sit *down*, Mr. Callaghan." Mr. Callaghan, fists clenched at his sides, sank down.

"—and I didn't want to go to prison as an accessory," Brian Coffey finished.

O'Hare, choking with excitement, nodded. The poor young fellow. He'd been living in anguish.

They were all getting up, exclaiming, milling. No one headed for the door; it was all too incredible, too thrilling. The murder of Lars Kasvi all revealed in detail right here! Just now! Not five minutes ago! And added to that, the incredible revelation that it was Mr. Desmond Moore who had killed him. Desmond Moore!

Inspector O'Hare, stunned and exhilarated, accepted congratulations. "Can you imagine," he heard Winifred Moore saying to Mr. Willinger, "my own darling cousin Desmond strangling that Finn and sinking him in the bog!" She gave a hoot of a laugh. "Frankly, I can imagine Desmond doing just that." She paused and added, low, "And worse. Worse." O'Hare felt faintly shocked.

Sheila Flaxton, congratulating O'Hare, said, "Life is so *star-*

169

tling, Inspector. One thinks one *knows* another person, but actually, one never . . ."

"One never does," O'Hare agreed and looked over at Maureen Devlin (three men, boundless sexual activities). Fergus Callaghan was standing beside her, glaring at Brian Coffey, who simply stood, looking uncertain.

O'Hare said to Sergeant Bryson, "Get that plaid horse blanket from the stable at Castle Moore. The technical crew in Dublin will analyze it. The yellow stuff, and maybe blood." To Brian Coffey, he said, "You'll give a deposition at the *Garda Siochana* in Dublin. I'll let you know the date."

Standing beside his desk, Inspector O'Hare leaned down and rubbed Nelson's shaggy head with rough affection, meanwhile glancing sidewise at the phone. When everybody'd cleared out, he'd phone Chief Superintendent O'Reilly at *Garda Siochana* headquarters and say crisply, "Concerning the murder of Mr. Lars Kasvi, I'd like to report . . ." And so on. Then he'd listen to O'Reilly, chief superintendent of the Murder Squad at Dublin Castle, congratulate him. Next, he'd call Lars Kasvi's family in Helsinki.

He snapped the cassette from the recorder. Evidence. He had to give Miss Tunet credit. Her knowledge of Gaelic and her clever taping of Brian Coffey's phone call to Oughterard had cracked the Lars Kasvi case. Maybe from now on he'd call her Ms. Tunet instead of Miss. A lot of the *Garda Siochana* in Dublin these days were saying Ms.

"Inspector?" Ms. Tunet was at the desk, such an innocent-appearing young woman, seemingly incapable of criminality. "Congratulations, Inspector." She was looking searchingly into his eyes. Did she expect him, because of her help, to call off the dogs?

"Thank you, Ms. Tunet." He felt a momentary regret that Torrey Tunet's charm concealed a thieving, murderous heart. She was clever. She had done him a remarkably good turn with her Gaelic and her cassette. But he could not turn a blind eye. He'd nail her yet for the murder of Desmond Moore.

"Thank you," he repeated, his voice flat, his eyes unblinking. At that, Ms. Tunet flushed and turned away.

"I'm off, Inspector." Winifred Moore came up, drawing on driving gloves. She and Sheila had come in the Jeep and were going on to Dublin to an art exhibit, Manet or Monet, she'd mentioned; O'Hare could never get them straight. One was water lilies.

The police station cleared out. Ms. Tunet, her shoulders stiff, her face like thunder, went off with Mr. Willinger. Mr. Callaghan, with a final infuriated look at Brian Coffey, left with Maureen Devlin. Only Brian Coffey remained.

"Mr. Coffey," O'Hare said kindly, "you'd better get some rest. You've been under a lot of stress." O'Hare thought he had never seen a young man look so exhausted. And his eyes! — As though he had not slept for days. Nights.

"I'll go along then," Coffey said.

"Do."

Through the front plateglass, Inspector O'Hare saw Coffey get on his motorbike, an expensive, new-looking bike. Coffey sped off.

54

A half-hour later, in the back room of O'Curry's Meats, Maureen Devlin and Finola and Fergus Callaghan were having a lunch of liverwurst sandwiches on brown bread, Finola's favorite. They had hot barley soup from Maureen's thermos, spooning it out of plastic cups, and a bag of pears.

There was only the stool, where Finola sat and the one chair for Maureen. So Fergus sat on a wooden crate. Out front, the shop was busy. Fergus could hear Mr. O'Curry, in a fine mood, joking with his customers. Mrs. Blake, the chemist's wife, was still there. She had come in to help Mr. O'Curry when Inspector O'Hare had requested that Mrs. Devlin be at the police station this morning. Mrs. Blake's pay had been deducted from Maureen's salary. Maureen had also paid Mrs. Blake two pounds extra to keep an eye on Finola. Finola always came with her to work now, sleepy-eyed and quiet; she sometimes brought a book, but other times just sat.

Fergus, spreading mustard on his sandwich, felt tremulous with worry and happiness. On the street, after leaving the garda station, Maureen had put a hand on his arm. "T'wasn't true, Fergus. Never! Never did I bed the Finnish man!"

"I know!" Fergus had cried out, rushing to comfort her — and had stood stricken when she drew back, blue eyes wide with shock.

"You *knew?*" She looked searchingly into his eyes; then

shook her head, a brief acknowledgment of something she saw. "It's all right, Fergus. Don't protect me. Don't hide it. I already know. But . . . You! You knew, how?"

"Well . . . ," he said; and there on the street he spilled it all out: the buried doll, the little shoe he'd found on Desmond's desk.

But now, spreading mustard on the bread, "Maureen?" It was painful to ask, he didn't want to ask, but he was going to. "When Brian Coffey said that about you and the Finn, you know"—he glanced sidewise at Finola—"ah, being together"—he realized he was blushing—"could you have said *then* that it was a lie, that you weren't even at the cottage; you were working at O'Curry's? You could've proved it."

Maureen said slowly, "But I couldn't've proved it. T'was the sixth anniversary of Danny's death. Mr. O'Curry let me off for an hour. I went to visit Danny's grave, but that was none of Mr. O'Curry's affair, so I only told him 'personal business.' As it turned out, I was alone at the graveyard; nobody saw me. So you see? And anyway, Fergus Callaghan, if I could've proved it, I wouldn't have." She looked at Finola, who was pensively eating the last of her sandwich. "Honey, will you get my shawl. It's on the hook behind the counter."

Finola gone, Maureen leaned toward Fergus. She said passionately, "Don't you see, Fergus? *I don't want them to know!* I don't care what they think about me! How many men they think I've slept with! So long as it protects *her.*" She gave a sudden shudder and hunched her shoulders and rubbed her arms as if they were cold. "Fergus, she *saw!* Finola saw that violence. *She saw it happen.*"

Fergus felt a chill.

Maureen said, "I won't let her be submitted to any more! She's already had more than a child could stand and stay sane. I've found someone in Dublin I can take her to for help. Meantime, I'll do anything to protect her."

Fergus thought how Maureen's every choice in life was like another chord of music that sank him deeper in love with her. "Well, then," he managed.

Back with her mother's shawl, Finola sat down and began eating the last of her sandwich.

"Finola," Maureen said, "your chin. I'll do it." She reached across with her paper napkin, tipped up Finola's face, and wiped mayonnaise from her child's chin. Finola, silky, flaxen hair ragged on her forehead, smiled at her mother. Maureen said, "There. It's all right now." But she stayed leaning forward a moment longer, smiling at Finola. For an instant, Fergus thought his heart would break.

55

In the garda station, alone with Sergeant Bryson, now that everyone had gone, Inspector O'Hare, pacing, gulped down a pork sandwich from O'Malley's Pub. He was too exhilarated to sit down. He had phoned Dennis O'Curry at the butcher shop and checked that Maureen Devlin had taken last Tuesday morning off for personal business. Very personal, O'Hare had thought wryly, hanging up. In bed with the Finn.

Then, ducks all in a row, he had called the *Garda Siochana* at Dublin Castle with the news of the solving of the Lars Kasvi's murder. Chief Superintendent O'Reilly of the Murder Squad had heartily congratulated him.

Happily, Inspector O'Hare edged a decent-sized bit of pork from the sandwich and fed it to Nelson.

56

Torrey drove the rented convertible back to Castle Moore,
Luke Willinger beside her. She wore dark glasses in case of
tears; she had pulled on an orange-and-black baseball cap that
a former renter had left in the glove compartment. The midday
sun made the hills and mountains seem to shimmer, or was it
because of tears? *"Chagrin,"* she said to Luke, "from the
French. Reflexive, in this case: 'to take on'; 'to fret oneself.' "
She looked ahead at the road winding between the hedges.
Already it was second nature to drive on the left side of the
road. "That cassette tape — I was a house cat bringing a mouse
to lay at my master's feet. Inspector O'Hare's feet. I had a
crazy hope that Brian Coffey would get so rattled under Inspector O'Hare's questioning that he'd make a slip. I thought
there was a chance he'd reveal something about the murder of
Desmond Moore in the stables. Something to help get me off
the hook. But it didn't work. Inspector O'Hare can't wait to
chew me up and spit me into prison."

"What d'you mean, reveal something?" Luke, one arm along
the back of the seat, the other on the door, had turned to look
at her. "How can Coffey know anything about Desmond's
murder? He was in Ballynagh at that Flaherty place, about
harnesses. He and the lad, Kevin."

Torrey kept quiet, watching the road. Her suspicion was too
ephemeral. But, damn it, *Brian Coffey knew something.*

She felt prickles of excitement down her back. Her foot went down on the gas pedal. The car shot ahead. The wind whistled. "God!" Luke Willinger said, "what's this? The Le Mans Four Hundred?"

But already she had gone beyond the speeding car. Already she saw herself in the woods. There was a pair of binoculars hanging from a peg in the back hall beside the mackintoshes. Tomorrow morning, early . . .

"What're you up to?" Luke Willinger asked.

"Nothing."

57

At one o'clock, Ms. Tunet, just back from Ballynagh, came into the great kitchen at Castle Moore. She had an orange-and-black baseball cap on the back of her head and her face was a little sunburned. "Something smells delicious," she said, and went sniffing around the pots on the big stove.

"You had a phone call from Boston, Ms. Tunet," Rose said. She dug the phone message from her apron pocket and handed it to Ms. Tunet, blushing a little at her handwriting. It was such a schoolgirl scrawl, though only those twelve words: *Your check for forty thousand dollars not yet received. Please fax intentions.*

"Thanks, Rose." Ms. Tunet read the message. She stood very still. Then she crushed the phone message and shoved it into her pants pocket.

"Pea soup for lunch," Rose said. "And cold beef."

"I'll be right there, Rose. I just want to get my sweater. I'm chilled."

"Ms. Tunet?" Janet had come in and was holding out Torrey's navy wool sweater. "Is this the one? Brian Coffey found it in the stable yard early this morning."

"Thanks, Janet." Hiding in the horse box with the cassette last night, she had felt stifled, had slipped off the sweater and tied it around her waist. Later she hadn't missed it. "I'll thank Mr. Coffey."

"Yes, ma'am."

Torrey said casually, "That's quite an expensive new motorbike Mr Coffey has, isn't it?"

"That it is, ma'am." Janet hesitated. "Mr. Desmond bought it for him."

"What for? To do errands?"

"Hardly, ma'am." Janet sounded definite. "Just that Brian was always saying he wanted a motorbike."

"I didn't know Mr. Desmond was that generous."

Janet said scornfully, "That he wasn't! Mr. Desmond was niggardly. So he must have liked Brian more than he liked the rest of us." Janet looked away. "Or something."

"Or what?"

Janet met her gaze. "Who knows?"

Torrey asked abruptly, "Did Mr. Desmond have a gun?"

"A gun?" Janet looked startled. "Not him! Mr. Desmond didn't care for shooting. Horses, yes. Hunting, no. He said hunting was too English for him."

"Too English?"

"Yes, ma'am. Mr. Desmond liked to quote Mr. Shaw about that. Mr. George Bernard Shaw, an Irish writer. About Englishmen going foxhunting. Mr. Desmond said that Mr. Shaw called foxhunters 'the unspeakable in pursuit of the uneatable.' Not that Mr. Desmond was a vegetarian like Mr. Shaw. Mr. Desmond would laugh and say, 'I like my lamb rare and my beef bloody.' "

"I see." Torrey looked curiously at Janet, the plain face, the intelligent, small eyes, the pockmarked cheeks. Janet seemed to her a woman who could be your friend, unexpectedly warm and compassionate, or cold-eyed and cynical to those she had no use for. She was, Torrey had noticed, gentle-voiced with Rose.

Winifred and Sheila were back from the Monet art show in Dublin in time for dinner. A chill had settled over Wicklow like a clammy hand. Janet had laid a sizable fire in the library. The wood smelled of hickory. The wall lights glowed. There was a plate of crackers on the mahogany table and a dish of smoked salmon bits and thin-sliced scallions.

Torrey, back to the fire, wore the one pair of wool slacks she'd brought to Ireland and two sweaters. She saw that the others were as warmly dressed: Luke Willinger wore a turtle-necked sweater and tweed jacket; so did Winifred. Sheila seemed wound around in yards of heavy shawls, a medley of maroons and greens.

Winifred, putting salmon on a cracker, said, " 'Poor is the family that can't afford one black sheep.' An old Irish saying. Funny, I always thought of my father as the one black sheep. Or myself. But not Desmond. I wonder who found him out . . . who slipped into the fold, at night while the shepherd slept, and with a knife — "

"For heaven's sake, Winifred!" Sheila's voice was a shriek. "Haven't we had enough for today?"

But Winifred, holding the cracker, said, "I can't wait to hear the fat lady sing."

Torrey said, "Neither can I."

58

By eight o'clock Wednesday morning, Kevin had finished his chores of watering the horses and filling the feed boxes in the stalls. He had swept the scattered bits of hay out into the stable yard. The morning smelled of rain, a fresh, invigorating smell. No use to finish painting the white fence around the field, though; painting needed a dry, sunny day. In the stable yard, he leaned on the broom.

"Get out the tarps and cover the hay. It'll get moldy otherwise; it's going to rain," Mr. Coffey said, coming up behind him. He was wheeling his gleaming new red motorbike into the stable yard. Mr. Coffey was wearing his black windbreaker and a cap. It was the first time Kevin had seen him unshaven; he looked funny with that red stubble on his white face. It looked raw. Mr. Coffey hadn't eaten his usual breakfast of boiled eggs, bacon, and bread. He'd only had coffee and had accidentally spilled some of it on the kitchen table. Janet Slocum had given him a sharp look. Janet didn't care for Brian Coffey; Kevin could see that. She was nice enough to Kevin, though.

Off went Mr. Coffey on his red motorbike. Kevin got the tarps from the storeroom. They were heavy canvas, a dingy gray. He was covering one of the bales of hay when he heard a footfall behind him.

"Good morning, Kevin."

He looked around, surprised. It was Ms. Tunet, the American woman. He was astonished that she knew his name. He felt flattered. She was wearing an old mackintosh, too big; the shoulders drooped. It was likely one of those from the back hall, the buttons missing, so it hung open. Beneath it, she had on dark brown corduroy jeans and a tan shirt, and a worn-looking, red webbed belt. Her short dark hair was covered by a bandanna, orange, with a blue design. She had tied it under her chin. She looked like any farm-working pretty colleen from back in Kerry.

She was smiling at him. "I saw you exercising Darlin' Pie yesterday, Kevin. I envy the way you ride. I do it so badly."

"Oh, no." He blushed. But it was true. He was a natural, like part of the animal. As for her, she'd never be able to do it right. It made him feel gentle toward her.

"Is Mr. Coffey about?" Her voice was husky soft, like Mary Ellen's in Kerry. He thought often about Mary Ellen.

"No, miss. He's gone to Eamonn Flaherty's, a harness place in Ballynagh."

"Oh." She bit a fingernail and looked about. "The stables are so big, aren't they? Pretty, too. That U-shape around the stable yard. But, after all, they're a castle's stables."

"Yes, miss."

"What're those two-story sections at the ends?"

"Mr. Coffey says they're more recent built, miss. Upstairs quarters, they were, for a chauffeur and a gardener."

"Well, it's all lovely." She was smiling at him again, a warm, friendly smile. "Doesn't Mr. Coffey live in one of them?"

"Yes, miss."

"The one nearer the castle, isn't it?"

Kevin studied the canvas tarp that he'd forgotten he was still holding. "No, miss. The other one."

"Well . . . I'm sorry I missed Mr. Coffey. Will he be back soon, Kevin?"

He gave a quick upward glance from the tarp. She had thrust her hands deep into the pockets of the big mackintosh;

her eyes were bright and she had a high color. She was edgy as a filly in cold weather.

"Likely in an hour or so, miss." He found he could not look her in the eye.

"I'll be back later then. Thank you, Kevin."

He did not turn to watch her go. He unfolded another tarp. Why was this American woman, Ms. Tunet, lying to him? An hour ago, crossing the stable yard, he'd glimpsed her, a still figure, watching the stables from the woods. It had been the flash of light on the binoculars that had caught his eye. He was famously keen-eyed, at least famous in Kerry for it.

So the American girl watching from the woods had seen Mr. Coffey zoom off on his motorbike, rackety-clack, out the stable yard and up the drive to the road.

She'd known Mr. Coffey wasn't there. So why?

At a sudden thought, Kevin half-turned and looked toward the upstairs quarters where Brian Coffey lived.

Torrey came into a low-raftered room with two casement windows that overlooked the hills to the north. It was a bed-sitting room with a worn carpet and comfortable-looking old furniture. She glanced hastily through a doorway on the left and saw a kitchenette with a dusty counter and stove and a tin wastebasket filled with empty beer cans. Next to the kitchen was a pocket-sized bathroom with a soiled cotton bath mat, the color of rust. The shower curtain was the same unfortunate color.

She turned and looked quickly about. Between the casement windows was a dresser, on it a couple of framed family photographs, groups of smiling people, women with babies, and shock-headed little redheads in knee pants. Devlins, surely. The family-proud Devlins of Oughterard. *Maureen's a whore.*

She pulled open the top drawer and rummaged, searching. Socks, crumpled underpants, a half-pack of cigarettes, an unopened package of condoms. " 'Hope springs eternal,' " she whispered aloud, whimsically . . . and felt a momentary shame;

everyone deserved his privacy. *But my life may depend on finding what I'm looking for.*

She searched quickly through the next drawer . . . and the next. If she could only find it, it would be a start. There was always a trail; you had only to find the initial starting point. She felt herself growing hot with tension and anguish. Besides, the raftered room was stuffy, the casement windows closed against the damp morning air.

Feverishly, despairingly, she looked about. No other place in which Brian Coffey could hide anything. Only this dresser.

She pulled at the bottom drawer. It was not locked. There was no lock, but she couldn't open it. She pulled harder and managed to inch it part way open. She saw then that the drawer was so full, its contents so heavy, that that had been the difficulty. With a strong, final pull, she had it open.

She gazed down at the jumbled contents. She picked up a steel watchband, so damaged that fixing it would be hopeless. She saw a Swiss army knife with a broken blade, a bent little picture frame with a cracked glass, a couple of tattered romance novels. There were bits of string, so short as to be unusable.

Torrey sat back on her heels. A pack rat! Brian Coffey was a pack rat. He was unable to discard anything, no matter how useless. She gazed at a broken, inch-long bit of pencil that rested on a girl's brassiere, pink, faded. She lifted the brassiere and dangled it from one hand. Where it had lain, she saw a snapshot of a freckle-faced girl with flyaway hair. She dropped the brassiere and turned over the snapshot; the date on the back was eight years ago.

Hopeless. Useless to find among this old stuff what she was searching for. She stirred the contents of the drawer with an indifferent finger, and her eye was caught by a grubby envelope. She opened it. Inside was a single sheet, an official document: Brian Coffey, Oughterard, County Galway, six months' probation, two years ago. Theft of a motor part. So a fellow thief! Brian Coffey had not been a model citizen. Had Desmond Moore known?

184

She put back the document. Beside it lay a toy pistol, hardly the size of her palm. Not likely real. Still, on the off chance that it was, she'd feel safer if it were kept out of Brian Coffey's hands. She slipped it into her pocket.

Give up. Look somewhere else, not in this pack-rat drawer of old stuff. And hurry up. *Get out of here.*

She shoved at the drawer to close it, but at that instant a small green envelope caught her eye. She looked at it in surprise. It contrasted oddly with the rest of the contents of the drawer, it was so clean and new looking. She pulled it out. She opened it. Two tickets to a horse auction in Cork. Her glance fell on the date of the auction. It was almost a week ago, Thursday, so the tickets had been unused.

Thursday. That Thursday, six days ago, was the day Desmond Moore had been murdered.

59

Now, now, no cutting up," Kevin said severely to Fast Forward, the chestnut mare. She was inclined to be skittish when he curried her. Kevin hardly had the words out when he heard the motorbike. Mr. Coffey returning.

Kevin stood still, holding the currycomb, one hand on Fast Forward's haunch. Apprehension slowly made a tight feeling across his chest. Did the American girl, upstairs in Mr. Coffey's quarters, hear the motorbike? He hoped so. Mr. Coffey was edgy lately, like ghosts in a closet were jumping out at him. Strange-acting, too. He sometimes disappeared into the woods for a half-hour or more. And he had sudden, ugly moods, where he had not had them before. He'd blown up yesterday, saying Kevin should've had the water buckets filled by noon, and here it was half after twelve. A bit frightening it was. It spoiled things for Kevin. He still admired Mr. Coffey for what he knew about horses, but he no longer liked to be near him.

In Fast Forward's stall, Kevin began slowly to pull the currycomb through the mare's tail, his head cocked, listening. He heard Mr. Coffey park the motorbike just inside the stable. Then Mr. Coffey came walking past the horse stalls. He stalked past Fast Forward's stall without even giving Kevin a nod or saying hello. His face was white and tense. He went in a beeline toward the end stable and up the stairs to his quarters.

60

Kneeling before Brian Coffey's dresser, Torrey was about to close the bottom drawer when she heard the footsteps on the stairs.

She'd been so absorbed she hadn't heard the motorbike returning. Only now did she seem in retrospect to hear its racket.

Too late! He was on the stairs. She had an intuitive realization that the boylike, innocent face of Brian Coffey concealed something dangerous. Dangerous, why? At once she knew: Brian Coffey was living in fear. His fear was as sinister as a knife, as lethal as the bite of a cobra.

Helplessly she looked about. No way out but the door. She ran into the bathroom, almost tripping over her flapping mackintosh, and stepped into the tub. The shower curtain was skimpy; it did not quite close.

In the mirror above the sink she saw Brian Coffey's reflection . . . saw him circle the room twice, walking jerkily, muttering to himself. Then abruptly he headed straight for the dresser, knelt down, and drew out that bottom drawer. He pushed aside his rat-pack collection and lifted a thick piece of newspaper that lined the bottom of the drawer. He drew something from beneath it, something flat, wrapped in a thin cloth.

At that instant, Kevin's voice came from the stairs. "Mr. Coffey?"

With a swift movement, Brian Coffey slipped the cloth-wrapped object in his hand under his black jacket, forced the drawer closed, and stood up. The expression on his face was so threatening that Torrey felt it like an icicle sliding down her back. He was an animal at bay, teeth bared.

"Mr. Coffey?" Kevin, from the doorway, said, "I . . . I put the liniment on Black Pride's foreleg . . . where the scratch from the fence was? But maybe you'd better look, I'm not sure . . ."

Brian Coffey gave a wild little laugh. "Ah, you're always — ! All right." He pushed impatiently past Kevin, shaking his red head in disgust. "Come on, then." He clattered down the stairs.

Torrey hardly breathed. Kevin stood looking around the room; his glance rested for a moment on the partly open bathroom door. For an instant Torrey fancied their eyes met. Then the lad turned and followed Brian down the stairs.

She was stiff with cold. For the last twenty minutes, since sneaking hurriedly from the stables, she'd been crouching on this wet stump in the woods, watching the stables. Waiting. Hoping. But she could be all wrong! It was just a guess.

She shivered. Her face was wet with the drizzling rain and her neck and wrists felt cold and clammy. She'd had no breakfast. She ached with hunger. The miserably wet weather made it worse. She imagined Winifred and Sheila and Luke Willinger at breakfast in the castle. Rose would have laid a fire in the grate in the breakfast room, a cheerful, warming fire. On the table would be hot biscuits and buttered scones, ham and rashers of bacon, lots of hot, fragrant coffee, and a pot of tea steaming on the —

There! Brian Coffey was crossing the stable yard. She went tense. He was heading toward the woods to her left. He wore his black bomber jacket and jeans and boots. He walked with a kind of single-minded purpose, his shoulders hunched against the drizzle. His red head was a dot of color in the bleak landscape of rain-darkened trees and gray skies. A red beacon.

The woods swallowed him.

Hunger forgotten, Torrey followed.

61

By nine o'clock Wednesday morning in Ballynagh, rain was falling and the sky was so darkly threatening that Sergeant Bryson turned on the wall lights in the garda station. Inspector O'Hare, arriving late, shrugged out of his wet raincoat. He had barely sat down when Sergeant Bryson smoothed out a crumpled bit of paper and laid it triumphantly on the desk before him.

"This message, sir. I found it in a wastebasket of stuff from Ms. Tunet's bedroom at Castle Moore. Someone's been pressuring her for money. Forty thousand dollars."

Inspector O'Hare put on his half-glasses and read the wrinkled note. He looked up over the rims of the glasses at Bryson. "The Moore heirloom necklace must be worth forty thousand."

"For sure, sir."

O'Hare rubbed his chin. The fax he'd received from North Hawk regarding Ms. Tunet, past and present, had indicated her current account in the North Hawk Savings Bank was eight hundred dollars. Never mind the other revelation about the young woman's moral character. A pity. "Desperate measures," he said softly. "Murder."

He glanced down at the crumpled paper, the schoolgirlish scrawl. "Who took the message?"

"Rose . . . Rose Burns, a maid at the castle. I questioned her. She said it was from Boston. A woman's voice."

Inspector O'Hare looked out at the rain. Never mind that he had awakened to miserable weather. He'd enjoyed a hearty breakfast of blood pudding, eggs, brown soda bread with honey, and strong black tea. He had also basked in the knowledge that the Lars Kasvi murder was solved.

Next on his agenda: the murder of Desmond Moore.

And now this message falling into his hands. Serendipitous. And yet . . . O'Hare felt a flicker of regret. Something about Ms. Tunet touched him, something clean and courageous, an untarnished something. Untarnished! That was a joke . . . considering this phone message alone. Rain pounded the window; he thought how it was raining on the hills and in the glens, and on the craggy wild mountains of Wicklow. A very sad rain, a rain like a shroud.

At his elbow, Sergeant Bryson said, "About the Lars Kasvi murder — I suppose the *Garda Siochana* will call this morning, confirming that the bloodstains on Desmond Moore's black-and-red-plaid horse blanket were Mr. Kasvi's?"

"I expect so."

62

In the woods, rain dripped. Under Torrey's wet brogues, the ground was soggy. But the dampness kept the twigs she stepped on from crackling. Still, she stayed well back from Brian Coffey. He was walking purposefully, unwaveringly, as though on an habitual path.

The woods thickened, then thinned. She heard voices, the clink of horses' hooves on an occasional stone, the jingle of a bridle. Through the trees she saw two riders, a man and a woman in yellow rubber ponchos single-filing their horses; they went on and disappeared into the mist. That must be the bridle path, Torrey realized. Ahead, Brian Coffey crossed the path. A few feet farther, he vanished.

Torrey, startled, stood shivering. Then she moved cautiously forward, placing her feet in their damp brogues as noiselessly as possible. A dozen steps, and she saw him.

He was kneeling on the weedy bank of a pond. His back was to her. He took what she thought of as "the thing" from beneath his bomber jacket. He unwound the cloth that had wrapped it. Leaning forward, using the cloth and a handful of grit from the bank of the pond, he began to rub what he held. He was muttering under his breath.

Torrey thought of runes of witches, yet knowing it was only Brian Coffey's muttering and the wraiths of fog drifting through the woods and dimming black branches of trees to gray that gave her such nonsense thoughts. Better to keep her head clear. She blinked her eyes to keep Brian Coffey's kneeling figure sharply in focus and took a step forward.

Under her foot, a twig cracked. Brian Coffey turned his head. Their eyes met. Then she saw what he had been washing and that he now held like a weapon. It was long and gleaming and dripping water from the pond, dripping clear water now, not blood, that gleaming kitchen knife.

Torrey stepped clear of the woods. No way now to retreat. She'd have to play it for what she could. She said, "You should have gotten rid of it. Buried it. Sunk it in the pond. Something."

He said, mechanically, staring at her, "It was too good to throw away."

Pack rat.

"Anyway"—he stood up, his grasp tight on the knife—"I'm safe now. I washed the blood off it that first day. And the next day, and—" His tone was defiant, triumphant, a winner's tone: *You can't catch me!*

She thought, *Yes, you washed the blood off that first day . . . and the next day . . . and the next. Lady Macbeth in a black bomber jacket: "Who would have thought the old man to have had so much blood in him?"*

"Why out here in the woods, in the pond?" She eyed him, curious, oddly unafraid. "You've got a kitchen sink, haven't you?"

"Ah!" His pale, freckled face was triumphant. "Sulphur! Sulphur in this pond; everybody knows that. The pond's full of sulphur. It kills. It does the trick."

"Sulphur?" She shook her head. "You can't ever get it clean enough, Mr. Coffey. The blood will show up. Because of DNA. Desmond Moore's blood. And maybe someone else's blood? It that it, Mr. Coffey? Desmond Moore's . . . and whose blood? Yours?" Was it true about blood showing up? She didn't really know.

His pale eyes widened. He shrank into himself; then he

snapped at her, "You can't know that! It's not true!" Yet she saw that he believed her. Like a desperate, cornered animal he sprang at her, the knife upraised, and she, stumbling back, thought belatedly how rashly, carried away with her triumph, she had trapped herself.

"*No!*" she cried out, and tried too late to pull the little pistol from her jeans pocket, hoping desperately that it was real and loaded. "*No!*" and in despair felt the pistol snag, caught on the edge of her pocket.

"Stop!" She struck out with her fist and felt the painful impact shoot up her arm as her fist struck his forehead. Then they were in a grotesque embrace. She clawed at his upraised arm. She smelled the acrid sweat of fear on his T-shirt beneath the bomber jacket that now in the struggle was half-wrenched off him. In mindless terror she sank her teeth into his shoulder, clinging to him, incomprehensibly, for safety. He screamed again and tore himself away. Then he was making a keening sound. He struck her on the mouth and she tasted her own blood. Their faces were close now. She saw the same mindless terror in his face. He raised his arm and she looked up to see the knife coming down on her.

63

Inspector Egan O'Hare was not happy. It wasn't because of the rotten, nasty, gloomy, cold, rainy morning, either. The sadness was like something in his bones, nothing he could help. Because after all, Ms. Tunet had brought it on herself.

The kettle on the two-burner electric began to whistle. The nine o'clock cup of tea.

"I'm opening another tea," Sergeant Bryson said. He tore open a fresh packet then leaned over and sniffed the brew; he always did that.

O'Hare looked distastefully at the phone. In a minute he would call Ms. Tunet at Castle Moore. He would request her to come in. He could see her entering the station, that jaunty, alive style of her. She would close her umbrella, she would tip her dark head, inquiringly, and—

And he would hold up the crumpled message from her wastebasket. "Forty thousand dollars. Quite a sum to come up with, wouldn't you say, Ms. Tunet?"

He didn't want to see it, Ms. Tunet's gray eyes go wide with shock.

Nevertheless. He reached for the phone.

"Uh-oh . . . ! Here comes the heiress," Sergeant Bryson said. He was standing near the door, glancing out into the street. O'Hara took a look, hesitated, and turned from the phone. A few minutes wouldn't matter.

"Greetings!" Winifred Moore strode in out of the rain. She wore a dashing tweed cape and a green suede hat. Sheila Flaxton followed with a dripping umbrella. Her pinched little face peered out of a plastic rainhood that was falling over her eyes. She wore a transparent raincoat over an an Irish wool sweater and long paisley skirt. Her nose was red. She nodded a good morning and sneezed.

"So, then!" Winifred Moore boomed out. "What's the word from the *Garda Siochana?* About Desmond's plaid horse blanket? Blood, or what? We couldn't wait, Sheila and I."

"We don't yet — " began O'Hare, but at his elbow the phone rang. He picked it up. Chief Superintendent O'Reilly.

"Good morning, Superintendent." O'Hare listened, gazing at Winifred Moore. "Yes. Thank you so very — Yes, you're very — I was lucky is all, Chief Superintendent. Thank you. Thank you. And to you, too, sir." He hung up. Cat with a dish of cream.

"Blood," he said. "Mr. Lars Kasvi's blood on Desmond Moore's horse blanket. And that yellowish vegetation on the blanket besides. Conclusive. I'm afraid, Ms. Moore, that your cousin Desmond, ah . . . that he . . . ah."

"No need to pussyfoot with me, Inspector," Winifred Moore said. "I knew my cousin only too well. Poor Mr. Kasvi."

"I'm sorry." For the thousandth time Inspector O'Hare wondered irrelevantly what they did in bed, Winifred Moore and Sheila. That is, if they really were. He wasn't quite sure. Whatever they did, it couldn't be as good as what he thought of as "the real thing."

"Blood? But he was strangled," Sheila Flaxton said in her high little voice. "So how could — "

"Blood from his nose," O'Hare said.

"Is that tea?" Winifred Moore had spotted the kettle on the electric two-burner and the can of tea. "African? My favorite."

O'Hare gave Sergeant Bryson a look, and Bryson poured the visitors each a steaming mugful.

The door opened. Fergus Callaghan came in. He clicked the button on his dripping black umbrella and it snapped closed.

He wore a mackintosh and a tweed cap. His face looked gray and tired, bags under his eyes. "I was just passing. Good morning. I was wondering — Any word yet? The plaid horse blanket, I mean."

Inspector O'Hare told him.

"As expected." Mr. Callaghan sounded depressed. "So I suppose . . ." His voice drifted tiredly away. He nodded to Winifred Moore and Sheila Flaxton. His glance strayed to the kettle steaming on the two-burner. Inspector O'Hare raised an eyebrow at Sergeant Bryson, who grinned, asked, "Tea?" and filled a mug for Mr. Callaghan. Mr. Callaghan nervously plunged his umbrella into the brass stand and accepted the tea with, Inspector O'Hare noticed, a shaking hand. Obviously Mr. Callaghan was not in top form.

The door was flung open. "Damn and hell!" Luke Willinger said impatiently as the door, driven by a gust of wind, slammed back against the wall. He yanked it closed and looked around. "Hello! What's this, a tea party? I thought I'd better report — I'm looking for Ms. Tunet. Her car's still at the castle, but she's disappeared. Anybody here seen her?" Mr. Willinger's jaw was tense, his eyes worried. He wore a black knitted cap and a red plastic raincoat over a black turtlenecked sweater with gray wool pants and heavy country shoes. "Damn and blast! I've looked for her on the hills and in the woods, even in O'Malley's Pub."

"Maybe she took the bus to Dublin," Winifred Moore said, "working with those conference — "

"She's not, for God's sake! I called the Shelbourne. One of the delegates has laryngitis. There's no meeting today." Mr. Willinger looked frustrated and angry.

"I saw her," Fergus Callaghan said, mug of tea in his shaky hand, "in the woods. A half-hour ago. I'd taken the bridle path on my motorbike. It's a shorter way to Ballynagh from Dublin. She was near the little pond by the oaks. She was talking with a man."

"What man?"

196

"Irish, by the stance of him, Irish somehow. I only saw his back. So I don't —"

"You can't tell if someone's Irish by his back," Sheila Flaxton said. "It's prepost—"

"Shut up, Sheila," Winifred Moore said. "Of course you can tell. I do believe that nationality, a specific culture, even a person's class can be—"

Inspector O'Hare did not hear the rest of Winifred Moore's comment. He was looking toward the door, which again had opened.

Maureen Devlin came in.

64

What is it? I have to get back to O'Curry's." Maureen Devlin closed the door behind her and looked questioningly from Inspector O'Hare to the others. "And she isn't even here!"

Inspector O'Hare blinked. "She? What she? I don't understand, Mrs. Devlin."

Maureen Devlin said slowly, "It's like yesterday, isn't it? All of you here." She wore her shabby black dress, with a gray shawl against the rain, but she hadn't even bothered with a scarf for her hair. Her face was pale and her damp, glinting, wavy brown hair brought the word *tresses* to the inspector's mind. Botticelli. Another painter in his wife's art books.

"She," Maureen Devlin said, "the American, that young woman staying at Castle Moore. Ms. Tunet. She telephoned me at O'Curry's. She asked could I come to the Ballynagh garda station."

"Called you when?" Luke Willinger demanded.

"Maybe twenty minutes ago. Mr. O'Curry was busy with customers. I had my little girl there. I couldn't leave her with no one to watch her; I had to call Mrs. Blake and then wait until . . ." She glanced at the wall clock. "She'll be all right, but I can't be too long. And there's my pay to think of."

"I'm sorry," O'Hare said. He felt as though someone outside him were running his life. "I'm not sure exactly—" He broke off. The sound of a motorbike reached them from the quiet morning street. The sound seemed to fill the one-room garda station.

The sound stopped. A moment later two people came in, blown about, wet with rain, looking as though they'd had a violent confrontation; and with enmity like a sword between them.

To Inspector O'Hare they momentarily looked like a young Irish couple who had had a violent quarrel; he was used to that, a tale of drink and broken crockery. Except that the girl, in a figured bandanna tied under her chin, was Ms. Tunet. She had a red welt on her neck, and her mouth was swollen and her face bloodless, so that her black-lashed gray eyes looked huge. The young man in the torn black bomber jacket and bloodied T-shirt, and with a white freckled face and red hair, was Brian Coffey. He had a wicked-looking purple contusion on his forehead.

Ms. Tunet looked around. Her gaze came to rest on Maureen Devlin in the worn black dress and gray shawl. Ms. Tunet said, "Mrs. Devlin . . . Thank you for coming." She lisped a little because of her swollen mouth. "I thought it was owed you to be here"—and at Maureen Devlin's blank look—"to hear who killed Desmond Moore."

Brian Coffey looked suddenly near collapse. Sergeant Bryson swiftly pushed forward the one sturdy chair left. Brian Coffey sank into it. He said shakily, as though in shock, "She spied on me! She stole my pistol! She's a thief! She stole—"

"It kept you from killing me!" The lisp made it sound incongruously like "kissing me." "Maybe I'm not the first person you—"

"She's trying to frame me!" Brian Coffey flung out his hands in appeal to Inspector O'Hare. "She might've shot me! In the woods! Then she told me, 'We're going to Inspector O'Hare with this. You washed it a dozen times but there'll be blood on it, on the handle and in the screws. Desmond Moore's blood. It's evidence you're hiding. Evidence in a murder.'"

An umbrella fell with a clatter, making O'Hare jump. The tea kettle began again to whistle; an unknown hand abruptly shut it off. O'Hare was conscious of startled murmurs, of Sergeant Bryson at his elbow.

The inspector looked at Brian Coffey's bruised face, "Mr. Coffey," he said, "blood on what? What's this about?"

At that, Ms. Tunet reached into one of the cavernous pockets of the drooping big mackintosh that hung almost down to her brogues. She pulled out something in a dirty cloth. "For your delectation and delight." She winced as she moved her swollen lip. She unwrapped the object and laid it on the inspector's desk. It was a meat knife, long and razor sharp. The handle had scalloped indentations to provide a good grip.

Brian Coffey plucked the wet T-shirt away from his chest; a rivulet of rain slid down one side of his opened bomber jacket. He said furiously, "She might've killed me! She was like on fire. I never saw a woman act that way. Not in Oughterard, not in Galway. Not even in Dublin."

At O'Hare's shoulder, Winifred Moore laughed.

"So then"—O'Hare leaned toward Brian Coffey—"this is the knife that killed Desmond Moore? Concealing evidence, were you, Mr. Coffey? Why? What's this about your blood on the knife?"

Brian Coffey said angrily, "That was all true! Everything I told you yesterday! Mr. Desmond killing that Finnish man at the cottage. But I couldn't tell you the rest. I couldn't because he'd say I was lying, making it up! But now because of her"—and he turned and glared at Ms. Tunet.

"He?"

"The next day..." He stopped. "The next day..." He looked at Inspector O'Hare.

O'Hare gave him an encouraging nod and said kindly, "The next day, Mr. Coffey?"

Brian Coffey looked back at Inspector O'Hare as though the inspector had wrapped him in a cozy blanket; and then he told it as though he and Inspector O'Hare were alone, two friends in the snug of a firelit bar, O'Malley's, maybe, confiding to each other over a jar or two.

"The next day, it got all strange." He'd been in the stable office ordering supplies. It was afternoon, and Mr. Desmond came in and told him something bad had happened: Fergus Callaghan had found out about him killing the Finn. "Now Callaghan is trying to blackmail me," Mr. Desmond said. "He wants ten thousand pounds."

Brian had been frightened. He was involved. "How could Mr. Callaghan have found out?" he'd asked Mr. Desmond, and Mr. Desmond had laughed a bitter kind of laugh. "He's close with Maureen Devlin, whore that she is. Lovers aplenty she no doubt has. Fergus Callaghan, for one. She must have told him. They'll share the blackmail money." Then Mr. Desmond said that Fergus Callaghan had telephoned him. Fergus Callaghan was coming to Castle Moore at two o'clock to collect the money. "I'll pay him off," Mr. Desmond said, "I have no choice. I told him to come to the stables. I don't want anybody at the castle seeing him. And I don't want you here, Brian. You're in too deep already." Then he'd patted Brian's shoulder and given him two tickets to the horse auction in Cork. " 'Take Kevin,' he'd said. 'You can leave at noon.' "

But Brian didn't go to Cork. And he only sent Kevin to Flaherty's Harness Shop with a list of the new supplies so he wouldn't be at the stable, and he'd told Kevin to wait there at Flaherty's for him to check over the stuff. Why didn't he go to Cork? He didn't know. But he'd felt something was off. He was scared, but he had to see. And he wanted Kevin by, not off in Cork.

So at half after one, Brian went up to the storage loft next to box four. It was musty, motes and dirt. He could hardly breathe. But he could see down into the stable.

"At two o'clock, Mr. Callaghan came." But right off it was strange. Mr. Callaghan left his motorbike in the stable yard and came into the stable. Sun was slanting into the stable from the row of windows above the boxes. Kevin had swept, but there were bits of hay on the concrete floor. The horses in their stalls were as usual, a little stamping and snorting, otherwise quiet.

"Mr. Callaghan wore country clothes, a shirt and light jacket and tan duck pants. His bits of gray hair were blown about by the wind.

"'What did you want to see me about?' Mr. Callaghan asked Mr. Desmond, as though he hadn't been the one to demand Mr. Desmond meet with him and pay him blackmail money.

"'Just one or two little things, Mr. Callaghan,' Mr. Desmond told him. 'They don't amount to much. For one, I seem to have misplaced a video. *Irish Gardens, Twentieth Century*. Did you happen across it when you were working in the library?'

"'A video?' Mr. Callaghan sounded surprised. 'No, that I didn't.'

"'No? You didn't by any chance happen to view the video?'

"Then Mr. Callaghan said something about how landscaping wasn't one of his interests.

"'So it isn't,' Mr. Desmond said back at him. 'Well, then ... a little shoe? In the library, did you happen across a little shoe? A doll's size shoe? Black patent leather?'

"At that, Fergus Callaghan clenched his fists. 'A little shoe? Yes, a little shoe!' His voice went all high and funny. 'A little shoe I found on your desk. God help you, Desmond Moore!'

"Then he called Mr. Desmond a pedo-something bastard, and he said, 'Brian Coffey lied, didn't he? Brian's a nephew to Danny Devlin. Brian thinking to protect the reputation of his aunt, Maureen Devlin, and not shame the Devlin family. Bad enough to the Devlins that Maureen is bringing up Finola a Protestant.'

"Mr. Callaghan's face had gone all flushed and fierce. He took a step toward Mr. Desmond. 'I saw Finola bury the doll in the woods! The doll is in my bureau drawer in my bedroom on Boyleston Street in Dublin. With both shoes on.'

"Then Mr. Callaghan—he was standing with his fists all clenched at his sides—Mr. Callaghan said in a funny voice, 'I know what Lars Kasvi saw through the cottage window.' "

"No! Please!" Maureen Devlin's voice rang through the station. "Stop!" She took a step toward Brian Coffey. "Stop!" Her fists were clenched to her chest; her face was agonized.

65

Sergeant Bryson moved quickly forward and took Maureen Devlin's arm. "Mrs. Devlin." She gave him an anguished look. "No!"

But she let him lead her back to the wooden bench beside the Coke machine. She sank down and put her fingers to her temples. Fergus Callaghan, beside her on the bench, was a stone image, eyes fixed on Brian Coffey.

Inspector O'Hare felt in the silence something almost tangible, a screen with the words *pedo-something bastard* and *doll* and *doll's shoe* floating across it. *I saw Finola bury the doll in the woods.* Finola, Maureen's little girl. Yes, even in Ballynagh. He glanced around. Winifred Moore, in her dramatic cape, looked fascinated, her russet color high, her eyes gleaming, Shelia Flaxton stood biting the handle of her umbrella, while Luke Willinger was looking toward Ms. Tunet, as though hoping to catch her eye.

As for Ms. Tunet, she was chewing one end of her bandanna, which O'Hare noticed at this odd moment, had a motif of peacocks. Turquoise. She shot a glance, somehow resigned, toward Luke Willinger and mouthed what looked to Inspector O'Hara like, "Oh, hell!"

"I'm afraid," Inspector O'Hare said kindly to Maureen Devlin, "Mr. Coffey will have to continue. If you would care to leave, Mrs. Devlin? Sergeant Bryson will be glad to escort —"

She cut him off with a wave of her hand, as though she were pulling aside a veil from before her face. Lovely blue eyes, clean jaw, sadness and forbearance. Funny, the things you notice about a person you've seen so often before. Odd. He turned to Brian Coffey. "Go on, Mr. Coffey."

So then, Brian Coffey went on. "Mr. Desmond in a nasty way called Mr. Callaghan a fool, an imaginative fool. 'You don't know what Lars Kasvi saw through the window,' he said, 'it is all nothing.'

"Then Mr. Desmond turned his back on Mr. Callaghan. He was holding his riding crop in his hand. He cracked it down on the half-door of Black Pride's box, and Black Pride reared and screamed. Mr. Desmond laughed and turned back to Mr. Callaghan. 'One of the servants, Rose or Janet maybe, could've left a doll's shoe in the library. Things get left about.'

"Then Mr. Desmond laughed again. He looked big and handsome and as though he owned the world as well as Castle Moore. He stared at Mr. Callaghan as though Mr. Callaghan was a serf in Russia on his estate and he could have him whipped if he wanted to. Like he had cossacks and such.

"But then Mr. Callaghan only gave a big sigh and said something about how he'd managed to get a copy of Mr. Desmond's Visa bill for the last six months, and he said, 'The June bill includes a purchase in Waterford. I know where you bought the doll.' "

To Inspector O'Hare, listening, it was as though with Fergus Callaghan's words, *I know where you bought the doll,* a looming wave had finally crashed. Ugly. Sad and ugly. The room was quiet. Maureen Devlin had put a hand to her throat; there was terrible pain on her face. No one made a sound; there was not even a shuffle of feet, only the rain spattering against the windows.

Inspector O'Hare looked back at Brian Coffey. "Go on."

Brian said, "That's when Mr. Desmond threw the riding crop aside and took out the knife. And I knew then that all the time, *all the time* he had asked Mr. Callaghan to the stable to kill him. He'd find a good-enough reason. He'd tell the police something. He was clever, oh, clever! And strong!

"He went for Mr. Callaghan's chest. Mr. Callaghan pulled a gun from his jacket pocket—he was no fool, after all—but he was too late. Mr. Desmond knocked the gun aside. It fell on the ground and went off, flying behind a bale of hay. The gunshot set Black Pride to rearing and screaming, and Black Pride, gone crazy, burst out of the box and took off like thunder. Startled, Desmond let the knife fall to the ground.

"For a second, Mr. Desmond and Mr. Callaghan stood frozen. Then Mr. Callaghan dove for the knife. At that, Mr. Desmond laughed like he was in charge, even lazy about it. Strange, it was, shivery, like he was playing some mean game with a cornered animal—a cat or a weasel or some such—and he went to put his foot in its riding boot down on Mr. Callaghan's hand that was picking up the knife, except that a stone or something turned under his foot and he lost his balance and Mr. Callaghan stood up with the knife.

"'I don't want to, but I will,' Mr. Callaghan said to Mr. Desmond, waving the knife around. He was all choked up. He sounded scared, like he didn't know what to do. He was backing away and holding the knife awkwardlike, like he hated even to touch it. 'I thought you might—So I brought the gun. In case you tried—As you did! As you did! It's you or me, isn't it, Desmond Moore?' His voice was way high, almost a squeak. 'You or me.'

"Mr. Desmond just smiled, the superior smile he sometimes does, and he said, 'Now, now, Mr. Callaghan, maybe we can figure this out. There are other ways. Monetary, perhaps?' He was moving closer to Mr. Callaghan, but I don't think he fooled Mr. Callaghan. Mr. Desmond had his eye on the knife in Mr. Callaghan's hand, and I could see by the way his shoulder moved he was going to attack Mr. Callaghan, grab the knife from him. The way Mr. Callaghan watched him, he knew it too, that it wasn't over.

"Then Mr. Desmond, as though like a sneer that he couldn't help, it had to come out, said, 'What's the difference? You sleep with the mother; I have *my* . . . proclivities'—and he made a sudden grab for Mr. Callaghan's wrist, with the hand that held the knife.

"At that, Mr. Callaghan made a terrible sound in his throat and raised his hand with the knife and drove it into Mr. Desmond's stomach. He must have struck something vital inside Mr. Desmond because Mr. Desmond just stood still for a minute then went down on his knees and fell sideways, blood spreading dark on his vest.

"That's when Mr. Callaghan dropped the knife, like he was throwing it away from him."

66

Stunned silence. Then, "Christ Almighty!" someone murmured. Willinger? Heads turned to stare at Fergus Callaghan. Inspector O'Hare, with shaking fingers, took out a cigarette, looked at the NO SMOKING sign on the wall, and put the cigarette back in the pack. He was hot and cold and unbearably excited. He flicked a significant look at Sgt. Jimmy Bryson, who moved to stand behind the bench where Fergus Callaghan sat beside Maureen Devlin.

"You saw . . ." Mr. Callaghan said numbly, looking across the room to Brian Coffey. "You *saw!*"

Inspector O'Hare was grimly pleased at Mr. Callaghan's helpless, hopeless look. Mr. Callaghan in his belted tweed suit, with his tie awry, ran a trembling hand through his gray hair. He looked old and tired. Inspector O'Hare, in contrast, felt stronger and younger than ever and well-prepared to deal with Mr. Fergus Callaghan, murderer, never mind the why of it. But first —

"Exactly why, Mr. Coffey" — and he leaned, tight-lipped with anger and exasperation across the desk toward Brian Coffey — "exactly why didn't you tell the gardai you had seen Mr. Callahan kill Desmond Moore?"

Brian Coffey ran a trembling hand over his face, which was filmed with perspiration. "I had a reason, all right! What happened then was — Mr. Callaghan got his gun from behind the bale of hay. He was going to go back, I guess, to get the knife. Just then I heard Janet Slocum calling out for Kevin, Janet coming toward the stables. At that, Mr. Callaghan turned and went away fast, stumbling like, running. But Janet Slocum never came after all. It was quiet, dreadful quiet.

"So then I came down from the loft, my legs all shaky. When I got close and saw Mr. Desmond, all bloody and dead, I got dizzy. I stumbled and tripped on the knife. I picked it up. I wasn't thinking, it was part of — As if like I was going with it to get help . . . like maybe to show them . . ." He shook his head. "I don't know. It was sharp and I cut my finger and it bled. Then I realized my fingerprints were on the knife. I could be accused of killing Mr. Desmond!"

Brian Coffey stopped. He looked from Inspector O'Hare to Sgt. Jimmy Bryson and back to the inspector. "I was scared, my blood being on the knife. I'd had a little trouble in the past, a bit of police trouble in Galway, in Oughterard. So I thought, better to hide the knife with my fingerprints and blood on it. Keep myself out of it, right? Nobody'd have to know I'd even been there.

"So I wrapped up the knife and put it in my motorbike pouch. I was afraid. . . . So then I went to Ballynagh, to Flaherty's, to meet Kevin, instead of running to tell the gardai what I'd seen."

Inspector O'Hare looked over at Fergus Callaghan, who sat staring at Brian Coffey and looking numb.

Brian Coffey's white freckled face with his bruised forehead looked exhausted. "Could I have a Coke?" he asked Sergeant Bryson. Bryson nodded and got a Coke from the machine next to Nelson's basket. He gave it to Coffey, who popped it open and drank thirstily, then wiped the top of the can. He looked over at Fergus Callaghan, a sullenly angry look, and turned back to Inspector O'Hare.

"Mr. Callaghan hates me. Account of what I told about Maureen Devlin. Her whoring. He's in love with Maureen. So when yesterday I told about Mr. Desmond killing the Finn, how could I go on and tell all the rest — about Mr. Callaghan being at the stable and what I'd seen? Mr. Callaghan'd say I was lying. He'd have let me go to prison."

A voice from among the listeners said softly, "Sure as there's a devil, there's an Irish ballad in this tale." Winifred Moore? A deep contralto. *Likely her.* O'Hare thought. He felt a stir of pity for Brian Coffey.

"Yes, Mr. Coffey. And the knife? What about the knife?"

Coffey shrugged. "It must've been a knife Mr. Desmond got from the Castle Moore kitchen. Expensive. Later in the woods by the brook I washed the blood off it. But it was too good to throw away. So I kept it." Gingerly, he touched the purple contusion on his forehead.

"After she caught me with the knife, Ms. Tunet held the pistol on me all the way back to the stables where I had my motorbike. 'Now get on the motorbike, with me on the pillion behind,' she told me. 'We're going to Inspector O'Hare. No shenanigans or I'll kill you.'"

Inspector O'Hare surprised himself by having to suppress a smile. He looked at Ms. Tunet in her bandanna of blue peacocks. "You said that?"

Ms. Tunet, one finger worrying her swollen mouth, gave him back a level look. "Wouldn't you have? I've got only one life."

"She said that because of the necklace," Brian Coffey said, "you're positive she killed Mr. Desmond. She told me, 'Inspector O'Hare wants my blood.'"

The inspector felt his face go red. He avoided looking at Ms. Tunet. He turned back to Fergus Callaghan. "Mr. Callaghan, we're taking you into custody. I'm afraid we'll have to—"

"You bastard!" Ms. Tunet's voice was a sob. O'Hare, outraged, jerked his head around. But Ms. Tunet was not looking at him. She was glaring at Fergus Callaghan, her chin thrust forward. "You would've kept quiet! You would've let me go to prison! All to keep it a secret! All to protect—All for *her!*" And she looked over at Maureen Devlin.

"Ms. Tunet," Inspector O'Hare said sharply, "The law is

concerned only with facts. And now, certain facts concerning Desmond Moore's murder have come to light."

"Facts?" Fergus Callaghan said. He straightened, folded his arms, and looked Inspector O'Hare squarely in the eye. " 'Tis facts you want, Inspector O'Hare? Facts, is it? The facts are that Desmond Moore and I had a money quarrel. He owed me for genealogical work I'd done for him. He wouldn't pay. He acted irrational about it, out of control. So when I came to the stable I brought the gun. I thought to defend myself if Desmond Moore tried — I didn't trust him. But to kill him? No! And with a knife? I wouldn't have!" He shuddered. "But that's the way it turned out."

Inspector O'Hare, pulling at his chin, regarded Fergus Callaghan. Here it was, the killer's confession. That's what had been wanted. He at last had the murderer of Desmond Moore.

As for Fergus Callaghan's motive, Inspector O'Hare slanted a glance at Maureen Devlin. He'd be a fool not to see that Fergus Callaghan would stick to his money-quarrel story. As for the doll, the little shoe, let them stay buried. For an instant, a flash, he saw his mother powdering over a purplish bruise on her neck, concealing it. He sighed and rubbed his chin.

Fergus Callahan said, "So off I went, back to Dublin, home to Ballsbridge."

"Well . . ."

In the silence that followed, Inspector O'Hare thought how different one silence is from another; how there is a silence in which you can hear a mouse in the wall; a silence in the horror of a motor accident, with people standing wordlessly by a person's body waiting for help; the bleak silence following a confession. "Well," he said, helplessly.

Maureen Devlin, as if roused from a trance, turned to Ms. Tunet. " 'Tis a good thing, Ms. Tunet, that you're a fighter. Fighting for your life, with all that about stealing the diamond necklace against you; the law believing that's why you killed Desmond Moore. But in the end, Mr. Callaghan would have spoken. Would have saved you."

Torrey Tunet gave Maureen Devlin a sidelong, skeptical

look and turned to Fergus Callaghan. "Mr. Callaghan?" And waited: peacock bandanna, mackintosh drooping from her shoulders, gray eyes questioning Mr. Callaghan.

Fergus Callaghan looked down at the mug of cold tea he still clutched, then back at Ms. Tunet. He blinked. "Oh, if *then!* Oh, yes. Yes. Of course."

Outside the garda station, Winifred Moore, striding toward her car, Sheila trotting beside her, tossed one end of her plaid scarf back around her neck. "Fishy. Smells to heaven. Knifed Desmond right through his shirt and vest? Fergus Callaghan hasn't the muscle. That's all belted tweed and shoulder padding."

Sheila clicked her tongue in exasperation. "Oh, Winifred! Brian Coffey wasn't lying! He told what he saw."

Winifred said, "Maybe what he *thought* he saw." Then, frowning, "But that's not quite it. There's a piece missing, Sheila. Something's off."

"You're not making sense," Sheila said.

"Ah," Winifred said, "there's more than fish in that bowl."

67

By midafternoon, RTE, the Irish National Television News, had shots of Fergus Callaghan emerging from the *Garða Sio-chana* headquarters in Dublin after being booked for the murder of Desmond Moore. It was reported that Mr. Callaghan had furnished bail and been released on his own recognizance. It was also reported that his counsel would ask for acquittal of the murder on the grounds of self-defense.

News reporters attempted to follow Fergus Callaghan, who drove off in a taxi that wove so fast and skillfully through the Dublin traffic that they lost him. At his Georgian home on Boyleston Street in Ballsbridge, the door with its bronze knocker remained closed. Phone calls went unanswered.

By two o'clock that same afternoon, news photographers from Dublin arrived at Castle Moore and jostled each other taking pictures of the vindicated American, Torrey Tunet, who, no longer thought to be a murderer, obligingly posed for them in a white shirt, jeans, and sneakers, standing in the stable before the splintered stall door of Black Pride, who placidly munched a bucket of oats and swished his tail.

As an added news story, they photographed the new owner of Castle Moore, the prize-winning poet, Winifred Moore, a forthright woman, whom they found in the great kitchen, teetering in a tipped-back chair at the kitchen table and devouring a currant cake topped with whipped cream. Ms. Winifred introduced the press to her English publisher, Ms. Sheila Flaxton, who was drinking tea and delicately picking currants from the cake and eating them.

At approximately the same time, in Dublin, in the office of Chief Superintendent O'Reilly of the the Murder Squad, Sergeant Fitzroy gave a grunt of disgust and placed the third anonymous letter before the chief superintendent. "Ahhh, no! The late Desmond Moore! Sick in the head, if you ask me. Handing out fake diamond 'heirloom' necklaces like penny candy. All to young girls he then used sexually. This letter's from a twelve-year-old. Barely literate. Says she got four pounds for it, poor little twig."

Chief Superintendent O'Reilly said, "Stick our heirloom 'evidence' in an envelope, Sergeant, and personally deliver it to Ms. Tunet. No apologies, mind. But it's hers. Mr. Desmond gave it to her. She might want to keep it as a souvenir of Ireland."

Several of the newspeople, after leaving Castle Moore, found their way to the old groundsman's cottage, having heard that a widow who lived there had been in some way involved with Mr. Callaghan. But they had no luck. The door, with its peeling green paint, remained closed. There was only the smell of fresh-baked bread. The photographers among them had to satisfy themselves with exterior shots: the dilapidated cottage with scuffed grass on one side, a scummy pond a few yards away, and a broken hedge, beyond which lay the access road.

From inside the cottage, Fergus Callaghan watched them depart.

Maureen was setting the table for a late tea: warm, crusty bread, a jar of ham paste, raisin buns, and gooseberry jam. Fergus, exhausted and feeling pursued, had arrived at her door on his motorbike barely a half-hour ago, coming through the woods.

They sat down at the table. Maureen, pouring the tea, said, "When I discovered about Finola, I stole a knife. Mr. O'Curry was having his afternoon lager at O'Malley's, his fifteen-minute siesta. I've a key to the butcher shop. I meant to kill Desmond Moore. Would I have? I was crying inside so hard, so hard! I was bewildered when I learned that someone'd got there ahead of me. When the police arrested Torrey Tunet, I thought she'd killed him. But I wasn't sure. It could have been . . . somebody else."

"Somebody else." Fergus nodded. "Me." Carefully, he spooned sugar into his tea. It was hard for him to get it into his head that he had killed Desmond Moore. At the stable, even hearing Janet Slocum calling and approaching as he stumbled away with the gun, he had looked back in the hope that by some miracle Desmond Moore had sprung to his feet and, dreadful as it would be, was coming after him.

Later, home in Ballsbridge, he had a surge of hope: maybe medical evidence would show that Desmond Moore had died of a heart attack before being knifed—something like that. But that hadn't happened either. The medical reports proved otherwise. So, one after another, each feverish hope died.

"Fergus, what can we do?"

He smiled at Maureen. "We can have our tea."

At Castle Moore, Winifred, teetering on the kitchen chair, was polishing off the currant cake when the girl came into the kitchen. She was about sixteen, slight and pale, with drooping shoulders and a waterfall of pale brown hair. Her face with its blue eyes had a look of vulnerability.

"This is Rose's sister, Hannah," Janet, who was peeling potatoes, said to Winifred. "She's staying a few days with Rose, in Rose's room. She got here an hour ago." It was already getting on to five o'clock.

"Oh, yes, Hannah. How do you do? Rose asked me about you. Yes, I think three days a week, twelve pounds, and doing the laundry, if that's all right with you, Hannah? Because Ms. Flaxton here"—and she nodded toward Sheila—"Ms. Flaxton and I will be constantly back and forth between England and Ireland, and we'll often be having guests."

"Yes, ma'am. Quite all right. Thank you very much, ma'am."
A smile quivered across the girl's pale face.

"And stand up straight," Winifred said. "Meet life head on.
There's nothing to be afraid of, Hannah. Take life by the scruff
of the neck and shake it about a bit. Right? Good for the
blood."

The girl gone, Winifred turned to Janet, at the potatoes.
"You were saying—About the knife?"

"Dozens of knives, generations of knives, in this kitchen."
Janet looked about at the immense oak cupboards, the tables,
sideboards, chests. "Whoever would know of a knife missing?
Or even a cupboard or a table itself?"

Sheila said, "I'll never understand people, how they can—
What inner—I don't have a nasty mind, Winifred, but the minute Brian Coffey mentioned a doll bought with Desmond's Visa
card, I took one look at Maureen Devlin's face and I twigged
it. How *could* he have?"

Winifred said, "I think I know what Desmond was about.
A sexual exploiter, all unleashed. With any excuse to justify
the evil in himself. Drumming up excuses for his . . . well, evil.
Desmond used past history to justify what he was doing. The
past hundred years or the past thousand years—the English,
the Vikings, the whomever, all the invaders of Ireland—it
didn't matter. It never does matter to people like Desmond.
Nothing strange about that pattern. We've seen plenty of it.
Some of it in uniform. Some not."

"But how could he—" Sheila began, but Winifred cut her off.

"Justifying! Desmond even had some cock-and-bull tale
about the Comerfords beating a stable boy to death! A stable
boy who was one of the Moores. How he could have convinced
himself of that when we Moores never left Sligo until we
shipped to America to keep from starving. Well, *you* tell *me!*
As for our being come-down aristocracy, hogwash! We farmed
our stony fields in northwest Ireland since—since God
knows—Cro-Magnon man. So much for that." Winifred gazed
off into space. She said softly, "Any excuse. Any."

Janet Slocum was alone at the kitchen table, just sitting and gazing into the basin of potatoes, only half of them peeled, when she heard someone come in. Ms. Tunet.

"Well, Janet," Ms. Tunet said, blowing out a breath, "the press has left, TV vans and all." She went to the sideboard and took a soda cracker from the wicker dish. Then she leaned back against the sideboard, crossed her sneakered feet, and looked back at Janet. "Now it's just us chickens."

"If it's tea you're wanting, Ms. Tunet, I can just—"

"No, thanks, Janet. Come on, Janet, tell me. I'm curious! Did you think I did it? Murdered Mr. Desmond?"

"Oh, Ms. Tunet!" Janet said. "How can you joke about yourself like that!"

Ms. Tunet laughed. "Oh, well!" She nibbled the cracker. "Did you? Did *you* think I killed Mr. Desmond?" She was looking hard at Janet.

Janet picked up a potato to peel. "Oh, no, Ms. Tunet! *I* didn't think so. And the police couldn't *prove* you killed him. 'Unsubstantiated evidence' *The Irish Independent* said. So I knew you'd get off and go away to America or foreign places. Out of Wicklow. Out of Ireland. Away from here." Fumbling, she dropped the potato peeler; it clattered against the basin of potatoes.

Ms. Tunet was looking at her. She'd finished the cracker and was whistling softly between her teeth, just leaning back against the sideboard and whistling. Then "That's right, Janet," Ms. Tunet said. "But it's different with Mr. Callaghan, isn't it, Janet? He's confessed to killing Desmond Moore. *He* won't get off. Or go off to foreign places. Or marry Maureen Devlin. No. Fergus Callaghan will go to prison. Or hang."

Janet just sat there, Ms. Tunet looking at her. Ms. Tunet's voice was soft and friendly. "Right, Janet?"

"I guess."

Ms. Tunet recrossed her sneakered feet. Janet, peeling the potato, could see them beneath her lashes; it was as though Ms. Tunet was settling in for something. Then Ms. Tunet said, very offhand, "Remember, Janet, that time when we were here in the kitchen, and you said that Mr. Desmond was 'niggardly' about money?"

"Down here in the kitchen?" Janet's mouth felt dry. She swallowed. "I don't recall exactly . . ."

"I do," Ms. Tunet said. "Particularly because you used the word *niggardly*. A very interesting word. Middle English, back then *nyggard*, equivalent to *nig*; in Scandinavian dialect, *niggard*. That meant parsimonious. Stingy. In Swedish, *nugg*."

Janet said, "I guess that's what I might have said."

"Stingy," Ms. Tunet said. "Still, Mr. Desmond gave that red motorbike to Brian Coffey."

Janet held the potato peeler still.

"If I remember," Ms. Tunet went on, and Janet, looking up, saw that Ms. Tunet was watching her, "when I asked why, since Mr. Desmond was so niggardly, you said, 'Maybe Mr. Desmond liked Brian Coffey more than he liked the rest of us.'"

Janet, after a moment, started to peel the potato. "Did I?

"Yes, Janet. Remember?"

"I guess."

Ms. Tunet reached around and took another cracker from the sideboard. "What're we having for dinner? Will that be mashed potatoes?"

"Scalloped. With a veal roast. Green beans with lemon and parsley."

"Sounds heavenly. It's so cool today." Ms. Tunet started to leave the kitchen. But after a few steps, she stopped and turned around. "Oh, I forgot! It was really sensational at the garda station this morning! You were mentioned, Janet—Did you know?"

"Me?" Janet asked.

"Yes. It was when Brian Coffey told Inspector O'Hare that he heard you calling and coming toward the stables just after Fergus Callaghan had killed Desmond Moore. But that then you never came after all." Ms. Tunet popped the rest of the cracker into her mouth.

"Did he?" Janet asked, "Brian Coffey? Yes, though about

that time — But that's right, I never went. I don't remember why."

Ms. Tunet said, "Poor Mr. Callaghan! Losing his head like that! And you know something odd, Janet . . . ?"

Janet held the potato and peeler suspended. "Odd, Ms. Tunet?"

"Yes," Ms. Tunet said, "I wouldn't have thought Fergus Callaghan'd even have the strength to do it. He's 'all belted tweeds and shoulder padding,' as I heard someone say."

Janet said, "Well, Mr. Callaghan doesn't *appear* to be strong. Still, you never — "

Ms. Tunet said, "Yes, of course. But such a pity, isn't it?"

Janet said nothing; she was giving the potatoes her full attention. She didn't look up when, a moment later, Ms. Tunet left the kitchen.

A nettle scratch that wouldn't heal and was beginning to fester. Turning ugly inside as well as out. Janet ran her fingers over her pockmarked cheek. It wasn't always fair the way life took you, swung you around like a cat by the tail, and threw you away. Except that, look now, this time it had not been her who at Castle Moore had been swung around and thrown away.

Ms. Tunet was onto it somehow. Onto something. Sensory, she was, or just putting different combinations together, like working on a puzzle, grabbing at bits, a word like niggardly, putting things in people's heads, like she'd done just now in the kitchen. But Mr. Callaghan'd get off. Self-defense. She'd lay a bet on it. But it was what was in a person's head that counted, what a person in his head did or didn't do . . . like what would be left inside Mr. Callaghan's head for the rest of his life? Not to mention her own head, where the nettle had already begun to fester. So, in a way, maybe she was glad of Ms. Tunet.

Janet bit a lip and got up. At the sideboard, she opened the drawer and took out a pencil and the ruled yellow kitchen pad used for making out the grocery list.

68

Ms. Tunet!" Rose called out, searching, near hysteria. Where was she? One minute she'd been posing for the news photographers in her white shirt and jeans; the next, she'd disappeared.

Crying out, "Ms. Tunet!" Rose ran into the bedroom and looked wildly about the empty room. "Ms. Tunet!" The bathroom? No, the bathroom was empty. But a damp towel hung on one of the gold hooks and the glass-enclosed shower walls were wet. Ms. Tunet had recently showered. The scent of a cologne whose name Rose did not know, infused the bathroom.

Rose ran out of the bathroom, out of the bedroom, and down the curved main staircase.

"Ms. Tunet! Ms. Tunet!" She was almost crying. She yanked open the door to the library and bumped into Mr. Willinger. "Hey there!" Mr. Willinger grabbed her arms. "What's wrong?"

"Ms. Tunet! Have you seen her?" Her face felt hot; she tasted salt and knew in shock that it had been too much for her, on Hannah's account — she had been crying. Because she might be too late, because of what Janet had told her Ms. Tunet had said in despair when she'd opened the envelope delivered by hand from the *Garda Síochana* and taken out the heirloom necklace. Rose saw Mr. Willinger through a haze. "Ms. Tunet! I must find her!"

She was astride what's-her-name — Blithe Spirit, Sweet Baby, Darlin' Pie — galloping across the fields. Either she or the mare was out of control; she was not sure which. She was free. She had fought and won. But there was the other war she had lost. She had failed. Unbearable, unbearably bitter that she would have to tell Donna, "Maybe in a year, two years, I'll have the money."

Luke Willinger had managed to survive that hideous time in North Hawk sixteen years ago. His mother had married again. Luke's kid brother, Josh, was a successful engineer. His thieving baby-sitter, Torrey Tunet, had not destroyed him. But Donna! Donna Lefebvre, with her paralyzed legs. "Maybe later on, Donna, I'll have the money."

For now, it was over. That one chance, with the surgeon from Texas, the eight-hour operation at Mass General in Boston.

She reined the mare to a canter, then to a walk. She had been riding wildly, dangerously. She was soaked with sweat, her hair plastered across her forehead. She was still in jeans, sneakers, and a white shirt. Around her neck was the Moore heirloom diamond necklace, the emerald below her collarbone. She had plans for it, for that necklace that had been hand delivered a half-hour ago from the *Garda Siochana* in Dublin.

High on a hill, she reined the horse to a stop. She looked west across the hills. She could see the woods that lay between Ballynagh and Castle Moore, the late afternoon sun gilding the leaves, casting shadows on the mountains. She narrowed her eyes, searching for the glitter of the lake, but the late afternoon had become warm and so humid that a low-lying mist hung over the lake, dulling its gleam to pewter. But there it was, down there to the left, her destination.

She guided the horse slowly down from the hills and through the woods toward the lake. She reached the lake and reined the mare to a stop. There, on the edge of the lake, was the little bathing hut. She looked along the shore and spotted the flat rock under which she'd hidden the necklace, outguessing Desmond Moore's sexual strategy. She was no innocent not to know a game or two. There'd been a particularly touchy time in Morocco, another in Beirut. There'd be more. She was twenty-seven.

She sat for a minute, quite still, gazing at the lake. Then she pulled the diamond necklace, that wretched fake, off over her head. She rose in the stirrups, straight backed, and with her head up she flung the necklace into the lake.

"Jesus!" Something flashed past her, dove, and was gone.

69

The bathing hut smelled of pine and was dim and humid. Torrey felt so exhausted that she collapsed onto the folding canvas stool. Her white shirt was damp with sweat.

"So . . ." Luke Willinger, five feet away, toweled his bare back, water still dripping down his legs. He looked like a primitive in a kid's TV series about a tribe of religious savages. He was barefoot and naked except for navy underpants instead of a loin cloth. Around his neck hung the diamond necklace, the emerald pendant against his chest.

"So," he went on, "Rose told me that when you opened the envelope from the garda and found the necklace, you said to Janet . . . Uh, let's see, I forget exactly—"

"I remember exactly. I said, 'This damned phony necklace! Worth maybe five pounds! I'll feed it to the fishes!'"

"Right. So—let's see. You'd gone off riding. I put on sneakers—"

"Oh, God! Get on with it! I don't care what you decided to wear. Is this a fashion conversation? What are we talking about?"

"Ah, yes." He grinned at her. With the towel, he tousled his wet hair. "Janet mentioned to Rose what you said."

"About feeding the fishes?"

"Right, again. When Rose heard that, she rushed around looking for you and ran into me. All tears and mottled face and having a fit. She'd switched the necklaces." Luke Willinger put a hand up and fingered the diamond necklace, grinning at her. "You threw tens of thousands of dollars into the lake."

Luke Willinger picked up his wet jeans between thumb and forefinger and regarded them distastefully. "Christ! As bad as wearing a hair shirt."

She sat staring at him, incredulous. "The real necklace? Why'd she do that? Rose."

"Who knows? I gathered she wanted — She was hiccuping and crying and bitter, but she wouldn't say, just kept repeating, 'I wanted the next girl to get the real necklace. She ought to have it! Whoever she might be!' "

Torrey said slowly, "And the next girl was me."

"Uh-huh. Desmond kept the real heirloom in the wall vault in his bedroom. Sometimes he didn't lock it; he was careless, especially if he'd been drinking, Rose said. She made the switch, putting the real necklace in the red leather case in the library."

"Oh, my. Oh, my." There, around Luke Willinger's neck and resting against his somewhat admirable-looking chest, was the miracle, the answer to Boston. She got up from the canvas stool. "Don't put on those wet jeans. Wait here and I'll bring you some dry clothes from the castle."

"Thanks." He took off the necklace, came over, and put it around her neck. She felt his fingers along her cheek. He smelled like the lake, the hut, and his masculinity. His hands moved around to cup her head, turning her face up to meet his kiss. *Ah, yes*, she thought, the warmth of his lips on hers. Ah, yes, yes indeed; kissing Luke Willinger was exactly the way she had dreamed it would be all those years.

70

It was raining when he reached Kilreekill on the red motorbike, the bike getting muddy and his black bomber jacket with rivelets of rain running down it and the neck of his olive turtleneck getting soaked. His helmet kept his hair dry, but what was the difference, so sick about it all, he was. How could it help any anyway when he got to Oughterard to his sister Eileen's? Because he couldn't tell her. But just to see Eileen for a little! Just to be with her in Oughterard for an hour, the two of them over a pot of tea; then he'd go back to Castle Moore.

So about the same time the newsmen and photographers were leaving Castle Moore, he'd wheeled the motorbike from the stable and put on the helmet and fastened it under his chin.

Through the rain he glimpsed a turn-off sign, not yet Loughrea, though. He touched the zippered breast pocket of the bomber jacket where he'd put the note. *"I came around the west corner of the stable. I saw you standing over him with the knife that Mr. Callaghan had dropped."*

He was on N6 now, already minutes from the roundabout at Loughrea, then he'd go up through Athernry to skirt Galway. His bomber jacket smelled sourly of wet leather. The rain was pelting down harder; it was only three o'clock but dark gray with the heavy rain. *"I saw what you did."*

He'd just gotten on the motorbike at the stable when she'd

come up. She was wearing her kitchen apron and handed him the note, no word, and had gone off. He'd revved up the motor, then with his feet on the ground for balance, he'd unfolded the note.

Ahead, he saw a road sign, but it was for a minor road, not the Loughrea roundabout sign. *"I'd thought to keep quiet about it. He deserved it. You don't know the half of what I've seen at Castle Moore."*

Raindrops slid down his nose, and his wrists were wet with the rain and getting raw, chafing against the black leather. It was pouring so steadily now that he could barely see the hills; cars and lorries had their lights on. *"I keep my eyes open. I know what Mr. Desmond did so you got to hate him."*

Part of the wet on his face was not rain. *"So I thought at first I'd keep quiet about at the stable, what I saw. But it's me I've got to think about, Brian. I can see that now. They've got to be told. It would go better for you if you're the one who tells. A confession. Like your conscience made you go to them."*

Him tell? *"And them knowing why, that would make them more lenient like."*

The wet on his face, so much more than rain. How many nights in bed he'd awakened with tears on his face; and he'd lie sleepless, in misery. It was why when Fergus Callaghan had stumbled away from the stable with the gun, and he'd come down from the loft and seen that Mr. Desmond, bloody as he was, was only injured and not dead — It was why, in sudden rage, he'd picked up the knife and driven it into the rotten heart of Desmond Moore . . . had done it because of what Mr. Desmond had done to him, done, and done, and done, then given him the present of the red motorbike, like paying a whore, one of the boy whores of Dublin. Because now he could never feel the same about himself as a man.

Mr. Desmond's blood had spurted onto Brian's black jacket and later he'd wiped it off, though some had gotten into a couple of cracks near the zippered breast pocket. He was glad it was there, like some secret, in revenge. Forever.

A gust of rain blew into his face; he blinked it away. *"But if you don't tell them, I will have to."*

Tell them? How could he ever confess, tell them why, for the shame of it?

Through the rain, he saw the sign for the Loughrea roundabout; a gas tank lorry snorted and rumbled close past the motorbike. In the rain, lights shimmered, reflecting everywhere, duplicating themselves on the shining wet road, the glistening sides of cars. The motorbike sputtered and he saw that he was out of gas. He tried to pull to the side, but his eyes were full of tears and shimmering lights. Out of the dazzlement a lorry loomed over him, and he cried out, "Eileen!" And for an instant there was the warmth and coziness of his sister smiling at him, and then there was nothing.

71

It was the first of September, the air crisp, sheep grazing on the hills of Wicklow south of Castle Moore. This morning it seemed to Rose, in the kitchen, as though the two murders of barely three weeks ago had never been. As for poor Brian Coffey! —

Rose slanted a glance at Janet Slocum, who was cutting up carrots for the stew. Janet was on probation; she had witnessed the murder of Mr. Desmond and kept mum about it. It was all proved by the note found in Brian Coffey's jacket pocket. Later they'd found Mr. Desmond's blood in a seam of Brian's jacket.

"That Janet!" — Rose had overheard Sheila Flaxton say to Winifred Moore right after — "thought she was God, I suppose!"

"No," Winifred Moore had said. "I'd say, more like King Solomon." And after Fergus Callaghan had been cleared, Winifred Moore ordered a dozen roses and had them sent to him from Rosary Florists in Dublin, though Sheila Flaxton said it was a silly thing to do. Then they'd gone off to London.

"Miss Winifred will arrive from London about seven tonight," Rose said to Hannah, who was grinding the herbs. "Back and forth from London like a shuttlecock! She and Ms. Sheila." She handed Janet the cover to put on the iron pot of beef, potatoes, and onions. "She's that fascinated with Mr. Willinger's landscaping."

Hannah, looking up from the herbs, asked, "The old groundsman's cottage near the hedge — where Mrs. Devlin and her little girl lived — now they've gone to live in Dublin, Mrs. Devlin marrying — Mr. Callaghan. It's for rent again, is it?"

"I suppose." Rose smiled at her young sister. Hannah blushed. She had filled out a bit, her fair hair shone, she seemed happy; she was going out with Sergeant Bryson every Saturday afternoon. Serious? She was seventeen; Jimmy Bryson was twenty-one.

Hannah, still blushing, changed the subject. "Mr. Willinger's going back to America tomorrow, isn't he?"

"So I am," Luke Willinger said from the doorway, coming in. "Smells like heaven in here."

"Kitchens do," Janet Slocum said. Mr. Willinger, in a sweater, country tweeds, and brogues, had a pencil stuck behind one ear. She was sorry he was returning to America. He didn't treat her like a criminal because of Brian Coffey. And she'd miss him at the AA meetings in Dublin. Unthinkingly, she raised a hand and touched her pockmarked cheek. Odd about Mr. Willinger and Ms. Torrey Tunet. The pair of them had been making love in Ms. Tunet's bedroom and even passionately in the woods and on the hills, once even in the vacated groundsman's cottage. It was known at the castle and even in Ballynagh; you couldn't keep anything from Ballynagh gossip. It had gone on for two weeks. But then —

"Is that Irish stew?" Mr. Willinger asked.

"Yes. The carrots go in next." But then Ms. Tunet had gone back to America. Did they plan to meet there? Would they marry?

"That's thyme, isn't it?" Mr. Willinger asked, poking a finger at a few green sprigs on the table. The look he gave Janet was acute, as though he had read her mind and closed a door. She looked away. "Yes, thyme."

———

At Mass General in Boston, the surgeon from Houston in the green surgical robe looked exhausted. He was sixty years old, with a lined, tired, intellectual face; it had been an eight-hour operation. Of the forty thousand dollars, he would come away with thirty thousand for that miraculous surgery. Mass General, including physical therapy, would get the rest.

"It went well, Ms. Tunet," the surgeon said. "That is to say, perfectly. She's a musician, isn't she? A drummer? Ms. Lefebvre?"

"Yes, Donna's Devils, that all-girl band." No more being hauled around in a wheelchair, in a van with a ramp, and playing just the snare drums. She'd walk. She'd have traps, she'd play percussion, right foot on the pedal, making the bass drum boom, left foot making the tophat cymbals clash. The dream of her life. The band was promising, it was an infant, still struggling, but it would grow. It would make a reputation, an income.

"Well, then." They smiled at each other, Torrey and the surgeon. There was no more to say. She watched his stocky figure retreat down the corridor.

Two days later, Torrey got off the bus at Logan Airport with a carry-on on wheels. Her ticket to Istanbul was in her jacket pocket.

In the international waiting room, she stepped into a phone booth and dialed Interpreters International. "Torrey Tunet. Myra Schwartz, please."

"One moment, Ms. Tunet."

Waiting, she thought wistfully of Luke Willinger, how, naked beside her in the groundsman's cottage, he had said, "After my stepfather's suicide, I had to redesign my life. I realized what I'd wanted all along was to redesign the landscape. I'd meant to be a psychoanalyst, out of gratitude to my stepfather." He had drawn a breath. "My own father had been a drunk. He died of it." And he said, blowing softly on her neck, "You changed my life. I didn't realize — I hated you. It is only now . . ." and he raised her body over him.

In the phone booth, she could hear the loudspeaker announcing a flight; not hers. Then, in her ear, "Ms. Schwartz is still on another phone. Please hold."

"Thank you." Waiting, she closed her eyes. Alas for her and Luke, the North Hawk past was inextricably tied to today, impossible to forget; the past would send out thorns. Making love, she had known it, had known it in the deserted groundsman's cottage, in the satiny whisperings in the bedroom of the castle, on the purple hills of Wicklow.

"Ms. Tunet? Ms. Schwartz says will you please hang on, she'll be with you in a minute."

"Okay, thanks." She felt for more change. Petty expenses didn't matter. She was seriously broke. Ten thousand dollars in debt. The Moore diamond necklace had turned out to be worth barely twenty thousand dollars. But she'd gotten the ten-thousand-dollar reward offered by Lars Kasvi's family. So that made thirty thousand, leaving her still owing ten thousand to Mass General.

"Torrey?" Myra Schwartz's voice on the phone, excited, elated. "Lucky you called! Hold onto your hat. I just got a go-ahead from my cousin Harry at Roget Productions. They like *Foreign Slang for Kids*. They hate the title but like the concept. They want an option."

"An . . ."

"An option, an *option*. Could be something they'd like to peddle to PBS. Who knows?"

Torrey swallowed. "How much? The option." *Ten thousand,* she prayed. For God's sake, *ten thousand*. She had only $233 in the North Hawk Savings Bank.

"Twelve. And could you work with them on it, they want to know. Part of the deal."

Torrey, dizzied, gave a wild little laugh. "Myra! My, God!"

"I'll call you in Istanbul when I get more from Harry."

When Torrey hung up, she was perspiring. She stepped out of the phone booth. Then she stood still, eyes wide. Languages had been her refuge from that tragedy in North Hawk, her escape. It had led to interpreting and finally to her concept of kids learning languages, starting with foreign kids' slang. It harked back to a six-year-old Spanish child she'd helped when she herself was only twelve. Kids and words. Weird.

"Excuse us. Sorry . . . sorry." A couple brushed past her, hurrying, pulling baggage on wheels, carrying magazines, children trailing. Beside Torrey, several people were gazing up at the Arrivals and Departures schedule; others dozed in chairs or read paperbacks. The loudspeaker was announcing a flight departure for Brussels.

"De nada," Torrey said softly after the couple. She fingered the peacock bandanna she wore at her throat, the one from her footloose Romanian father. But now—introducing kids to foreign languages. Only an option, but a start. If it wasn't Roget Productions, it would be another outfit. She could, for instance, work on language projects anywhere. Anywhere. Even—

Her eyes widened. She was seeing the deserted groundsman's cottage in Ballynach. The Finn had been murdered there; yet she and Luke Willinger had made love there. The cottage. So . . . suppose a new roof, freshly painted walls, a sparkling bay window. She saw herself in the cottage, munching a buttered hunk of soda bread while working at a pine-smelling desk that held a computer and fax; she saw herself on-line in Ballynach talking to Roget Productions in New York. Talking to any company in the world. She laughed with pleasure. "Why not?" she said aloud. "Why not?"

"Flight 347 for Istanbul now boarding." The loudspeaker.

Her flight. Her last job for Interpreters International. Smiling, tickled with herself, Torrey picked up her carry-on, walked out to the departure gate, and boarded the flight for Istanbul.

232